King's Champion

by

Martin Doktár

Published by New Generation Publishing in 2016

Copyright © Martin Doktár 2016

First Edition

The author asserts the moral right under the Copyright, Designs and Patents Act 1988 to be identified as the author of this work.

All Rights reserved. No part of this publication may be reproduced, stored in a retrieval system or transmitted, in any form or by any means without the prior consent of the author, nor be otherwise circulated in any form of binding or cover other than that which it is published and without a similar condition being imposed on the subsequent purchaser.

www.newgeneration-publishing.com

 New Generation Publishing

1. LONDON

The King was alone in this his most private space. A small room, little more than a closet really, located in a part of Buckingham Palace avoided by staff and never seen by visitors. He'd insisted on having it constructed when he ascended to the throne - a special communications chamber. Secret in the sense that only a handful of the country's most senior intelligence officials and of course the PM, the Home Secretary and their closest mandarins were aware of its purpose. The Palace staff knew that their monarch from time to time would seclude himself behind the small but solid door with its impressive electronic triple-security lock, but they could only guess what he did inside. The same applied to the Royal Family.

Soundproofed and virtually impossible to penetrate with listening devices, the room was stacked with computers. Some hooked into specific connections via secure fibre optics, others accessing the Internet in more or less untraceable ways. But one computer had no outside link whatsoever. It contained His Majesty's private intelligence files, most of which he received by hand on memory cards.

His eye caught the clock display as he pushed in the card that had denied him sleep and driven him to sneak about his own palace like a furtive intruder. It was 3:23 am. Not for the first time was he reminded of Shakespeare's line in Henry IV: *Uneasy lies the head that wears a crown.*

The file had arrived the previous day by special messenger from MI5, but he hadn't yet had the time to digest it properly. The implications were too immense, too unsettling and beyond what ought to be thinkable in this day and age and in this country – *his* country!

As he read on with intense concentration, deftly navigating through the material, the heat of the room became almost unbearable and he found it hard to breathe. The smallness of the confined space together with the dire information on the screen caused him to feel an anxiety that he immediately resented. This must be what claustrophobia feels like, he reflected.

Stop it! Stay focused!

The facts mercilessly added up to everything he had sensed and feared. Together they formed a threat scenario of staggering proportions, and there seemed to be no glimmer of hope, no hint of a solution. If *he* didn't enter the battle, no one would. In a deep and profound sense he was the nation's ultimate guardian. Seen in the light of what had been sacrificed in two world wars, he might even be the final defender of liberty in Europe. He *had* to find a way to act!

For several minutes he remained deep in thought. Finally, having come to a decision, he reached down under the desk and opened a drawer. In it was a small and well-worn leather notebook. The King picked it up and flipped though the scrawl-filled pages until he found the entry he wanted. The heading read: *When the chips are down*. Then the name *Metcalfe*, the letter *R* and an obscure anonymous email address.

He carefully entered the email address into his most secure Internet connected computer. Then consulted his tablet organiser for details about his schedule. Finally, with a sense of purpose outweighing his apprehension, the King typed a short message and pressed *SEND*.

2. BHUTAN

Running was a sublime pleasure. He could let his mind relax and empty itself of all content except a keen awareness of his own body. He felt the blood flow faster through his arteries and his lungs extract precious oxygen from the thin mountain air. His heart pulsated with ample power, driving his muscles as hard as required. He was so fit and so in tune with his surroundings that he could run hard through this brutal terrain without consciously thinking about his steps.

The pain would come eventually, when he pushed himself close to, or slightly past, his physical limits, but he dismissed it as insignificant. There were so many harder tests he had to endure. In the beginning they had been forced on him, but for a long time now he had submitted to them because he wanted to. Discipline was everything. No longer imposed on him of course. How could it be? To impose discipline you had to possess credible means to punish disobedience. Who could punish *him*, and by what means?

He smiled as he saw the creek nearly full of water. So much better than standing under a shower. In just a few seconds he shed all his clothes and quickly submerged himself in the chilling mountain stream. Gripping a boulder to help him stay under the surface, he held his breath for as long as he could while he thought about what lay ahead for him that day.

Most of the morning was set aside for finishing his weekly crisis analysis. No particular region in focus, just a total assessment of the state of global stability. Or more precisely, lack of stability. He had several specific facts that needed verification, but they shouldn't require more than an hour of straightforward hacking.

Then he would work on his physical strength and pain resistance for two hours. Because it was Thursday, there would be no firearms practise. Instead, the late afternoon and evening were reserved for his master class at the monastery.

Normally the students were granted the opportunity as reward for dedication and progress. They came by special invitation from several of the martial arts schools in the country. Sometimes, but not always, they were competition winners. Today was different however. There was to be one guest only. A kung fu master, who had travelled secretly – and illegally – from China to do battle with him.

Although he looked forward to the experience, it dismayed him that his own reputation had spread so widely. Maybe agreeing to the master classes had been an error in judgement, but at the time he had not felt he could refuse. The classes were a way of paying the Lama back for all he had done for him over the years.

The kung fu master's visit had been requested and arranged by the Lama. Everything discretely prepared through the unofficial network that connected Bhutanese monasteries with those in neighbouring Tibet. He would have to wear the brown contact lenses he sometimes used to disguise his piercingly blue eyes. He kept his red blond hair dyed black anyway, and was careful to colour his eyebrows and eye lashes. Being a *round eye* in this part of the world was conspicuous enough. Revealing his genetic heritage would have been senseless. He would use his Chinese code name "Pan", but avoid being drawn into serious conversation. Perhaps the guest was exactly what he claimed to be - a kung fu enthusiast dedicated to his art. Or perhaps there was more to this unprecedented visit.

3. LONDON

Sir Hugh Canderton walked into his office in the colossal Ministry of Defence building in Whitehall. He briefly reflected on how his offices kept getting smaller the longer he postponed his final retirement, but at least he had a well equipped desk with all the tools of the trade, and some pretty young thing had just given him a cheery *Good morning Sir Hugh* as he passed her on his way in. He might well be the oldest person in the building, and there were preciously few who knew what his responsibilities were, other than show up three days a week and sit behind his desk for a few hours before entertaining other assorted old-timers over lunch, but he could not imagine the day when he would be out of the game completely.

Sir Hugh may have looked like a caricature of a Whitehall civil servant in his dark suit, severe spectacles and impeccably tidy grey hair, but there was nothing placid or complacent about his personality. Those few colleagues who knew him well respected him as a deeply dedicated man, who believed passionately that a country's only real assurance of liberty was its ability to defend itself.

For twenty six years he had served as the MoD's key non-military link to the intelligence community. Almost every crisis that caught the attention of British Intelligence involved military options and implications. These needed to be analysed, evaluated and put in an overall MoD context - meaning cost and resource allocation. There was always an abundance of competent officers and intelligence operatives who could put together impressive contingency plans for military action. Unfortunately for them, the plans often failed the test of Sir Hugh's unflinching realism. By the time he reached retirement age and was given his current somewhat nebulous position, he had made very few friends in the building, but not a lot of enemies either.

With surprising dexterity for a man his age, he attacked the computer keyboard and checked the accumulated messages on his secure server. Nothing that required his *interference*, as friendly advice from yesteryear's intelligence scion would inevitably be perceived. No matter. It gave him more time to review the multitude of specialised news services he could still access.

He was about to sign in to the first of these, when he hesitated and instead with meticulous care opened a small but very secure looking safe. From its contents, which were mostly documents but also included a 9mm Browning Hi-Power automatic pistol, he withdrew an early generation iPad. This device never left the office, and was turned on only briefly. It had only one purpose.

Like a priest performing a religious ritual, Sir Hugh plugged the iPad to its equally old charger and waited a minute to make sure there was enough juice in the circuits. Once he pressed the power button, the iPad booted up like it had only taken the briefest of naps. Moments later it was connecting to the outside world.

He gasped when he saw the message. With a sense of incredulous foreboding he started to read it.

Mr Metcalfe, can you meet me 3pm October 6 at the Mayfair Hotel, Manchester Suite. R.

Years too late! he thought to himself. Or maybe it wasn't. In any case, the protocol was still valid. Somehow it had been passed on. And it meant Sir Hugh was coming out of retirement.

4. BHUTAN

The visitor was called Chenwei. He looked a bit older than *Pan* had expected, but displayed the wiry powerful build of a martial arts fighter. He had brought a young assistant, whom he referred to only as Gao. Full of deference both towards his superior and the hosts, Gao barely lifted his glance from the floor until Pan happened to look at him during the preliminary stretching, and found himself eyed with great intensity.

The monastery's gymnasium was full to capacity, but there were no spectators from outside the walls. The Lama understood Pan's aversion to anything resembling fame and had banned outsiders from the event, while giving all his monks permission to attend. No cameras or electronic devices of any kind were of course permitted.

Once the Lama had given his speech and formal pleasantries been exchanged, the two combatants sprang into action. Pan's first priority was always to gauge his adversary's strengths and weaknesses. One must never underestimate an opponent!

Though considerably shorter, he found Chenwei very strong, almost his own equal in terms of pure muscle power, not that in mattered a great deal. In kung fu, the quickness of movement was far more important than physical strength, and the visitor delivered his blows and kicks with explosive suddenness and virtually no warning. Not being able to read the opponent's game, Pan had to rely entirely on reflexes to block the flurry of attacks coming at him. Not a problem as such – he knew that his reaction times were exceptional – but it was fascinating to face a fighter who didn't seem to give away any of his intentions.

Time to test the visitor's defences. Pan unleashed a flurry of blows, and calmly noted how Chenwei parried them. As he bloke off his attack and stepped back, he thought he saw the kung fu master's eyes change their expression slightly as he started to believe in his own superiority. Convinced that Pan had nothing he could not handle, the man became increasingly confident. Gradually his moves turned more showy and choreographed. His feet seemed to rarely touch the ground as he jumped and twirled. Excited shouts and gasps of astonishment from the spectators soon filled the room.

Pan admired Chenwei's athleticism, but actually found the attacks easier to deal with now that his opponent was playing to the gallery. Rather than go along with the leaps and jumps he remained firmly on the ground, while deftly staying out of trouble with highly effective turns and blocks.

Whether Chenwei was tiring or not, he suddenly changed tactics and went back to his initial direct approach. He launched a fierce attack that forced Pan to step back several paces while adjusting to the new momentum. He felt he had to make a decision. Sending the kung fu master back to China defeated was not an option. The loss of face could have repercussions on the Lama's connections with Tibet. On the other hand, he didn't want to concede the match to a fighter who, for all his skill and energy, was not truly in his class. So he set about to create an honourable draw.

Using his super-human reflexes in a controlled manner, he stepped in close and engaged Chenwei in a whirlwind of blows and counter blows. Every time his opponent retreated a step he followed him closely, keeping up the pressure. When Chenwei increased his punching rate, he responded in kind.

A collective intake of breath could be heard in the room as the two fighters became a vision of limbs in motion faster than any of those present had ever experienced. Pan knew that he could step it up further if he needed to, but not by much. This was the toughest martial arts opponent he had come across, and it was good to know that he had nothing to fear from him.

Just then, he heard a noise that shattered his calm composure. The unmistakable sound of an electronic camera taking a picture. The device itself was probably set to silent mode, but the mechanics of the release button still make enough of a noise for him to notice.

Only a phenomenal reflex saved him from Chenwei's next blow. Then he extracted himself from the toe-to-toe with a half somersault of his own and used his peripheral vision to locate the one person who could have taken the photo – Gao.

Chenwei's assistant looked furtive, with neither hand visible. Whatever device he had used was now hidden away. Another split second decision. Make an issue of it or not?

Pan assumed a neutral position and then slowly bowed to his opponent.

'I regret that is all the skill I have, Master Chenwei,' he said courteously. 'You have tested me to my limits. Thank you for this honour!'

The visitor must have been relieved, but didn't let it show. Instead he gave a broad but cold smile.

'It is I who am honoured, dear Master Pan. You fight well. I hope to see you in my country soon.'

'It would be a great pleasure,' Pan responded, and at that moment decided that Chenwei and Gao would not leave Bhutan alive.

5. BHUTAN

He allowed himself four hours of sleep that night. Knowing the target's schedule helped. The kung fu master and his assistant would be driven in the monastery's old Toyota Land Cruiser to a point where they could approach the Chinese border on foot. No doubt they were being met on the other side, but their return would at least have the *appearance* of a clandestine crossing. That meant leaving the Monastery for the three hour drive at 2:30am. Using his motorbike instead of a four-wheeled vehicle, he could make the trip in half the time and be comfortably in position despite leaving an hour later than his quarry.

The bike was a specially adapted cross-country racer. The same unique eye to hand coordination skill and reflexes that served him so well in martial arts enabled him to drive at break neck speed over seemingly impossible terrain. There was no need to overtake the Land Cruiser, as his route to the destination was quite different, and significantly shorter. He used an infrared headlight and wore corresponding IR goggles that enabled him to see ahead without himself being visible in the dark.

The Monastery driver had made this run many times before, and Pan knew that he was unlikely to deviate from the normal route. Nevertheless, he felt a touch of relief when he saw the Land Cruiser approach and come to a stop at the usual spot.

Chenwei and Gao lost no time setting off towards the Chinese border. They didn't turn their heads to watch the young monk behind the wheel execute an awkward three-point turn and drive off. Instead they fell into a steady pace, not quite a running, but not really walking either. The road ceased to be drivable at this point, but the path was clearly visibly in the emerging twilight of dawn. This was one of not too many routes through the mountain range. It followed a long gorge that flooded after heavy rains, but otherwise remained passable.

Pan remained hidden behind the protruding boulder he had chosen as protection. Moments after the two Chinese passed him, he stepped out behind them, raised his noise-suppressed pistol and shot Gao in the head.

Chenwei spun around immediately and only needed a second to take in the situation. He had an AK-47 strapped to his shoulder, but bringing into a firing position was not an option with Pan only a few steps away. Instead he gave a nod of thoughtful respect.

'So you guessed,' he said.

'Your friend was careless with his camera,' Pan responded. 'And I think you took my DNA."

Chenwei shrugged. 'It was easy.' He half glanced behind him. 'They are expecting me back, you know.'

'Yes of course. It is too bad, but makes no difference. Why did you come?"

Another shrug from the kung fu master. 'We heard about you. We keep track of dangerous men.'

'Who are *we*?'

'That I can't tell you. Don't prolong this conversation. Do what you came to do.'

Pan took a couple of steps closer. 'Turn around,' he commanded.

Chenwei remained still. 'I prefer not to.'

'Turn around and slowly lower your rifle to the ground.'

With a wry smile the man from China obeyed. Once the AK-47 was on the ground, Pan stepped forward and kicked his legs from under him. Then he held the gun firmly against the back of Chenwei's head.

'I'm going to search you for weapons. Move and I shoot you in the head.'

He found only a knife, which he threw behind the boulder where he had hid earlier. Then he stepped back and allowed Chenwei to get up. The man was rattled but composed.

'Shooting me unarmed is not brave,' he spat, then stared in evident disbelief as Pan lowered his gun, removed the magazine and ejected the chambered round. He tossed the gun after the knife.

'Why?' Chenwei asked.

'It would be dishonourable to shoot you like a criminal.'

The kung fu master bowed slightly before he spoke again. 'It is good of you to give me a chance, but it makes no difference,' he said. 'I know you are invincible for me. Thank you for showing me respect back at the Monastery.'

There was no further need to speak. The two men adopted fighting positions and approached each other slowly. Chenwei moved first. He knew that his only chance was a deception followed by a lethal attack. Unfortunately for him, Pan knew it too.

The deception was a quick feint to the right. Pan pretended to go for the block, but didn't. Instead he immediately sprung inside Chenwei's follow-up blow and exposed the adversary's chest to a quick stab of his own. He struck with precision and devastating force just under the heart. The kung fu master was rendered helpless for the precious second it took Pan to shift into another move. No longer classic kung fu, but pure British Special Forces unarmed combat. He felt Chenwei's neck snap, and let the dead but still spasming body drop to the ground.

6. LONDON

Sir Hugh made a point of arriving exactly on time. He stood for nearly a minute outside the Manchester Suite until his watch reached 3:00 precisely. Then he rang the bell and saw the door open instantly. Two men in suits stood beyond the threshold and eyed him carefully. One of them spoke in the half deferential, half challenging tone of a policeman or soldier.

'Your name, Sir?'

'Metcalf,' responded Sir Hugh. 'I trust I'm expected.' The suit stepped aside, as did his partner.

'Please go right in, Sir. We'll be on the outside.'

They let him pass between them before stepping out into the corridor and pulling the door shut. He proceeded warily through a small hallway into a dimly lit reception room. In the far corner he perceived a man standing. Then a familiar voice spoke to him.

'I know you! You're Sir Hugh Canderton, right?'

'Indeed. At your service, Your Majesty.'

The King indicated a couple of easy chairs and they seated themselves.

'I had no idea who would come. You are Metcalfe of course?'

'I am, Sir. Or at least I was. It's been a long time since I used that name. May I ask how you knew?'

The King leaned forward and Sir Hugh saw his face clearly in the light from a table lamp. There was something disturbingly weary about his face, although he was still very much a man in his prime. His handsome features that evoked such affection amongst his subjects looked strained, and his normally open and sincere eyes appeared unsure and unsettled.

'My grandmother once spoke to me very candidly,' he began. 'She said that there might come a day when I was king and matters got out of control. A major crisis that I couldn't handle on my own, but couldn't ignore either.'

He hesitated and looked directly into Sir Hugh's eyes.

'I've had your name and the method for contacting you written down in a secret place, but never thought the day would come, so to speak.'

'How may I be of assistance, Sir?'

The King nodded thoughtfully and took a deep breath before speaking. 'It's now over four years since the great financial meltdown. Nothing has improved. All of Europe is in depression. Every one of the major countries struggles to maintain even essential public services. We don't dare say it in public, but it's a fact. There is no growth, unemployment is rampant and civil unrest . . . Well you follow the news.'

Sir Hugh sensed that he should weigh in. 'Large scale immigration and economic stagnation are often a toxic mix,' he offered. 'And plummeting living standards lead to increased crime rates. These are very difficult times.'

'How did we get here?'

Sir Hugh wasn't sure if the question was rhetorical or not, but decided to respond.

'In economical terms, it was always unsustainable to have less and less industry while the public and service sectors expanded. Unless living standards were allowed to deteriorate of course, but that was politically unacceptable.'

The King understood. 'That's the great weakness of our democracy,' he said. 'Very few politicians have the courage to face their voters on platforms that involve read sacrifice and hardship. And those who do aren't elected. When a democratic society deteriorates, the populists and extremists benefit.'

'You are thinking of the L&O Movement, Sir?'

It was obvious than the King was acutely aware of the political crisis that Sir Hugh knew only too well. Eroding buying power, soaring unemployment, crime, terrorism and ethnic strife had reduced support for the traditional political parties to a point where only feeble broad coalition governments could be formed on a parliamentary basis. Such ineffective governments left the field wide open for extreme opposition parties. These normally cancelled each other out because they fought against each other for the same dissatisfied voters, but that had suddenly changed.

In amazingly short time – less than two years – most of the anti-establishment parties in Europe had formed an unofficial, but highly effective umbrella organisation - the Law & Order movement. In the UK, the populist opposition had now largely merged into a newly formed party called the Law and Order National Alliance, or LONA for short. However, bloggers and many journalists soon started referring to this home-grown version of L&O as *the Longbows*, due to the party's chosen symbol – a longbow of the kind used by English archers to defeat the French army at Agincourt in 1415.

'The PM has privately told me that he expects the coalition to break down in the next couple of weeks. If that happens he'll have to ask me to dissolve Parliament.'

'And LONA would do well in a snap election.'

The King sighed. 'They would do more than well, Sir Hugh. Based on my information, they'd get an overall majority in Parliament and Neil Nelson would be the next Prime Minister! The end of British democracy.'

'Hitler didn't even have a majority when he took control of Germany in 1933,' the older man observed. 'It was enough that the Nazis became the largest party in the Reichstag.'

'Exactly. I can't let it happen, Sir Hugh!' The King spoke calmly but with great determination in his voice.

'What will you do?'

'I first thought I might speak out as head of state. Strongly reject LONA and the *so-called* Law & Order movement. Announce that I refuse to dissolve Parliament. That would force a public showdown. I know it would break with political tradition and constitutional practise, but considering what's at stake I'd risk it. Except...'

He paused and seemed unable to find the right words to continue. Sir Hugh cleared his throat tactfully. 'Your Majesty?'

'The Met's Protection Command has let me know that should the monarchy be drawn into crisis during the prevailing political climate, they wouldn't be able to keep me or my family safe.'

'I find that statement bordering on treason, Sir!'

'Of course it is. But there's more. Apparently LONA has several contingency plans for how to get rid of me if I become a problem. A *spontaneous* riot led by armed agitators escalating into the storming of Buckingham Palace. A *terrorist* strike during a royal function or aimed at my helicopter.'

He reached across and handed Sir Hugh a data card. 'This is a copy of material given to me by the sole senior person at MI5 of whose loyalty I'm still certain. I'm hoping that by sharing it with you, I'm giving you what you need. You have to be aware what's going on in and behind LONA so you can take – well, action.'

His expression lingered somewhere between hope and doubt. Sir Hugh understood him completely.

'Sir, rest assured that the old man you see before you is not the sharp end of Operation Metcalfe. I'm merely the custodian of a secret weapon, which may now be unleashed if Your Majesty gives the order.'

'Tell me more, please' said the King.

7. LONDON

As a veteran of countless intelligence briefings, Sir Hugh knew how to present complex information succinctly.

'In the 80's I worked a great deal with MI5 in Northern Ireland,' he began. 'Many operations required close coordination between undercover activities and military deployment.'

'I've heard a lot about what went on in those days,' the King interjected. 'There must have been some hard choices.'

'Indeed Sir. There were times when we threw away the rulebook. As in this case. There were many strong personalities in the PIRA, and sometimes they clashed with the leadership. MI5 were tracking an exceptionally dangerous terrorist – I'll leave his name unmentioned – but he kept eluding them. So they used an infiltrator to spread the word that the man was in fact an informant. It seemed that PIRA bought the story, and we learnt that they were sending a team to take him out. At the last minute however, they called the attack off. Our infiltrator disappeared and was never found again. However, by following the hit team we were able to locate our target.'

The King shifted in his seat. 'I guess arresting him wasn't on the agenda,' he suggested. Sir Hugh met his glance. 'No Sir, it wasn't. Instead we made it look like PIRA had gone through with the liquidation. Or that some other faction had stepped in. We deliberately didn't make it clean and professional. The location was a remote farmhouse, so our squad opened up with every automatic weapon they had, then threw in enough grenades to obliterate everything inside.'

'How many were killed?'

'Our target had two comrades with him, plus his girlfriend and – this came as a total surprise – their two year old son.' Seeing the King's shock, Sir Hugh quickly continued. 'Incredibly, the boy survived unhurt. He had taken cover inside the stone fireplace, and we didn't find him until we shifted through the rubble. He was covered in soot, but otherwise barely scratched.'

'What happened to him?'

'He had to disappear, so we quickly invented a new identify for him and arranged for him to be adopted by an inspector in the RUC, a man called Clifford. Inspector Clifford was an RUC legend, and so hated by the PIRA that we were looking to pull him out anyway. He and his wife left the UK and never returned."

'Where is this going, Sir Hugh?' The King frowned and looked ill at ease.

'We discovered that the boy hadn't survived by chance. He had, and still has of course, extraordinary gifts. Even as a two-year old, he spoke clearly and had a large vocabulary. He explained to us that he had seen what was happening and quickly hidden in the only safe place available.'

'He explained? But he must have been in shock!'

'That's what first made me realise that he was exceptional, Sir. He was a bit shaken by the explosions, but otherwise completely calm and collected.'

'Not crying for his parents? That's unbelievable!'

'I thought so at the time, yes. I remember prodding him about them, and he just looked up at me and said *People die in war.*'

'So *he* is in fact the weapon you mentioned?'

'Yes, indeed. His other talents include phenomenal eye-to-hand coordination, near-eidetic memory and practical intelligence of the highest order. He's been trained in secret by intelligence and military experts, and confidentially tutored in computer science, physics, chemistry, engineering, history, philosophy and literature. Plus he speaks at least ten languages.'

'Where exactly is he?'

'The Cliffords were re-settled in Canada, but the boy never got on with his stepparents. When he was fourteen, he disappeared and we thought we'd lost him until he made contact himself two years later. From Bhutan! He's still there, in a remote part of that remote country. Completely off the radar, but with electricity and satellite connected broadband.'

'But by now this Mr Clifford must be in his forties!'

Sir Hugh nodded. 'Thirty-eight in fact. But his name isn't Clifford. When we constructed his new identity, we used the name of an orphaned Northern Irish boy who'd died in an accident. My man's official name is Sean Brendan Coyle, but no one calls him by his first names.'

'Am I right to say that *Coyle* is a sort of sleeper agent, and you're his handler?'

'Sleepers are usually embedded under cover in hostile territory, but essentially yes. Coyle was extensively trained as I explained, but he's never become operational.'

'Who authorised it all? And how is he being paid?'

'At the time, the priority was hushing up the operation that killed his parents. I took what I'd discovered about the boy to friends in MI5 and it was agreed that Clifford's relocation package would be made extra generous.'

'Operational control? His training?'

'We set up a small committee, of which I'm the only surviving member. I was always the sole handler, and I engaged the, shall we say, *mentors* on a very strict need-to-know basis. None of them fully understood what we were training Coyle to be.'

'What *did* you turn him into?' asked the King, and Sir Hugh considered his words carefully before replying.

Finally he spoke. 'An un-stoppable assassin.'

8. BHUTAN

In the basement computer room of his modest looking house, which despite its humble appearance was built with security in mind, Coyle – aka Pan – ran a decryption programme that turned the latest message from Sir Hugh into clear text. As he read it he nodded thoughtfully while reflecting on how good the timing was.

His return from the border region had been uneventful. The sight of him riding his motorbike was commonplace to the villagers, and it was unlikely that anyone noticed that he had been gone for quite a while.

He had taken great care to remove all traces of the ambush. The bodies of Chenwei and Gao lay in a ravine, where anything but an extensive search by hundreds of police or soldiers would fail to find them. Unfortunately, the two would be missed by their masters, and even without proof of foul play the fact that the pair had disappeared during a mission to feel him out would arouse suspicion. More than likely another mission would be authorised – probably one less subtle in nature. If they already suspected that the reclusive westerner was some kind of clandestine operative, the loss of two agents would make them determined to find out more. This might be an excellent time to get out of town.

We should meet Oct 9 in Paris to discuss a project back home. Can you be at the café at noon? Better pack a full bag.

Unless he was very much mistaken – and he rarely was – after over twenty years of preparation and waiting, he was finally being called into active duty. He sent a brief line agreeing to the rendezvous, and then began the meticulous process of cleaning house. It meant making sure that no pertinent information about him or his associates could be discovered in his absence. He had no idea for how long he would be away, or even if he would return at all. Nor did he really care.

9. HAMPSHIRE

The leader of LONA was not a tall man, but he was broad shouldered and had a way of leaning into you that most people found intimidating. Certainly Bill Utley felt unsure in his presence, and struggled to get his points across.

'But it could backfire,' he argued more weakly that he should have. 'Neil, you have the voters behind you already, you don't *need* another big terror event.'

Nelson looked at him with a mixture of amusement and contempt. 'How can we sell Law & Order is we don't have enough lawlessness and disorder!' He turned to the third man in the room. 'You're with me on this, Barry?'

Barry Vickerton allowed his enormous frame to sink into a leather chair before responding to his boss. 'It's tough for Bill. He has to spend time with those crazy bastards to keep them on side. I just keep the money coming.'

Nelson heaved himself up on his antique mahogany desk to that his legs dangled above the floor. 'That's not what I asked. Do you agree with me, or don't you?'

Vickerton pushed his right thumb and forefinger deep into his pudgy chins in a gesture of contemplation. 'As a matter of fact, I agree with both of you,' he said smoothly. 'A high profile terrorist strike could be useful, but only once the coalition has broken down and an early general election been called. Otherwise we risk bringing the Government parties together again. They might be inspired to show a front of *unity in the face of terror*, or some crap like that.'

Utley pounced weasel-like on the opportunity to divert the subject. 'What's our best guess on election timing?'

The party leader reached out and pressed an intercom button. 'Have Rita and Bonnie pop in,' he said to the machine. Turning to his two associates, 'They need to be in on this.'

Rita Ridgewood arrived first. LONA's Head of Security and Intelligence cut a tall and striking looking figure in a dark blue business suit. Her raven black hair was severely tied back, giving her an air of overstated but undeniable authority.

Moments later she was followed by shorter, blonder and shapelier Bonnie Stevens, her sharp political skills cunningly hidden behind her secretary-of-your-dreams looks.

Nelson wasted no time on pleasantries. 'Bonnie, when will the limp-dick in Number Ten run out of options? What's your latest take?'

The party's Chief Whip took the time to drape herself across a leather chesterfield before answering. 'The RTP holds the key, now that the Scots and the Welsh have ruled themselves out. If Brian pulls his support, the coalition's finished.'

'Great, but I don't like the RTP's popularity getting a boost,' said Nelson. 'It might just make it necessary to take them into *our* cabinet.'

'I'm not sure that wouldn't be a good thing,' Bonnie countered. 'Then it wouldn't look like a pure LONA government.'

'And we own them anyway,' Vickerton pointed out. 'Hell, we created them!'

Nelson was not entirely convinced. 'There are too many sincere idiots in the RTP. They'd be a problem once we actually start to govern and they realise that our idea of law and order is just a bit different from theirs.'

'Nothing we couldn't take care of,' Rita Ridgewood stated with a thin smile. She looked over at Bonnie, who nodded but looked less convinced.

'We'd have to be careful to keep up the image of a united cabinet,' she said.

Nelson made his decision. 'Too risky,' he declared. 'We use the RTP to bring about the election, but once that's in the bag it'll be pistols at dawn as far as we're concerned. Are we clear on that everybody?'

He looked around the room and received the acquiescence he had expected. Turning to Bonnie again, he gave an order. 'Make Brian Atkins understand that if he can't pull his party out of the Government within one week, we'll stop the money flow. See how far they get without L&O funding!'

'I'll see that he get's the message,' she promised in a tone a little too neutral for the leader's liking.

'And make sure you keep Bill in the picture,' added Nelson. 'In case he needs to give old Brian a bit of special *inducement*.'

Bonnie saw Bill Utley's sly face suddenly become alert. 'Just let me know what you need, love,' he said in her direction but more for Nelson's benefit than hers.

'Great, that's settled then,' said the Great Man. 'Anything else we need to discuss while we're all here?' As he spoke, it struck him that the only one of his inner circle missing that Saturday morning was Steve Henderson, LONA's public relations expert and keeper of their valuable connections to other Law & Order parties in Europe. But at the moment he was away in Brussels of course.

Rita Ridgewood responded to his opening. 'Remember how I've been doing risk analysis with our *friends* in the intelligence services and the police?' Nods all around.

'Something come up?' Nelson inquired.

'I've been running down all unexplained operations or agents. Most are a waste of time of course. Usually a bureaucratic error of some kind. But we want to know if there are assets out there than could be a threat to us.'

'And you found something?' Nelson guessed.

'Something very hush-hush was funded from 1987 to 2009. The payments were supposed to be untraceable, but then nothing is ever completely hidden from the accountants. Our people found the trail.'

'But that's a long time ago,' observed Nelson. 'What makes you think it matters today?'

'There was a rumour. The kind you find in Whitehall about anything that's *really* secret. Well, first of all it seems this project was managed between some senior career officers and unnamed *pillars of society*. The service heads were kept in the dark, and so were the governments of the time.'

'Unusual, to say the least! But you said there's more?' Nelson's interest was evident.

'Yes, according to my latest information, when the payments ended it seems someone else took up the slack and continued to fund the project out of his own pocket.'

'An individual? Who'd do that?'

'Would you believe Henry Elliott?'

'You mean *The* Henry Elliott of football and construction and logistics and fuck knows what else? What's in it for him?'

'Let's connect the dots as I see them,' replied Rita with thoughtful calm. 'Henry Elliott is a household name, and amongst the twenty or thirty wealthiest individuals in the country, but he's never endorsed a political party. He's turned down knighthoods, OBE's, honorary doctorates – you name it. Yet he's into charities in a big way, and he's taken an obscure old football club all the way to the highest division and two FA Cup finals.'

'So?' Bonnie voiced her bewilderment.

'Say old Elliott is a blue-eyed humanitarian idealist, and say there was an intelligence operation designed to be a safeguard against political takeovers or coups. Say this operation lost it's funding, and going to the government wasn't an option.'

Bonnie smiled at her. 'Henry Elliott would be the ideal person to contact. Can you prove it?'

'Not in a legal sense, but enough for us. That's why I've already acted on it.'

'What does that mean?' snapped Nelson. He was getting irritated at not seeing the full picture.

'The money trail ends in an interesting place,' Rita pressed on. 'It so happens that the rumours about the *operation* mentioned the same rather exotic location – Bhutan.'

'What the hell is that?' exclaimed Nelson. 'An island in the fucking Pacific?'

'Bhutan borders India and Tibet – which is of course part of China,' Bonnie informed him. 'Small independent nation with lots of mountains to hide in.'

Rita continued. 'Thank you Bonnie. Unfortunately none of our domestic sources knew of any asset there that would fit the picture. So I passed the information to Nagelmann. He asked the Chinese for help, and after some poking around – well, they came up with an intriguing individual. Apparently British, living since many years – no one knows exactly how long – in a remote village up north near the Chinese border. He's well known to the local monastery, where he gives martial arts lessons.'

'Interesting, but hardly conclusive,' said Nelson, but Rita barely missed a beat.

'That's why we asked the Chinese to find out more, and they did. They sent in two undercover agents to take a good look at this martial arts guy and get enough to positively identify him. Finger prints, DNA, a photo or two.'

'And?' Nelson leaned forward in a pose of anticipation.

'The agents never returned, Neil. They vanished completely.'

After a couple of seconds, Nelson broke the silence. 'Maybe we need to have a word with Henry Elliott,' he said.

10. PARIS

The café was across from Gare Saint-Lazare, and part of a long list of pre-agreed rendezvous points that Sir Hugh had suggested and Coyle duly memorised in the early years of their unusual association. Now the intelligence veteran sipped a super-strong double espresso at a corner table while he waited for his protégé to appear. Looking out of the window, he sighed at the dismal weather. In principle, Paris could be at its most beautiful in October, the changing leaves enhancing the city's many parks and boulevards with their symphony of golden and red hues. Unfortunately, it didn't work on a wet and windy day like this.

'Hello Uncle,' said a familiar voice, and he turned around to see Coyle standing there. They hadn't met for over eight years, but aside from some deepening lines around the eyes, Coyle looked the same. His lean frame and erect posture tended to make him taller than he actually was. But he moved with the graceful smoothness of a much smaller man. And it was impossible to guess at the remarkable strength contained in his body.

'Thanks for coming. You're punctual as always.' Sir Hugh wished he had expressed himself with more warmth, but Coyle somehow didn't invite emotions. He lowered himself into the lacquered wicker chair offered.

'Present for you,' he said as he pushed a small aluminium briefcase towards his host's feet. 'Or rather for my sponsor. Please give him my best regards and thank him for the loan.'

'The loan? What do you mean?'

Coyle smiled. 'I know Mr E provided the funds with no strings attached, but I always chose to think of it as a loan to be repaid.'

'Coyle, for heaven's sake, how did you know who it was? I never. . .'

'Told me who he was or how you persuaded him. Sure, but it wasn't a hard thing for me to discover. I've had certain *training* as you'll recall, Uncle.'

'So what's in the briefcase?' asked a deflated Sir Hugh.

'Bearer bonds, diamonds and some platinum bars. Total value about twice what our benefactor paid me over the years. I thought he might like having a secret liquidity reserve in these troubled times.'

'But how on earth did you manage to get this amount of money? It must be over two million!'

'I rounded it up to three, actually. Well, I've been at it for some time. My activities have been self-financing for the last eight years, but since the subsidies kept coming I thought I might as well invest them wisely. Once you have a decent start capital, making it grow isn't that hard really. At least not in my part of the world.'

As a white-aproned waiter glided over, Coyle ordered a glass of Badoit mineral water and Sir Hugh opted for another espresso. When the waiter left them, the older man went on the offensive.

'You really mean to tell me that you speculated with the money given for your livelihood and operational expenses! That's totally unacceptable!'

Coyle's calm demeanour remained unruffled. 'Unacceptable in what sense, Uncle? Legally? I don't think so, since we're sort of *above* the law here anyway. Ethically? Isn't my established mission to remain available and fully primed should a crisis requiring my services occur? Once you switched from *institutional* to private funding, I knew I had to take precautions in case the money dried up altogether one day. What I've done is *secure* my operational availability. That has to be entirely in the spirit of our original compact!'

The civil servant in Sir Hugh was suddenly at odds with the pragmatic intelligence officer. In the end, the latter came out on top.

'So you're in no need of further funding? And you're a hundred percent operations ready?'

'Yes on both accounts, Uncle. What do you say we press on?'

'All right then, Coyle. I need you to. . .' he hesitated a moment looking for the right word. This left him open to an interruption.

'Save British democracy. Yes, that much is obvious.'

Sir Hugh looked stunned. 'How could you possibly guess that?'

'I make it my business to know what goes on in the world, especially back home. What else could have brought you to this point after so many years of – *idle preparedness*?'

Sir Hugh drained the last dregs of his espresso before speaking only slightly louder than a whisper. 'I need you to take out the leadership of LONA,' he said.

'Says who?' Coyle asked with a hint of disapproval.

'I met with the King. The authority for the mission ultimately comes from him.'

'Did the King tell you to have Neil Nelson and his bunch eliminated? No, I didn't think so,' he added seeing Sir Hugh's shocked expression. 'I bet he wants you, meaning me of course, to save the nation from being taken over by Law & Order Fascists.'

'The LONA Longbows *are* L&O Fascists!'

'But the solution isn't to kill off the leadership. It may at some point be *part* of the solution, but it's not the main item on the menu.'

'Then how do you see it?'

Coyle spotted the waiter approaching with their order, and held off commenting until they had been served and the man was out of hearing range.

'My take is this,' he began. 'The three traditional main parties are now so weak that they can only govern in a Labour led coalition that also includes two of the, shall we call them *protest* parties, Voice of Islam and the Rightful Tory Party. Now it seems the Twits have had enough and will bring down the Government.'

When Brian Atkins led his group of thirty-two disgruntled Conservative backbenchers out of the party fold and formed the RTP, he failed to anticipate that the initials lent themselves to subversion by pundits and political opponents. Almost immediately, the Rightful Tory Party became known as the Righteous Twits Party, or just the Twits.

'The PM is an idealist, and with the deteriorating situation in the country everyone is rushing to distance themselves from him,' explained Sir Hugh somewhat superfluously.

'The Twits don't want to be part of a government that in their opinion does nothing, which means an early election and most probably a working majority for LONA. You want me to intervene so that doesn't happen.'

'Absolutely!'

'But *how* I do it is up to me. I won't be micromanaged by you or anyone else. So let's forget the Assassin job title and take as read that I possess broader skills.'

Sir Hugh looked started for a second. Then he seemed almost embarrassed.

'Look Coyle, I think I understand. All these years of training and nothing else! I mean, you never did a mission and never killed anyone of course. Now I'm suddenly asking you to step in at the sharp end. To be honest with you, I wouldn't have wanted to go this route, but when the King contacted me I felt I had to try.'

Coyle had to laugh. With an effort, he composed himself and smiled gently at his old mentor. '*You* may not have sent me on any missions, but I've completed plenty. Nineteen, to be precise. I took some initiative, you see. It seemed a waste of resources to only study and train.'

'You mean you've been working as a hitman? That's outrageous! But it explains the money.'

Coyle shook his head sadly. 'No I haven't been killing people for money,' he stated. 'But I have in fact disposed of several so called hitmen, who were all in one way or another working against British interests. It came with the territory?'

'What damned territory, Coyle?'

'About seventeen year ago I decided that remaining purely theoretical wasn't an option if I wanted to become the sort of operative you told me to be. So I started freelancing in support of British military – Special Forces mostly – operations in Iraq and Afghanistan. Later on some other countries as well, as you can imagine. All in all it was very educational, and I liked that fact that I was helping out our chaps.'

'How exactly?'

'When I'd came across an operation that looked like it might turn into a clusterfuck as the squaddies say, I'd position myself where I could provide fire support if needed. And yes Uncle, it was usually needed.'

'Nobody knew you were there?"

'The ones I did battle with got a pretty good idea, but of course they didn't know I wasn't British Army in the strict sense.'

'How many did you kill?'

'Not sure. Sometimes I used explosives, and they make counting difficult. Say two to three hundred. I *am* rather good at it, but then you always knew I would be.'

11. LONDON

The MI5 man's first impression of Henry Elliott was not what he had expected. The tycoon looked like a lorry driver forced to wear an expensive suit. Bulging at the midriff, balding on top. Only the eyes revealed the entrepreneur's true nature. They were steady, confident and utterly intelligent.

'So how can I be of service to MI5, Mr Carpenter?' he asked in his distinctive baritone.

They were seated in Elliott's corner office in the City, overlooking the river as it wound its way towards Greenwich and ultimately the North Sea. Dennis Carpenter looked every inch the archetypical senior official. Not a hair out of place. His patrician ancestry and prestigious education were written all over him, along with countless hours at the squash and racquet club. He had an appointment arranged by Thames House and wasn't kept waiting on arrival.

'Oh it's fairly routine, Sir. We're trying to fill in some blanks.' As he spoke, he knew from something in Elliott's eyes that he had made a mistake. Personal visits from MI5 officers of his seniority level were never *routine*.

'Go on then. I'll tell you what I can.'

'We're looking into old off-the-books operations across the intelligence services. The idea is to ensure that we know what became of our assets, and of course the money.'

'I see. A lot of off-the-books stuff was there?'

'Oh, more than people think. Usually for very good reasons. But after a while, the need for total secrecy may no longer be there, and we want to create a record of what happened.'

Elliott's face revealed nothing at all. 'I'm afraid you have me at a disadvantage, Mr Carpenter', he said. 'You wouldn't be here if you didn't think I have something to tell you, but I can't for the life of me think what that might be. I've never had anything to do with the intelligence services.'

Carpenter decided to go on the offensive. 'But since 2009 you've been funding *Mountainside Conscience*, an environmental research group in Bhutan, through a freight-forwarding company you own in India. A company you actually acquired in 2009. One might speculate as to why you bought Raginder Pesh Logistics, since they never seem to have made any profit.'

'Then please speculate.'

'I'd say it's likely that you bought Raginder Pesh as a vehicle to fund whatever people were posing as environmentalists in Bhutan. We checked it out, and the group doesn't exist. It never did.'

'They must have existed, if we're supporting them.'

Carpenter allowed himself a thin smile of satisfaction as he moved in for the kill. 'No Mr Elliott, it was always just a front for an intelligence operative under very deep cover. An agent to be called into action only if very specific conditions were met.'

He was pleased to see the businessman nod his head thoughtfully.

'Yes, that would make sense,' Elliott admitted. 'Funding an agent in the way you described would be clever, but then it could be about almost anything. Even ordinary embezzlement by my local management. I'll certainly look into it.'

The MI5 man refused to be diverted. 'Believe me Sir, we *know* there's an undercover agent behind Mountainside Conscience and that you've been funding him.'

Elliott seemed unperturbed. 'Then why are you *really* here?'

Carpenter played his last card. 'To be absolutely honest, and off the record, I came to warn you. The agent has gone rogue. And we believe he's covering his tracks by killing anyone connecting him with his past. That would put you high on his list!'

Suddenly Elliott's substantial frame roared with laughter. He gathered himself before speaking. 'Well, thank you for the warning, Mr Carpenter. I guess I'd be worried if I really knew this mysterious agent of yours. As it is, even if this Bhutan outfit turns out to be as bogus as you claim, I had no idea that my money was being misused.'

'That won't necessarily stop him coming after you, Sir.'

Elliott got up from his chair to signal that the meeting was coming to an end.

'As I'm sure you know, people in my position get a lot of threats,' he said, extending his hand to the MI5 man. 'We throw away a two goal lead against Arsenal and before you know it there's a mob throwing Molotov cocktails at my front door. I assure you, I've got myself more than enough security to protect me from your mountain man from Bhutan. If he exists, which I quite frankly doubt.'

Dennis Carpenter left the building feeling that his mission had been a waste of time. *Well maybe not.* Henry Elliott hadn't asked for the agent's name. It would have been embarrassing if he had, since Carpenter didn't know the name either, but by not asking, the famous businessman had more or less confirmed that he was *aware* of the mysterious agent.

12. GWENT

DS Joanne Stack steered her dented and dated Golf though a worsening drizzle up a pothole riddled Welsh country lane. Daylight was rapidly fading, and she briefly considered turning back. Looking at her reflection in the side window, she cringed. Not exactly vain, though most men found her attractive, she took pride in her appearance, and seeing her normally lustrous blond hair with its natural curl falling limp and greasy and crying out for a wash made her sigh. She knew that a look in a proper mirror would reveal lines on her face that weren't truly there yet, but hinted at what she would look like if she didn't start working less and sleeping more.

It would be an exhausting drive back to Cardiff after she had done her devoted daughter bit for her dad, and he wasn't even expecting her for heaven's sake!

Well, she was almost there really. And she could do with a break after what had been a thoroughly crap day. Sent out by DCI Wainwright to interview a potential witness in a suspected vehicular homicide case, she had wasted three hours with a terrified middle-aged woman, whom someone had intimidated so severely that she could hardly string a sentence together, let alone provide cohesive testimony. When it occurred to Joanne that she was within an extra hour's drive from her retired soldier dad's remote old farmhouse, it seemed an opportunity to redeem both the wasted day and herself as the elusive only child of a widowed man living alone.

Not that former SAS Staff Sergeant Mike Stack was either needy or vulnerable, but he was seventy-four years old and despite his claims to the contrary she sensed that he was quite lonely now that her mother was no longer alive.

The final track leading to Mike Stack's house was over a mile long and seriously bumpy. Mindful of her not-too-healthy muffler and exhaust, she shifted down and crawled the last bit. As she reached the yard, she was surprised to see a white Ford van parked next to her dad's truly ancient Land Rover.

It was quite dark by now. She stepped out of the car and noticed that there was only a faint grow of light from inside the house. Looking at the old cowshed, she saw that the main door was slightly ajar, and the inside looked fully lit up.

She was debating with herself which building to approach first when she heard the shot. A single powerful crack that she immediately identified as a weapon being fired. And it came from inside the shed.

Fleetingly grateful that the new CID regulations required her to be armed at all times, she pulled out her compact but powerful Glock 26 pistol and ran to the door. The opening was too small to pass though, so she pushed against the frame hoping that the hinges wouldn't squeak. They didn't, and she stepped inside and saw the trap door in the floor. It was open and she could see steps leading down into a cellar she had no idea existed.

Down on her hands and knees, she made her way to the edge of the trap door. Leaning forward and fighting hard to control her breathing, she peered into the cellar.

Relief flowed through her like delayed pain when she saw her dad standing – very much alive – next to a workbench. His rugged but still handsome face beamed with enthusiasm and seemed ten years younger. The space in front of him was covered in weapons parts and the tools of an experienced gunsmith. He was removing a set of ear protectors from his head.

'Dad, what the hell's going on here?' she shouted as she hauled herself down the steps. He turned around with a sheepish look in his eyes, like a boy caught smoking.

Then, out of nowhere, a fist of steel grabbed her right hand that still held the gun, and before she could react, she had stumbled a few steps forward into the middle of the room. Spinning around, she found herself staring into the face of a man with piercing blue eyes that seemed completely at odds with his jet-black hair. He was handsome in a severe way, with a lean and thoughtful face, and he held her Glock in his left hand. Not in the manner of a weapon, but as an object to keep safe.

'Your daughter, the detective?' he observed rather than asked.

Her dad had recovered his composure by now. 'I didn't know she was coming!' he stated the obvious.

It was time for her to take the initiative. 'DS Joanne Stack. Can I have my weapon back please?' She kept her voice steady and professional.

'Perhaps,' he said evenly, but showed no sign of handing her the pistol. 'I'm Coyle. Mike, can I ask you to explain about me?'

Still embarrassed at having his secret cave exposed, the former Staff Sergeant spoke quietly. 'He's a secret operative. Deep cover. I've kept his arsenal in case...'

'I'd need it one day,' Coyle competed his sentence. 'That day happens to be now. We were just fine tuning the Sako TRG-42 over there, to be on the safe side.'

Joanne groaned when she saw what was clearly a military issue sniper rifle. 'You can't have weapons like that!' she protested. 'Dad, you know it's totally illegal.'

Coyle said, 'They're not his guns, Joanne. They're mine. And I have them because I need them.'

His calm infuriated her. 'Then I have to take you in.'

'You're arresting me?'

'I could. You forcefully disarmed a police officer. My weapon please!' He held out her hand towards him.

'I don't think you identified yourself as a police officer, so that point is probably mute, but you're right about my weapons. Strictly speaking they're certainly illegal. But then I'm not really operating within the law.'

Seeing that she was still demanding her Glock back, he smiled and for a moment came over as quite charming.

'Okay, I'll make a deal with you. I'll let you take me in for questioning or whatever, but first you have to shoot me.'

Before she could react he had moved in on her and put his right arm around her shoulders. Gently, but with irresistible momentum he moved her across the room to where there was a rectangular hole in the wall. Taking the Glock by the front end, he thrust the butt into her hand, but kept hold of it so that his left hand covered the muzzle.

'Now the gun is pointing into the sandbag we just used for live firing. Keep it there so we don't get a nasty ricochet, and fire through my hand. If you do, I'll be your prisoner.'

'You're mad!'

'No, I'm just showing you that I'm in a serious line of business. You either pull the trigger, or forget what you've seen here.'

Coyle's right arm still held her in a vicelike grip, but she felt the gun against the palm of her hand and her forefinger connected with the trigger. A slight pull and a 9mm bullet would smash through his left hand. 'Dad?' she appealed with a side glace.

'Do what you have to do, love,' he responded.

She felt a surge of anger at both men, but mostly at the smug stranger. Without further hesitation she took a sharp breath and pulled the trigger.

13. GWENT

They were sitting in Mike Stack's main room, which was a cheerfully functional mix of kitchen, library and noncom mess. Joanne stared at Coyle.

'What *are* you?' she wondered out loud, and wished she could stop shaking. Knowing you're in a state of mild shock was one thing, overcoming it was another.

'As a very young boy I came to the attention of some senior figures in British Intelligence. They discovered I had certain special talents, and decided to help me develop them to their fullest potential.'

Special indeed! Joanne relived the moment she fired her gun only to find that he had shifted his hand with inexplicable speed from the muzzle in time avoid the bullet, then brought it down to effortlessly relieve her of the weapon while the recoil still vibrated up her arm. *Impossible!*

'Over time, they decided to keep me hidden away in a far away location as their secret weapon of last resort. I was to be used only in an extreme emergency. You dad very kindly taught me how to make the most of firearms. He was my favourite tutor.'

'Thank you Coyle! That's nice of you to say,' Stack interjected. Towards his daughter he said, 'I've never seen anyone shoot like this fellow. He can acquire a target, aim and fire in less time than, well, *possible* really. And he never seems to miss!'

Joanne said, 'I believe you! But what's the great emergency?'

Coyle smiled drily. 'You really have to ask that, doing what you do for a living! How are things at work these days? Enough crime to keep you busy?'

'Crime's out of control, everyone knows that!' Joanne snapped at him.

'Ever asked yourself why that is?'

'Bad economy, no jobs, no prospects, everything getting expensive, lots of people are desperate.'

Coyle waved his hand dismissively. 'Doesn't it seem to you that a lot of what you'd normally call random violent crime has actually become quite *organised?*'

'Well the gangs are behind most of it.'

'And who's behind the gangs?'

'What do you mean? They're gangs. They have leaders.'

'Okay, let's say they do. How many of these leaders have you seen arrested, convicted and sent to prison lately?'

Seeing hesitation in her eyes, he pushed on. 'Would it be wrong to say that most of the times you've gotten close to nailing a major gang leader, the investigation has either been interfered with or failed for unexpected reasons?'

'It happens,' she argued evasively.

'You bet it happens! And the reason is that a large number of senior police officers, and their superiors in the Home Office, are being paid off and controlled by LONA and the Law & Order Movement!'

'You can't possibly prove that!'

'Actually I can.' Coyle held up a small data card, which he proceeded to insert into the small computer in front of him.

'This is a copy of data given to me by the man who first discovered me and turned me into what I am today. He in turn got it from a top level source in MI5 through a *special conduit.*'

Despite her simmering anger and reluctance to give in to Coyle's persuasion, Joanne soon found herself absorbed by the secret report.

'As you can see, L&O have been funnelling enormous amounts into Neil Nelson's party. The Longbows then use the money to fund underworld activity as well as political terrorism. But worse still, to control vital individuals in the civil service, the armed forces and the intelligence services. Even many rival politicians are ultimately in LONA's pocket.'

'Where's all the money coming from?'

'I have a theory about that, but let's talk about it later. For now, do you agree that we're at war, so to speak?'

'How can so many people keep their mouths shut?'

'If you read on, you'll see that the Longbows have a squad of ruthless enforcers. Former Special Forces men, ex-MI6 operatives, even criminals. They crack down on anyone who steps out of line. If this works with criminals and terrorists, imagine how effective it is with politicians and civil servants!'

Joanne felt herself go pale. 'This report – who was it written for? Your *special conduit?*'

Coyle nodded. 'His Majesty our King,' he confirmed. 'He trusts me to save the nation. Will you help me, Joanne?'

'What do you need from me?'

Coyle held her glance for about a second. 'Can you ride a motorbike?' he asked.

14. GWENT

Coyle's phone buzzed gently. He looked at it in surprise, since the only person who had the number was the man who had given it to him in Paris, Sir Hugh Canderton. They had agreed to communicate in the next few days using pre-paid and unregistered phones. But the caller's ID was withheld.

He pressed reply the reply button and made a low grunt.

'I wanted to say thank you for the valuable briefcase,' a confident male voice said. 'Do you by any chance recognise my voice?'

'I do,' Coyle replied. 'You must have seen our Mutual Friend.'

'Yes we met earlier today. He filled me in on what's happening. Unfortunately someone else came to see me the other day. I thought you should know about it.'

Coyle didn't like where the conversation was going. 'About me?' he asked.

'He claimed to be MI5. Quite a big cheese judging by his card. The point is, he knew about the subsidies. I stonewalled him of course, and in the end he came out and said they knew you were an off-the-books operation and that you'd gone rogue. That you might even be coming for me.'

'Then it's a good thing our Mutual Friend set the record straight.'

'But it's a damn nuisance that they're aware of you.'

Coyle was processing the information and Henry Elliott gave a *hello* to see if they were still connected.

'Yeah, I'm still here. Look, could you do two things for me please?'

'I'll do my best.' Elliott's voice was still both warm and confident.

'You must have a picture or some video footage of the big cheese in question.'

'Yes, of course.'

'Could you email it to me, along with the information on his card? Use an email account that can't be associated with you.'

'I can do that. Where do I send it?'

Coyle rattled off an obscure address from memory. 'You'll also get am email from me,' he continued. 'But not from the address I mentioned. I'll send it to your main business email account.'

'I'll read it to you.'

'No need, I have it. The message will look like unbreakable code, but don't bother trying to decipher it. It's fake. The only legitimate content will be tomorrow's date and the time 17:15 hrs.'

'What happens then?'

'Have your driver drop you at the northeast corner of Berkeley Square. Then, with only one or two bodyguards in tow, pretend to head for a secret meeting somewhere in the area.'

'With you?'

'That's what I want them to think, yes. I'm betting on them monitoring your normal lines of communication. But what you actually do is walk around the block in a full circle once, then stroll around briskly anywhere you like in Piccadilly or Mayfair for thirty minutes. When the time's up, have your car pick you up again and take you home, or wherever you're actually going.'

'So you won't be there?'

'Oh I'll be there all right, but you won't see me. I'll be taking a good look at the opposing team.'

15. GWENT

Joanne had been absorbing every word.

'Do you really see me as part of all this?' she asked.

'Done much surveillance work?'

'As a matter of fact I have. But no, I don't ride motorbikes.'

'Pity. It would have been useful. I've got two of them in the van. Bought them in France, where I collected the van itself from a friend.'

Joanne grasped the idea. 'Surveillance cameras!' she exclaimed.

'Exactly. The whole country is full of them. But a helmeted driver on a motorbike is pretty anonymous. And it's the quickest way to move about if you know what you're doing.'

'What about number plate recognition?'

'It works both ways. The authorities can track you, but you can throw them off the scent by switching plates a lot. I'm not looking for permanent anonymity, just an operational time advantage.'

She realised that she was becoming caught up in his sense of purpose. 'There's not much time to get to London and set up an operation,' she said.

'I gave us just enough time,' he replied. 'Keep in mind that they won't know where Elliott will get out of his car, but we do. That means we don't need to do a lot of recce in advance. We'll spot them when they arrive, but they'll have no way of knowing that we're expecting them.'

'So what do we do now?'

'If you're onboard, I suggest we leave here early tomorrow morning in my van. You'll have to call your superiors and ask for a week's leave. Will that be a problem?'

Mike performed a contrived cough. 'My health is getting worse,' he said with a wink at his daughter.

'That'll do it,' she agreed. 'I'll call right away in fact.'

Coyle nodded. 'And when you're finished, remove the SIM card and battery from your phone and leave it behind inside your car. I have a spare phone you can use, but for close quarters communications we'll rely on digital battlefield radios. They're unobtrusive and secure because of their short range, unless there's someone close by with a very clever scanner.'

Joanne thought for a moment. 'Is there any way we could stop by at my flat in Cardiff?'

'Not really. Why?'

'I could pack several sets of clothes. And I've got a couple of wigs that I've used before when doing surveillance.'

Coyle only considered the idea for a moment. 'No, we go straight to London,' he decided. 'You'll have enough time to shop for those things when we get there. You'll be in the right area. Just buy all you need. It'll be on me, of course.'

'Right. Anything else?'

'No, just spend some quality time with your dad; then get some sleep. We leave at 6am.'

'What about you? What'll you be doing?'

'Preparations,' he said curtly and started working the computer keyboard.

'Aren't you exposing yourself by connecting to the web from here?' she protested.

'Not the way I do it,' he assured her, and seeing her doubtful expression, decided to enlighten her.

'Earlier today I placed a special kind of wireless router outside. It enables me to connect using a satellite. From anywhere in the world.'

'Your computer still leaves a trace!'

'Yes, but it's very well hidden behind lots of cut-outs and deceptions. Whoever takes the trouble, and more importantly, the *time* to break through everything will find that I'm part of a secure communications system connected to the National Security Agency of the United States.'

'But you're not NSA, right?'

'Of course not, but they make a fantastic cover. At least as long as they have no idea that I'm piggybacking on their satellites.'

16. LONDON

Dennis Carpenter was uncomfortable. First because he had overestimated the need for warm clothing, and moving quickly through the streets on foot made sweat run down his back. Second because he wasn't leading a team of his choice.

Had this been an MI5 operation, all his assets would have been thoroughly trained specialists in covert surveillance and threat interdiction, but as things were he had to work with men who were no doubt lethal enough, but operationally quite limited. And there was the nagging question of whether the Longbow enforcers would defer to him as field commander if they found themselves in a tight spot.

He tried to comfort himself with the reassuring thought that he had twelve serious professionals at his disposal against Elliott, his single bodyguard and the mysterious man from Bhutan – if and when he showed himself. The key would be to remain unspotted until they could identify the target. Once the man revealed himself, his fate would be sealed.

Operational communications were less than ideal, but so far working all right. Each man had a Bluetooth earpiece with microphone connected to a mobile phone, and the phones were linked to each other in a simple conference call. He kept getting brief reports from his agents as they rotated their positions to reduce the risk of detection.

It was twenty-six minutes since Elliott left his armoured Mercedes in Berkley Square and continued on foot. It had taken Carpenter's team only a couple of minutes to organise themselves after leaving their own vehicles, and at least one of them had never lost visual contact with the burly tycoon.

Carpenter was pushing his way along a busy Avery Row when a fellow pedestrian suddenly turned and hit him hard in the midriff. Gasping for breath, and in considerable pain, he felt himself dragged into a doorway.

The attacker's hands moved expertly all over him, removing his handgun, phone and the little taser he carried as backup protection. Then a piece of string was slipped over his head, and he felt something at the end of the string fall into the small of his back, under his coat.

'You know who I am,' said a steely, precise and utterly emotionless voice into his ear. 'I've just attached an explosive device to your neck. I'll detonate it by remote control if you put yourself outside my line of sight. Are we clear?'

The question was emphasized by a sharp stab at his left kidney, and he nodded reluctantly.

'Now stand up properly and talk to me like I'm an old acquaintance. If you don't play along I'll have to terminate you.'

With an effort the MI5 officer straightened himself and for the first time took a proper look at his attacker. The man was about his own height, around six two, and maybe slightly heavier in a muscled way. His face was partly obscured by the hood of a fashionable outdoor jacket and a peaked cap, but the visible part revealed a strong clean-shaven chin, a long straight nose, and a thin-lipped mouth set in unflappable determination. The deep brown eyes were cold and penetrating. Carpenter glanced down the street hoping to see his nearest operative.

'You're on your own,' Coyle informed him grimly. 'I took your backup guy out of play. Now this is what's going to happen. You'll walk up to Bond Street tube station and catch the Central Line towards Ealing. I'll be with you all the way, but not right next to you. If you speak to anybody or try anything else to attract attention, I'll blow your spine to pieces. Same if you escape, or we just *happen* to get separated. So it's very much in your interest to play by my rules. Don't even think about removing the device! It'd take you much longer than I need to press the little button in my pocket.'

Carpenter considered his only remaining option, throwing himself at his abductor while they were still standing close enough for hand-to-hand combat, but the man's easy confidence dissuaded him.

Instead, he tried speaking to him. 'What do you want from me?' It didn't come out right. Too weak and frightened.

Coyle gave a predatory smile. 'I want information. Don't worry, it'll be in both our interest. Now get going and don't attract attention to yourself by looking stressed and unhappy. Act normal. Surely they taught you how to act normal!'

'Where do we get off the tube?'

'Ah, now you're thinking properly. Notting Hill Gate.'

'And once we're out of the station?'

'I'll make sure you don't get lost.'

17. LONDON

Being a woman had its advantages, she thought as she saw her reflection in an Old Bond Street shop window. Two hours of *no-holds-barred* shopping at Harrods had provided her with an array of clothes and accessories, and she was putting them to good use. It had been Coyle's idea that she should buy a grey wig. Grey! Well, it worked. She suddenly looked middle age. As long as she remembered to curb her normally springy and athletic way of walking.

She wore black slacks under a half-length reversible jacket that had cost a bundle. Dark green on one side, a beige and blue pattern on the other. After ten minutes in pursuit of the men hunting Coyle, she slipped into a ladies' store, where she hid briefly between clothes racks and changed her appearance in seconds. Jacket reversed, the grey wig replaced with a dark auburn one, and no longer wearing fashion sunglasses, she emerged from the shop a different person.

Makeup helped as well of course. Unlike Coyle, whom she had observed applying small amounts to subtly alter his features – making them less distinct – she had the freedom to use as much colour as she wanted. Her normal light cheek and forehead freckles were now totally hidden, and she had given herself much more pronounced eyes and eyebrows. A chance encounter with a friend was highly unlikely, and she felt sure that no casual acquaintance would recognise her.

Picking out Dennis Carpenter from Henry Elliott's security video was easy. He started out with the confident swagger of a fit and powerful man in full control, but as Elliott led him through the busy shopping streets in an erratic manner, she saw frustration gradually creep into his demeanour. Even so, she had to admit that he was a very good-looking man.

The LONA thugs were harder to identify, and she couldn't afford to make a mistake. She finally settled on one, who just *couldn't* be anything else. Expensive but ill fitting suit. Heavy build, a face that looked vaguely east European, eyes hidden behind sunglasses. The man walked with the easy gait of a soldier or athlete, and he had an earpiece stuck to his head.

She told Coyle over the radio, and he confirmed that he too had spotted her man, and pegged him as part of Carpenter's squad.

'Stay with him and let's be lucky,' he told her. 'I'm about to knock out one of his colleagues, so be careful in case they start running all over the place.'

Not taking for granted that her target was entirely preoccupied with Elliott and the possibility of Coyle showing up; she hung back a bit and kept as many pedestrians as she dared between them. It turned out to be a prudent decision. The man suddenly turned and scanned the street behind him. He was clearly troubled by something.

Joanne looked at her watch and realised that this was when Elliott was supposed to end his walkabout and get back into his car. She saw the thug lift his hand to cover his mouth, as he spoke feverishly into the earpiece microphone.

They've lost Carpenter, she thought. *Coyle's done it!*

Now the team was leaderless and confused. Elliott was leaving the area without having made contact. What should they do? Carpenter had to make the call, but he wasn't talking to them.

A man of similar general appearance ran past her and up to his colleague. The two of them had a brief but agitated conversation before setting off together at a quick pace. Joanne followed, betting that the men were rattled enough not to notice her.

After a hectic few minutes, she saw them join another group at the corner of New Bond Street and Grosvenor Street. Judging by the gestures she observed, this was where Elliott had been picked up by his driver. A debate seemed to rage, and several more men joined the group. In the end, she briefly counted ten team members, before a large SUV pulled up and five of the men climbed in. About a minute later, another SUV appeared, and Joanne groaned inwardly. If they all drove off she would have no chance of tailing them.

Fortunately, two men were left on the sidewalk. They walked off at a brisk pace along Grosvenor Street, their body language conveying that they were, well, she thought *pissed off* described it rather well. Presumably they had heard about one of their group being ambushed.

She followed at what seemed a safe distance. The two turned left into South Audley Street, and a few blocks later right into Deanery Street. Having lost visual contact, she broke into a run and tore round the corner just in time to see her targets disappear through an inconspicuous door into a large building to the right.

She walked right past until she reached the corner of Park Lane. Looking at the front of the building, it all made sense. She tried the radio, but Coyle was out of range. Instead, she pulled out the phone he had given her and sent him a text message.

Two of them went into the staff entrance of the Dorchester Hotel.

18. LONDON

The self-catering apartment hotel was a short walk from Notting Hill Gate tube station. Coyle had booked in for a full week under the name John Morton, and collected the key while Joanne did her shopping. They weren't staying here of course. For their London base, he had selected a conventional business style hotel in Earls Court. There was parking for the van, and a constant flow of people to ensure that no one paid them much notice.

'First things first,' he said to the increasingly fidgety Carpenter after closing the door. 'Are you carrying any kind of homing device that could lead MI5 here? It's in your best interest to tell me. Believe me, you won't survive if there's even a hint of trouble.'

This was the first real test. Would Carpenter be rational or emotional?

'My phone,' he sighed after a brief hesitation. 'Even turned off, it has a tracker.'

Coyle was pleased. 'No problem then. I left it on the tube. Nothing else?'

'An embedded microchip. But it's only effective if someone with an active sensor is pinging this building or very close by.'

'Then we won't worry about that either. It'll be some time before your MI5 buddies start to wonder what's become of you. The Longbows are going berserk of course, but I don't think they're very good at this.'

He saw the mention of the Longbows register in Carpenter's mind. The man was tempted to say something, but changed his mind.

Coyle pressed on. 'Yes, of course I know about your freelance arrangement with Nelson and his cohorts. Now turn around and let me remove the cord from around your neck. No need for explosives now that we can sit down and have a civilised chat.'

Carpenter glanced at the offered upholstered chair. Then he made his move. It was to be expected. Coyle would have thought the man wet beyond belief if he hadn't given it a try. From his limited perspective it was the only real alternative to surrender.

The backhanded blow to Coyle's throat was well-disguised and hard enough to seal the fight right there. Had it connected.

Carpenter's brain didn't register Coyle's movement, but suddenly his world seemed turned on its head. He was lying flat on his face, his right arm held behind him in a way that caused excruciating pain.

Coyle spoke into his ear. 'Would you like to end it right here? Just nod your head if you'd like to be dead. It'll be my pleasure. If not, this is what's going to happen. We'll get up, brush ourselves off and forget this little episode. We'll have that nice chat I mentioned. You okay with that?'

Carpenter emitted a grunted *yes*, and Coyle pulled him to his feet. Then relieved him of the explosive bundle, which was actually a harmless fake. But Carpenter didn't know that. As he settled himself into the chair, the MI5 man recovered a measure of composure.

'I won't tell you anything,' he declared.

Coyle eyed him evenly. 'That's up to you of course, but I'm not sure non-cooperation is your best option.'

'Then what is, if I may ask?'

'Well, consider the facts. From what I've already said it's clear that I know you're a senior MI5 officer, and it doesn't scare me one bit. It's also clear that I know you're on the payroll of LONA. For some reason you and your Longbow pals decided to pick a fight with me and look how that turned out.'

'I don't know why they…'

'No of course you don't, you're just hired help. But that means you really only have four options and only one of them is good for you personally. So either I kill you, or

Nelson's goons kill you for being incompetent, or your MI5 masters deal with you for being a traitor, or...'

Coyle paused, knowing that this was the key moment. If Carpenter was a hardened professional, he would clam up. But if he was the weak corrupt man he appeared to be, he would break. He would go for option four, personal advantage.

'What's the fourth alternative?'

Coyle grinned like he had met a good friend at a party. 'You talk to me. Then you disappear. You must have plenty of dishonest money stashed away. Take it and run before they know what's happening. Get on a plane and don't come back.'

'But my family! I have a wife and two sons at Oxford!'

'So send them tickets. Whether they join you or not is up to them.'

Coyle observed the man resign himself to what he had to do.

'What do you want to know?' Carpenter sighed.

Coyle fixed him with a hard stare. 'First we're going to talk about your hit team today. LONA enforcers rather than MI5, I gather?'

A dejected nod. Coyle thought about the text message he had received from Joanne while on the tube train. It confirmed what he had been able to guess from the wallet of the man he had intercepted in the street before making his move on Carpenter. He'd knocked the guy out with a swift blow to the neck, dragged him behind an illegally parked delivery lorry and given his right knee a kick that would keep him out of action for weeks.

'I know they're working under the cover of hotel security. Makes sense, when you considering all the terror threats and street crime promoted by LONA. Most hotels must have been taking on extra security.'

'Yes. So?'

'There's got to be a company that organises these security men. Keeps them on file and contracts them out to hotels and other vulnerable establishments. But also passes them their orders for LONA missions. And that company is Hammersmith based Highgate Security Services, right?'

A vaguely defiant shrug. 'You seem to know everything already. You don't need me.'

'Oh, but I do Dennis! I need details. Lots of details! Lets start with who's in charge of Highgate, and who's their main contact at LONA?'

Much less hesitation. 'Grant Whitmore runs the show. He'd be taking his instructions mostly from Rita Ridgewood. Maybe Bill Utley as well.'

'Nelson himself?'

'No, he'd never expose himself. Everything's done through others. Nelson can't risk being compromised. He'll be the next Prime Minister.'

'Another very good reason for getting the hell out of the country. Now, you're going to describe in detail the layout of the Highgate headquarters, all the security protocols in place and all the weak spots as you see them. Your professional analysis, so to speak.'

'You're going to hit them there?'

'You bet I am! And I'll give you a very good incentive to help me succeed.'

The MI5 man started to sneer, but controlled himself. 'What incentive?'

'Before I leave, I'm going to put you to sleep with a special injection. Provided I'm back to revive you with an antidote within twenty-four hours, you'll wake up with no ill effects. But if I don't return, you'll pass into an irreversible coma. The best you can hope for is lingering on life support as a vegetable until your organs give out. So think sharply Dennis! This has got to work!'

19. LONDON

The dashboard digital clock read 20:17. It had been a long day for Joanne, but somehow she didn't feel tired. She had know Coyle for just over twenty-four hours, and in that time he had evaded a bullet, set up an ambush in the heart of Mayfair, knocked out a professional hitman and kidnapped a senior MI5 officer. Now she was watching him in the van's mirror as he approached from behind on one of the motorbikes, a super-fast Kawasaki road racer.

She had parked the van close enough to have a line of sight to the modern steel and glass cube that served as base for Highgate Security Services, yet far enough away not to attract attention or show up on security cameras. Her mission was, once again, to observe what happened and warn Coyle of any unexpected developments.

The Kawasaki swung confidently onto the pavement in front of the building's front door. Coyle strode up a couple of concrete steps and pressed a call button. After a while a bored male voice muttered something through a wall speaker, and a small red light indicated that a camera was active.

Coyle held up the package he was carrying.

'Delivery for Grant Whitmore,' he announced.

'The office is closed,' responded the speaker. 'You'll have to come back tomorrow.'

'Look mate, I'm not doing this again. It's not my job. I mean, this ain't a regular delivery. This Carpenter bloke gives me two hundred quid in cash to get the package here in twenty minutes. It's seems real urgent to me, but if you don't want it...'

The lock buzzed and Coyle pulled the door open by its brushed steel handle. Stepping inside and passing through another set of doors, he found himself in a black leather, glass and steel lobby. A heavy looking man in uniform emerged from a side door.

'You look like Fred,' Coyle observed. Confusion gave way to apprehension on the guard's face.

'How'd you know?' he blurted.

'Dennis Carpenter said the fat stupid one is called Fred. Seems you're so out of shape they can only use you for night duty. He also said you sit and watch porn all night but you're too lazy to even jerk off.'

Rage suddenly clouded whatever judgement the man possessed, and Coyle was on him before he could decide how to attack. First a blow to the stomach to keep things quiet, then a knee to the chin. Fred collapsed and looked like he would be out for a while, but Coyle took the precaution of securing him to a sturdy door handle with his own handcuffs. Before leaving the reception area he pulled out a roll of duct tape and applied a strip over the unconscious man's mouth. He also tore open the package he had used to gain entrance. It contained a silencer-equipped Heckler & Koch MP7 carbine and three 30 round magazines.

Thanks to Carpenter, he knew that Whitmore's office was on the third and top floor in the southeast corner. He'd made a sketch of the building's layout and memorised it.

Taking the lift was rarely a good idea, so he opted for the stairs. The door leading into the third floor working area was locked, but Fred's key card took care of that. Past a small lobby with some workstations, a brightly lit corridor led across the building.

As he moved silently towards Whitmore's corner office his hearing registered an unexpected noise. With extra care, he approached a door marked Managing Director. Yes, there was definitely someone inside. That was why the corridor lights were still on.

No point in being shy. He pulled the door open and stepped inside in one swift motion. The man behind the desk was definitely Whitmore. Carpenter's description had been vivid as well as accurate. Built like a bulldog, but with the face of a shrewd barrister. Ex-army, though not Special

Forces. Lieutenant Colonel Whitmore had been an overly assertive supply and logistics officer. And now he was forcing Coyle to change his plan.

20. LONDON

'Who the fuck are you and how'd you get in here?' Whitmore barked, but Coyle spotted the alarm in his eyes. Perhaps the way the intruder held the MP7 had something to do with it. Relaxed yet professional to the point of implying that putting a couple of rounds through the seated man's heart would be entirely routine.

'Oh, I had a quiet word with Fred and he let me in. Told me to go right up.'

'Fred!'

'He's an idiot by the way. You should never skimp on basic security. Not in your line of business!'

Whitmore got the picture and produced a grim smile. 'Why are you here?' he asked.

Thinking furiously, Coyle decided to improvise. 'I've come to send a message,' he announced calmly.

'Seems I have no choice but to listen to it.'

'Two messages actually. Firstly, I don't appreciate that MI5 clown Carpenter mounting an operation against me and using your goons as muscle.'

The penny dropped. Whitmore suddenly looked a bit more respectful.

'What's happened to Carpenter?' he enquired. 'You messed up Gregor's knee, but otherwise he seems okay. Except not knowing what hit him.'

'I often have that effect on people. Including Carpenter, but he's been very helpful of course. Didn't require much persuasion.'

'You're shitting me!'

Coyle made Whitmore push back in his work chair so his hands were visible. Then he placed his own phone on the desk and played part of the video he had recorded of Carpenter before giving him the injection. To ensure that the MI5 man fully grasped he had to disappear, he had made him talk about the various LONA leaders by name, and explain how they ran their scheme of political extortion mixed with financial incentives for those who cooperated. Carpenter even explained how intimidation beatings and lethal hits were arranged through Highgate.

When Coyle ended the video Whitmore was pale with suppressed rage. 'Is that your second message?' he snarled. 'That Carpenter's a traitor!'

Coyle carefully pocketed the phone before replying. 'No, that's not the message,' he said. 'The message is that Nelson and his lot have become a liability. We're switching our support to the Rightful Tories.'

'The fucking Twits! No way! Wait a minute. Who the hell are *we* in this? Who do you work for?'

'My name is Markevich, and as you've probably guessed I work for those in favour of law and order in Europe.'

'And what do they want?'

'I just told you. They're switching from LONA to RTP. You and Highgate are finished as of now. You'll wind up whatever legit business you have and disappear, the lot of you. I'll be handling the enforcement side myself.'

Somewhere in Whitmore's head his pompous side won out over his fear and anger. 'You'll so full of shit, you're choking on it!' he said contemptuously. 'I guarantee you won't leave this building alive!'

Coyle chuckled. 'According to Carpenter, you've got fifty-four enforcers, including the rapid response team you keep on round-the-clock standby down on the first floor. Make it fifty three since Gregor won't be doing much heavy lifting for a while. And you've got some regular security guys like Fred. That may be enough to intimidate key individuals in British public life, but I rather fancy my own chances against them. Especially when you consider who's backing me.'

Without giving Whitmore a chance to respond, he grabbed the notebook computer on the table and looked at the screen briefly.

'Looks interesting! I'll take this with me if you don't mind. Just be so kind and write down your password on a piece of paper.'

'Fuck off!'

'No problem, I will. I'll leave with the password and you'll still be alive. Or I'll leave without it and you'll be dead - the way a bullet in the brain makes you dead. Your call, Grant.'

For the second time that day Coyle's icy calm triumphed over his adversary. Whitmore grudgingly, but in the clear precise handwriting of a military bureaucrat, wrote down his password. Coyle turned off the computer, then restarted it and made sure the password was correct. Then he shot Whitmore in the right foot.

21. LONDON

Joanne's battlefield radio crackled into life, finally breaking the tension she had been enduring in the van.

'On my way down to the troops,' Coyle's digitally enhanced voice informed her.

'You're behind schedule,' she remarked. 'Anything wrong?'

'No, but a slight change of plan. Whitmore was working late in his office. I saw it as an opportunity.'

'What opportunity?'

'Sorry, no time to explain. I've got to work fast before he frees himself and set off the alarm.'

'Why didn't you secure him?'

'I did, but only well enough for about ten minutes. Remember, we *want* the alarm to go off.'

Joanne hadn't forgotten, she just didn't like the idea. 'Be sure to tell me when to get moving,' she said, and got a quick '*I will*' back.

So far Carpenter's intelligence had been spot on, but Coyle took great care while he descended the steps and closed in on the standby team's quarters. There was a security door that looked solid enough, but evidently wasn't sound proof, for he could hear what had to be a loud action movie playing on the other side.

Fred's key card did the trick again, and once he was inside the room Coyle moved with ferocious intensity and speed.

It was a matter of numbers. There were supposed to be eight enforcers, and not only did he have to get them all, he had to allow for plus or minus a couple – this might be a special night.

Six men were slouching on two large sofas and a leather recliner in front of a state-of-the-art home cinema system. Only three of them had even registered his entrance, while the others remained fully engrossed in the film. Those who had noticed him didn't look concerned, merely curious with a hint of irritation. Well, that would soon change.

He picked off the three alert ones in less than two seconds. The suppressed shots were nearly drowned out by the movie sound, but of course the men cried out and thrashed about on the furniture. Their colleagues' first reactions were directed at them rather than Coyle, and he made the most of it. Because there was movement in the room and the targets were further apart this time, it took him almost four seconds to put a precisely aimed bullet in each man. He went for knees and lower legs. Shots that incapacitated but didn't kill. The last of the six tried diving behind the sofa, and was rewarded with a bullet up his right buttock into the hip joint. He wouldn't be walking anytime soon.

This is where things got serious. Where were the other two, or three? Did any of the wounded men have a gun on him?

There was an open door to the side, and a mean looking character come rushing through while reaching behind his back. Coyle fired twice. First into the man's right shoulder, then his left leg. Before he hit the floor, Coyle had snatched away the gun and was moving through the doorway himself.

He registered a toilet door ajar, the light on inside. A noise told him there was someone on the other side. There was no way to handle this in a surgical way, so he flipped the MP7 to full auto and dropped to one knee. Pushing the silenced muzzle through the crack in the door, he fired a low burst.

A crazed roar sounded and then he heard the eighth enforcer tumble to the floor. A quick glance inside confirmed that the man was alive, but out of action. Time to move out, but first a quick sweep of the remaining rooms. They were Spartan sleeping quarters with military style cots, but all were empty. The Highgate response team was at standard strength. No more, no less.

As he re-entered the entertainment lounge, two of the wounded men there showed signs of getting themselves together, so he shot one in the right arm and hit the other one over the head on his way through the chaos. Moments later he had closed the security door behind him and was running down the stairs.

Bypassing the ground floor, he continued downwards into the underground garage. There were three SUVs and a top-of-the-line BMW, and he swiftly put a bullet in every tyre, but the cars were not his main objective here. He examined the mechanised security door that allowed vehicles in and out. As he had expected, it was designed to be operated by remote control from the cars, and probably from the reception area as well. Three quick shots shattered the box containing the motor and control electronics. Another took care of the power cable. If anyone wanted to drive in or out, they would have to manually crank the heavy door open. Unless they used explosives, which was unlikely.

Coyle scanned the area to ensure that he had not missed anything. Then he returned to the ground floor. He nodded to Fred as he passed him in the lobby and bent down to pick up his motorcycle helmet, but decided against putting a bullet in the guard's leg. The unfortunate man was in enough trouble already.

22. LONDON

As he emerged from the building, Coyle spoke to Joanne on the radio. 'I'm out. Head for the pickup point.'

'On my way,' she acknowledged and got the van moving within seconds. She made a right turn into a side street and soon lost sight of the Highgate building in her mirror. Driving carefully to avoid attracting attention – although who noticed a white van anyway – she swung a left at the next corner, and then took another turn right into a small industrial parking lot. Moments later she heard the throaty sound of Coyle's motorbike approaching.

Loading was a simple operation thanks to the narrow metal ramp Coyle had procured for the van. All she had to do was open the rear doors, pull the ramp out and secure it with a push bolt. Coyle drove up the ramp without hesitation and killed the engine.

'Let's go!' he shouted. 'I'll close the rear.'

She was still standing on the outside, but quickly climbed back into the driver's seat. By the time she turned the ignition key, she heard the back doors slam closed.

They had agreed that driving back the same route would be a risk not worth taking, so instead she took a circuitous route that nevertheless brought them to within two minutes brisk walk from the Highgate headquarters.

Although she was far from happy about it, her involvement in the attack ended at this point. She brought the van to a brief stop, heard the rear doors slam again, and knew that Coyle had left the vehicle. He would have discarded his motorcycle helmet and leather outfit, and exchanged the MP7 for a weapon more suitable for what he was about to do next.

She pulled off the curb and drove off towards their hotel in Earls Court, while gratefully noting with that there seemed to be no police sirens bearing down on them.

23. LONDON

Urban sniping was one of Coyle's most refined skills. As he had revealed to Sir Hugh, he had practiced on some of the most vicious modern battlefields in Iraq and Afghanistan, but he had stopped short of telling his mentor just how brutal some of his self-imposed missions had been.

Selecting your position was a crucial element. There had not been enough time for thorough recognisance of the area, but Coyle had been able to indentify a spot that he thought would do, and that was where he headed. Less than three minutes after leaving the van, he climbed a fire ladder onto the roof of an empty looking warehouse with a direct view of the target area.

He too reflected on the lack of sirens. Just as he had anticipated, Grant Whitmore was not calling the authorities. Instead he would be summoning his own troops from all over London - meaning the just short of fifty enforcers still fit for action. Not all of them would be within range of course. Some would be out of town or otherwise engaged, but the majority would be on their way here to secure their headquarters and take stock of the damage.

For several reasons he had not selected a real sniper's weapon. He was close enough to hit what he wanted with a lighter and more flexible gun, there was no need for high penetration ammunition, and finally he appreciated the operational advantage provided by the Heckler & Koch MP5SD's integral silencer. In automatic mode the weapon had a cyclic rate of 800 rounds per minute, but he planned to fire single shots aimed to perfection with the help of an attached light-enhancing telescope sight.

The first group arrived in a Land Rover Discovery with darkened side windows. It drove straight down the ramp that led to the garage and stopped just short of the disobedient door. Coyle once more checked that the street was clear of pedestrians. Then he punctured the two tyres that were visible to him with quick shots. Four men poured out of the vehicle with drawn weapons. Two had automatic pistols; the others swung police style shotguns around in vain attempts to find a target.

He shot all four in five seconds. Leg hits in each case. One man seemed slow to get the message, so he sent him an additional round through the right elbow as encouragement.

Two of the wounded men fired their weapons, making the situation a noisy one. Could not be helped. It might actually help by diverting attention from him.

Two more SUVs came heeding their master's call. Both stopped behind the Land Rover blocking the garage entrance. Coyle waited until everyone was in the open before he engaged. Nine men fell in agony as limbs were torn into and bones shattered by 9mm bullets. Several further shots rang out as the enforcers attempted to fight back without a clue about who or where their enemy was. A single bullet passed close enough for him to take notice, but there was no follow up.

Methodically he ensured that all visible tyres were shot out. The longer it took to make the cars usable again the better.

A large Mercedes arrived, but before its passengers had gotten out, it was followed by three more SUVs. There were suddenly eighteen targets running around trying to make sense of what had happened to their fallen comrades. Coyle kept his breathing calm and rhythmic while he picked them off one by one.

In the end, three of the enforcers seemed to grasp enough of their predicament to take cover where he couldn't hit them. Well, this operation was never going to be total perfection anyway. He considered calling it a night, but then a further Mercedes arrived, and a minute later yet another SUV. Targets not to be ignored.

There were four men in each vehicle, but in no hurry to join the mayhem. The street was blocked by now, so the Mercedes started performing a three-point turn. Unfortunately the SUV was too close by now and hemmed in the Mercedes. Coyle tested the windows and discovered that only the Mercedes's were bulletproof. That left the men in the SUV vulnerable, and he quickly put slugs into their shoulders and upper arms.

Now completely blocked in, the Mercedes crew decided to get out and head for the building. Coyle thought it revealed poor tactical awareness, since he had bounced a couple of shots off the windows making it clear that he was not firing high-penetration rounds. There were four of them, and they collapsed on the pavement after running only half a dozen steps.

At last he heard sirens. The Highgate lot's frantic shooting must have been reported, and police cars were on their way. It was time for Coyle to make an orderly withdrawal. He eased himself back to the edge of the roof, keeping himself in deep shadow all the way. Then he climbed down the ladder and walked into a back alley.

24. LONDON

Their hotel room was quite large, but Coyle had avoided booking a suite in order to make their visit less conspicuous. He had explained to Joanne that since he was the only one with fake identity documents, the reservation had to be made by and for him. She was there as *Mrs David Baker*.

When they checked into the room earlier in the day she had noted that he had at least arranged for twin beds. Wrapped in a brand-new bathrobe she lay on one of them in a paradoxical state of hyper-anxious exhaustion. The battlefield radio made a noise and she pulled it to her ear.

'You awake?' Coyle asked calmly. 'I'm on my way up.'

'I'll take the chain off the door,' she responded automatically and swung her legs off the bed. Moments later she heard his pre-arranged knocking signal on the door, and opened it for him. He stepped inside and the moment the door closed behind him she flung her arms around him in a tight embrace.

Coyle looked genuinely puzzled. 'Is something wrong?' he asked. 'Are you okay?'

There was concern all over his face and she suddenly felt very silly. Stepping back she said, 'I'm fine. It's been a long day, that's all.'

He looked into her eyes and detected her vulnerability. 'Sorry, I didn't think. This is all a bit new to you.'

She released her grip and took a step back. Holding up a large plastic bad, he smiled disarmingly. 'I brought some Chinese food,' he said. 'We need to eat. Then sleep.'

He moved into the room and she followed, pulling the bathrobe tighter around her.

'How did it go?' she asked and thought she sounded like a wife inquiring about her husband's day at the office.

Coyle was by the mirror, removing his brown contact lenses.

'They came even quicker than I expected,' he told her. I'd tied Whitmore just hard enough to give me time to take down the standby team and block the garage entrance. Once he had freed himself he raised the alarm and summoned the rest of his hired guns. But of course there wasn't anything they could do. They were sitting ducks as they could not get into the garage.'

'How many were they?'

'I counted thirty nine arriving. Three managed to take cover so I couldn't get at them, but the others are out of action.'

'You shot thirty six of them!'

'In the street, yes. Another eight inside. Plus Whitmore himself. All of them will require medical care and weeks of recuperation before they do anything physical.'

'What the hell are you, Coyle? Some kind of robot?'

'I told you before. It's just something I'm good at. I need less time to aim and fire than other people.'

'And you don't miss!'

'The only reason for missing is not aiming properly.'

'Yeah, that's the *only* reason.' She sat down on the nearest bed. 'So how many enforcers are left?'

'Carpenter said there were fifty four, so that leaves ten. No make that nine. Gregor won't be doing much running about either.'

'Who's Gregor?'

'The goon you spotted in the street before I lifted Carpenter. The one whose knee I busted. Whitmore told me his name.'

'Nine of them against you. Not much of a contest then.'

'Oh, I doubt they'll fight. Highgate Security is no longer a threat, and that means we can start phase two.'

'What's phase two?'

Coyle placed the bag on the only table in the room. 'We'll discuss the details tomorrow. But right now let's eat and sleep. The prawns and noodles look promising, but I think the duck may be a bit dry. See what you think.'

25. LONDON

Neil Nelson awoke with a start. On the nightstand his mobile was making a soft but persistent noise. Shit, he shouldn't still be here! A discrete fuck was one thing, waking up in a extramarital bed another altogether. His image as a respectably married man was an asset he could not afford to compromise.

As he turned and reached for the phone, his movement pulled part of the covers from Bonnie Stevens's full and sensuous body beside him. A pale beam of outside light fell on her left breast with its perfectly formed nipple. In this low light it appeared dark, but he knew it was in fact delicately and deliciously pink.

She was still wearing her white lace-trimmed knickers. Those damned knickers! She insisted on wearing them to bed and keeping them on throughout their lovemaking. He was allowed to touch them on the outside, but not pull them down or slip even a single finger inside. When she finally considered the foreplay over, she would pull the crotch aside to let him enter her.

It annoyed the hell out of him, but at the same time it was an incredible turn-on! He couldn't get enough of her, although he had never seen her completely naked. Or maybe because of that.

The display told him the caller was Rita Ridgewood. The time was shortly before midnight. She wasn't calling for a chat.

'Talk to me Rita,' he said, making an effort to suppress feedback from the generous quantity of expensive wine he had consumed earlier.

The LONA security chief spoke sharply. 'We have a situation, Neil. You need to get down to Party Headquarters at once. I'm calling the whole senior team.'

Nelson was still groggy from interrupted sleep. 'What's going on?'

'There's been an attack on Highgate. Someone took out most of our active force. We're severely exposed security wise.'

'What? Who's attacking us?'

'That what we've got to figure out – before anything else happens! Can you be ready in five minutes?'

Nelson agreed, then hung up. Bonnie was now awake and flipped on the bed light.

'What's the problem?' she asked in her languid after-sex voice.

'You'll get your own call from Rita any minute now. She'll explain and probably take you along with her to Party HQ. I'm heading there now.'

He got out of bed, grabbed his crumpled clothes and stumbled into the bathroom to piss and get dressed. Rita would have alerted his personal security men already, and they would be ready to whisk him away in the armour plated Jaguar he used as his main personal transport. Fuck, she probably knew exactly where he was! Which was the same high security building in Chelsea Harbour where she lived herself.

26. LONDON

The rapid clatter of keys penetrated Joanne's sleep. Half opening her eyes, she became aware that the room was no longer totally dark. Then, turning her head, she saw Coyle bent over the computer he had brought with him from Highgate, his face a mask of intense concentration.

'Don't you ever sleep like a normal person?' she groaned at him.

Unperturbed, he smiled happily. 'I get by on less, I suppose. It's helpful in operational situations.'

'What's so important you've got to do it in the middle of the night?'

'Oh, I wanted to have a crack at Whitmore's secrets while the other side is still in disarray. Catching him at his desk was a major stroke of luck!'

His fingers were tapping away uninterrupted while he talked. Clearly he was no stranger to multi-tasking.

'What've you discovered?' she asked, and at that moment realised she had abandoned the desire to go back to sleep.

'Just as I thought, Highgate handles personal security for Nelson and his closest lieutenants. That's why nine enforcers didn't come to help out Whitmore. He's got over a hundred run-of-the-mill security personnel on the books, to make the business look ordinary. But anything to do with LONA is enforcer territory.'

'Does that mean you know where all the Longbow bigwigs live?'

'And eat and play! You bet! If I were an assassin they'd be easy targets.'

Joanne first wondered if he had meant it as a joke.

'You're saying you're *not* an assassin?' she exclaimed.

'Not primarily, no. I only kill when it's the only, or at least the optimum, solution to a problem. I could easily have left all or most of the targets last night dead, but I didn't.'

'Why was that, actually?'

'Dead people make more noise.'

'Beg your pardon?'

'The media would have been all over it. Not even LONA can suppress a massacre in the middle of London. But there won't be a lot of headlines about a bunch of security guys getting shot in the legs. It's in our opponents' interest to play down the affair as much as possible.'

'Because you kicked their asses?'

'Because Nelson doesn't want it known that Highgate is his weapon of intimidation. Partly because he'd be exposed legally, partly because the people living in fear of him might think they're off the hook.'

Joanne sat up in the bed. 'What happens now that Highgate's been disabled?'

Coyle rewarded her with a look of respect. 'That's exactly the right question. Nelson will have to rely on his friends in crime and terrorism. And thanks to Whitmore and his computer, I know exactly who they are.'

27. LONDON

The atmosphere in the conference room was tense to the point of incendiary. Rita Ridgewood was in control, but only just. There was too much uncertainty in the air, too many alarming thoughts floated in what passed for discussion but was really a shouting orgy.

Finally Grant Whitmore arrived. One of the still fit enforcers pushed his wheelchair into the room, and everyone gathered around the man with the heavily bandaged foot.

Everything said and done in Whitmore's office was recorded. There were three concealed cameras and several microphones. After a brief fuss with technology, the LONA leadership could follow the entire spectacle, from Coyle's sudden entry to his calm departure.

Whitmore paused the recording shortly after the intruder's entry. 'As you can see, he kept his balaclava on after taking off his helmet. Even Fred would not have let him into the building wearing a helmet.'

'His face looks asymmetrical,' observed Rita Ridgewood. 'Disguised to defeat facial recognition software, you think?'

'Yes, probably. The police are trying – low key mind you – but nothing so far.'

'And no fingerprints either!' Nelson concluded while pointing at the man's gloved hands. 'Okay, let's have it all.'

They continued to watch the recording, but as soon as Carpenter's voice came on, order broke down in the room and once more it seemed everyone was talking at once. Nelson brought his fist down hard on the conference table.

'Shut the fuck up!' he roared. 'We need to listen carefully.'

Bill Utley agreed, but could resist adding his own statement. 'The cowardly prick!' he spat.

Soon the extent of Carpenter's treason was clear to all. 'We'll get him, Neil!' Rita stated, her voice cold venom.

Nelson held up his hand like a traffic warden. 'Sure, but he's not top of the shit list right now. That guy is! Whoever the fuck he is!'

Coyle had now gotten to the point where he announced that Law & Order were shifting their support to the Rightful Tories.

Nelson exploded. 'No fucking way! This isn't happening! I'll strangle that piece of shit myself if I have to.'

Finally a name! The intruder said he was called Markevich.

'You check it out, Grant?' Rita asked, but the response was unhelpful.

'Markevich rings no bells with anyone I know,' Whitmore conceded.

'His accent isn't east European,' Bonnie observed. 'Quite neutral, but he sounds rather British to me.'

'Why should he give his name unless there's something behind it?' Nelson argued. 'He's taunting us by coming out in the open like that.'

'It's got to be a bluff!' Rita countered, but Nelson stopped her. He wanted to take in the rest of the recording.

'I didn't have a choice, as you can see,' Whitmore explained as they saw him caving in and giving Coyle the password to his computer.

Nelson watched in a daze as Coyle shot Whitmore in the foot and then swiftly tied him to his office chair and left the way he had come.

The Highgate chief was embarrassed, but pushed on. 'The next video feed is from the response teams quarters.'

After only a brief pause, they were treated to the sight of *Markevich* interrupting the enforcer team's movie evening. A staccato symphony of expletives erupted amongst the LONA leadership.

'That's just not possible!' Nelson blurted out. 'Nobody can shoot like that! The man's a fucking robot!'

'Extraordinary!' Rita agreed. 'That man is *very* dangerous!'

Whitmore flipped to the next video file. 'This is what he did to my men as they were arriving,' he explained. 'He'd disabled the garage gate so the cars were stuck on the outside. Then he just – well have a look!'

The outside video was less sharp, and did not show the shooter himself, but the way the arriving enforcers were picked off one by one was graphic and frightening.

'That can't be just the one guy!' Nelson protested, but Whitmore shrugged in deflated disagreement.

'There were only shell casings from one weapon,' he informed them. 'And all the shots seemed to come from where we found the casings. We can't be sure Markevich was she shooter, but it's unlikely he brought his twin brother along for the outside part.'

Nelson knew he had to act decisively.

'I need Bill, Steve and Rita in my office now!' he announced. 'The rest of you, stay and discuss how we can keep this shit as low profile as possible with the media. Bonnie, think about whether we need to say something as a party.'

He marched out followed by the three he had chosen for the follow-up. Bill Utley, the former criminal lawyer turned politician and now his master's link to organised crime. Steve Henderson, an academic destined to become Foreign Secretary in a Longbow government. And cool dangerous Rita Ridgewood, the most ruthless of them all.

Not waiting for anyone to sit down, Nelson addressed Henderson first. 'Steve, I want to go and see Hannes right away. Tell him what's happened, and make sure he knows we don't think he's behind it.'

Henderson's high balding forehead creased itself in concerned wrinkles and he stroked his neatly trimmed beard. Behind his thick glasses, cold intelligent eyes displayed a shrewd awareness of what might lie ahead.

'What if he *is* behind Markevich?' he asked quietly.

'Then you'll sense it. Or he may even tell you. But I don't think it's the case. It can't be!'

'What else should I tell him?'

'That I want a meeting in person. As soon as we get things calmed down a bit here. I need to look him in the eye and tell him we're in control.'

'I see. Okay, I'll leave first thing in the morning.'

'Good, now go join the others. You don't want to hear the rest of this conversation!'

Henderson got the drift at once and made himself scarce. The Leader waited until the door closed before speaking.

'First of all, Highgate and Whitmore are finished. We write them off.'

Rita appraised her boss carefully. 'You sure about that, Neil?'

'Yeah of course I'm fucking sure! Whitmore turned out to have no more balls than Carpenter, and now that Markevich has got his computer Highgate's totally compromised.'

'So he's out of the loop?' she prodded.

'As of right now and immediately! Nothing confidential goes his way! But you do need to work with him to manage the police and the media fallout from all this.'

Bill Utley's weasel-like face broke into a cruel smile. 'And longer term?' he enquired with obvious subtext.

'Use you imagination Bill! He knows too much about us to have a long life expectancy. But listen up both of you! We have one great priority now and that's to get this Markevich cunt whatever it takes.'

'Of course,' concurred Rita. 'But it's got to be done under the radar.'

Nelson was warming up. 'You start pulling strings with the police and the intelligence services. And Bill, you get word to your *friends* outside the law. Money is no object. I want Markevich dead!'

Utley's shrewd smile got wider. 'I say we have a frank and open discussion with him first.'

'It would be useful to know who hired him,' Rita weighed in, but Nelson overruled them both.

'We've all fucking seen what he can do with a gun!' he erupted. 'Weren't you paying attention? You don't take chances with a man like that! You shoot him on sight and you shoot to kill!'

28. LONDON

Sir Hugh Canderton was approaching the front steps of his impressive place of work when he became aware of a young woman bearing in on him from the left. Well, she looked quite young although her hair under the silk scarf was silver grey. Despite the early hour and overcast sky she wore sunglasses that effectively concealed her eyes.

'Sir Hugh, could you spare a minute? I'm Joanne Stack, Staff Sergeant Stack's daughter.' She spoke with the distinct diction of someone familiar with police and military work.

'Of course, how nice to meet you!' he responded and took her extended hand. As he did so, her grip became surprisingly firm.

'Our mutual friend wanted you to have this information,' she said and pressed a small item against his palm.

Annoyed that it had taken him so long to recognise tradecraft, Sir Hugh secured what he realised had to be a data card.

'Thank you so much! How is you father?'

'He's very well, but no longer operational,' she replied, smiled and detached herself. He watched her walk off and felt a sense of foreboding mixed with anticipation. Coyle was moving faster than he had dared to expect.

Once in his office, he hurriedly pulled out the same old iPad he used for Metcalfe messages. There were no messages from "R", so he inserted Coyle's memory card and soon saw text forming on the screen.

Dear Uncle, the operation is taking shape. LONA have been using Highgate Security as front for the enforcers who instilled and maintained loyalty amongst the corrupted. This has now been dealt with, and some highly informative files have come into my possession. The following persons are certain to be on LONA's payroll, so

I suggest you make discrete efforts to sideline them as much as possible.

There followed a long list of people in the police, the intelligence community and in several ministries. The Home Office dominated, but quite a few MoD employees were on the list as well.

There were too many names to take in at once, so he skipped to the end of the message, where Coyle requested a favour.

You will have met Joanne Stack. She is being very helpful to me, but working on this while on temporary leave is not ideal. Could you pull some strings to have her reassigned for a couple of months from Cardiff CID to a suitable London based unit? It must be headed by someone reliable, who will let her operate unsupervised!

Yes, Sir Hugh could do that. Still, he checked the list of traitors to make sure that DCS Clara Miller wasn't among them.

29. SLOUGH

For Bogdan Konev business was not only good; thanks to the protection arranged by Bill Utley, it was excellent to the point where his only challenge seemed to be getting on tactfully with the other major players in drugs distribution and prostitution. This meant sharing the market, but there was enough to go around, and the overall climate of ever-deepening economic crisis played right into their hands.

Every businessman needs an office, and Konev's was in the back of a particularly seedy sex club in Slough, just outside the M25 and an easy taxi ride from Heathrow Airport. At the *Lokal*, there were few restrictions to what a patron could enjoy as long as he paid the stipulated rate. Perverts came here from afar, because Konev guaranteed discretion as well as high quality *product*. It was not his only club, but he considered it his flagship.

The Lokal was only marginally useful to Utley and LONA – although it was an excellent place to trap certain people in compromising (and blackmail enabling) situations – but Konev's well-organised army of thugs served as a useful complement to Highgate. There were some deeds that Grant Whitmore's enforcers preferred not to have on their consciences – or résumés.

The Boss and one of his regional managers sat around a glass table, on which they had spread several pages full of numbers. Despite their protected status, it made sense for them to keep internal accounts on paper copy rather than risk computer secrecy being penetrated.

As a concession to the early hour, just after 9am, there was only coffee and no alcoholic drinks on the table.

There were two doors: a massive official entrance that would take heavy explosives to force, and a secret backdoor leading into a stairwell and ultimately into the back alley.

Konev heard the code being punched into the front door lock and looked up to see one of his bouncers coming through the narrow opening. He looked unsettled, and Konev felt a sudden stir of alarm.

Then a man dressed in a black leather outfit appeared behind the bouncer, and sent him crashing to the floor with a swift kick to the back of the knee.

'What are you doing you imbecile?' Konev shouted in Russian. He was Bulgarian himself, but most of his club bouncers were Russian and he was fully competent in their language.

'Don't worry about him, he didn't have much choice,' said the intruder in equally immaculate Russian and nudged the door closed behind him.

Konev was the product of a tough career in crime and not easily rattled. 'Who the hell are you?' he demanded, but then his eyes widened as he spotted a compact carbine with attached silencer in the man's right hand.

'Sorry, we haven't been introduced,' Coyle said in a friendly voice. 'I'm Markevich. We need to talk.'

He saw no sign that the name was familiar to the Bulgarian. Good, it meant that word hadn't reached him yet.

The gun made Konev cautious, but he made an effort to seem in control. 'I'm busy with my associate here,' he declared with a meaningful gesture towards his guest.

Coyle shot the man in the head and he slumped backwards in the chair. Less than a second later another muffled shot bored into the skull of the bouncer, who was struggling to get up.

'That should clear your calendar.'

It was all about intimidation and effect. Seeing two of his men casually killed drove home a powerful message. *This is serious, so pay attention!*

Konev half raised both hands in a gesture of submission. 'Take it easy! What do you want from me?'

Coyle pulled the third chair from the table, turned it around and sat down so that there was space between him and the Bulgarian. He held the gun in an easy confident manner.

'You understand that if we're *interrupted*, I'll have to kill you?' he said and Konev nodded.

'No one will disturb us,' he stated in a flat voice. 'But what is your problem with me?'

'I want to avoid *having* you as a problem,' Coyle responded, still sounding reasonable but with a slight hardening of his tone. 'Very soon now, your Longbow friends will tell you to hunt me down and kill me. If you attempt to do so it will be very unprofitable for you.'

'Ah!' Suddenly Konev put the pieces together. 'You're the one who attacked…'

'Highgate yes! They're finished. Just a handful of serious guys left, and they're scared shitless. No threat to me and no threat to you.'

'But LONA have power. They control everything!'

Coyle shrugged away the argument. 'Bribed loyalty only goes so far, my friend. We'll be making sure it gets less and less safe to take Nelson's money.'

Konev snorted. 'He'll be in power soon. Then he won't need to bribe people.'

'Thanks for mentioning that, Bogdan. What do you think a Longbow regime will mean for people like you?'

The question seemed to surprise him. For several seconds he projected only confusion and hesitation.

'I bet you thought you'd be given permanent license to print money, but that doesn't make sense if you bother to think it through properly.'

A hint of defiance appeared across Konev's hardened face. 'Then how do *you* figure it?' he asked almost petulantly.

'All you have to do is look at what happened in Hungary, Bogdan! There are seven countries across Europe where L&O parties are included in the government, but Hungary is the only one where L&O is actually the *ruling* party.'

'That will happen here too!'

'If you're too stupid to follow a simple line of reasoning, I'll have to shoot you.'

The Bulgarian stiffened, but didn't raise his voice. 'So what happened in Hungary?'

'In the other six countries, those where L&O is still trying to secure real power, the crime situation keeps getting worse. But in Hungary, the L&O government at once cracked down on organised as well as occasional crime. Brutally, but effectively! Today you can drop a wallet full of money on a park bench in Budapest and collect it the following morning untouched. Unless some honest citizen finds it, checks your address and brings it to you door.'

'You're saying it's not in my interest to have Nelson as Prime Minister?'

Coyle rewarded him by lowering the gun a fraction. 'Now we're making progress,' he said. 'Nelson is using you and your colleagues to created a feeling of lawlessness and insecurity in the country in order to get elected. Once he *is* elected he needs to show that he can deliver on his promises. He knows who you are, where you are and what you do. What could be easier than putting you out of business?'

'Not possible! We all know too much about him!'

'Don't disappoint me just as I'm beginning to like you, Bogdan! Or I *will* have to shoot you and all this will have been a waste of time.'

'What do you *want*?'

'I want you to think, Bogdan. Nobody who knows anything sensitive will be tried in a court of law. The more important you are to LONA now, the quicker you'll be dead once they come to power.'

He could see the message penetrating. Konev blinked nervously while he tried to find a new angle, but Coyle pre-empted him.

'And as a first small step towards your redemption, I want you to cut off all cooperation with Nelson and his people as of this moment.'

A proud man used to having his own way, Konev had to adopt a posture of self-worth.

'I'll think about it,' he said.

'Let me give you an added incentive,' Coyle proceeded. 'Should I learn that *any* criminal group with roots in the eastern part of Europe continues to do dirty work for the Longbows, I'll hold you, Bogdan, personally responsible.'

'You can't!'

'Look, you're lucky to get this chance. By right you should be dead by now. Don't fool yourself into thinking you can protect yourself against me. Do you doubt for a second that I'll come back and kill you if you don't do as I say?'

As Konev looked straight into Coyle's eyes the man seemed to shrink. 'No, but how can I control the others?'

Coyle got to his feet. 'That's you problem, and since your life depends on it, I suggest you give it your full attention. You know the people you need to speak to, and you know the message.'

He walked over to the backdoor, found the hidden handle and opened it. Turning around, he addressed the Bulgarian again.

'I'd make sure those bodies disappear if I were you. Or maybe you'll want to keep them around to show to your friends and colleagues in case they think I'm not for real.'

30. HEATHROW AIRPORT

The motorcycle enabled him to dash through the morning traffic to Slough, but had very limited luggage capacity. He pulled into a space in the parking building between Terminals 2 and 3; then quickly removed his helmet and leather gear. Underneath he wore a tracksuit in which he could pass for a very casual holidaymaker. He stowed away the biking outfit, including boots. Then, very carefully to avoid observation by human eyes or surveillance cameras, the gun. He left the helmet attached and padlocked to the handlebar. It would not fit into either of the bike's fibreglass lockers, so he had to risk leaving it exposed.

Ten minutes later he had made it over to Terminal 1, where he used a British Airways automatic check-in machine as David Baker. With boarding pass and passport held ready, but no luggage except his phone, he passed through security into the departure lounge. Here he picked what looked like the best store selling men's clothing and set about turning himself into a serious looking businessman. It was a swift, if not inexpensive process. Only the shoes remained, but he got a sturdy yet elegant pair of black brogues from the shop next-door.

According to the information board, his flight was on schedule, but he had almost an hour to kill before takeoff. He carried his purchases into one of the toilets to change. He stuffed all he had been wearing and all the labels and packaging material into the biggest of the paper bags from the men's shop and left it in the stall rather than risk attention by shoving it into a trashcan. He emerged back into the departure area wearing a light raincoat over a conservative grey suit, complete with white shirt and elegant but non-descript silk tie.

When the departure gate was announced he headed there immediately. With most people using automated check-in, you couldn't keep track of who lined up to fly, but in the end every passenger had to turn up at the gate. That was where he would identify his target.

31. LONDON

First there was only a gradually growing sense of nausea. Then he became aware of light way too bright for his eyes. Even so, his confused mind struggled to find a firm footing in reality.

Once he realised that he was also very thirsty and suffering from a pulsating headache, the memories started returning with brutal clarity.

'Fuck!' croaked Dennis Carpenter, and rolled over to his side so he could look around the room. He was on the floor – Markevich hadn't taken any extra trouble over his comfort – but he could move all his limbs freely. Slowly and stiffly he struggled to his feet.

Right in front of him, on a low table, he spotted the explosive device his abductor had placed behind his back to keep him compliant. There was a handwritten note protruding from underneath. Gingerly he lifted the device and picked up the note.

Thank you for your help Dennis! You will by now have grasped that the drug was not as drastic in its effects as I led you to believe. If you look at the "explosives" you will find that they are made of soap, but there was no way you could have known that yesterday. So no need to feel either stupid or angry to the point that it would cloud your judgment. All my other warnings to you are very much real and valid. Your friends at LONA know the extent of your treachery, and your official employer will soon start putting the pieces together. Therefore, if you want to give yourself a chance of survival, do as I suggested and disappear at once. Sincerely, Markevich.

The nausea became overwhelming as his heart went into overdrive. That sour sinking feeling that precedes vomit invaded his stomach and he staggered towards the bathroom. Finding the light switch cost him precious seconds and he made it neither to the toilet nor the sink.

Sinking to his knees, he threw up a vile organic substance on the tiled floor.

32. ZURICH AIRPORT

Steve Henderson was tense but highly focused on his task as he emerged from the secure area into the arrivals hall of Zurich Airport. He scanned the crowd for a piece of cardboard with his name on it, and was pleased to find it without difficulty. The greeter was a powerful looking young man in a bulky leather jacket. Quite so, Henderson reflected. Hannes Nagelmann was always security conscious and picked his staff well.

'Welcome to Zurich, Mr Henderson,' the man said, while he raised a phone to his ear in a smooth practiced movement. 'I'm calling the car to the front. Follow me please.'

Ah, Swiss efficiency! Already the visit was going well, and he intuitively knew that his mission would be successful.

Outside, the weather was cool but dry and Henderson took a grateful breath, the way one does after spending too long in airports and planes. He saw Nagelmann's chap wave at a black people carrier, which swung over and stopped just a few steps from where they were standing.

The young man proceeded to open the sliding side door, and at that moment Henderson felt his right arm seized in a vicelike grip just above the elbow.

'I'm Markevich. Play along or you're dead!'

The voice that spoke into his ear was clear, emotionless and confident. A glance at the man's face reconfirmed the impression, and Henderson allowed himself to be steered towards the now open door.

Coyle spoke rapidly in German to the greeter and the man behind the wheel. Both nodded and the greeter responded with something that sounded respectful before sliding the door closed and taking his own seat up front. The people carrier moved off the curb into traffic.

Keen to keep Henderson off balance, Coyle leaned close to him while reapplying his grip on his arm. He had had to release him briefly as they climbed onboard.

'I told them we're going to the meeting together. To be clear, I'm not armed, but breaking your neck or crushing your windpipe would be no problem at all.'

LONA's Head of Public Relations and Foreign Contacts stared at him. 'You – you were on the plane,' he remembered. 'How'd you know I was. . . ?'

'Courtesy of Grant Whitmore. His computer's given up a treasure-trove. Including your travel agency booking account.'

'But this trip wasn't planned!'

'Oh, I figured Nelson would send someone right away, and you were the most logical candidate so I looked for a new booking.'

Henderson went quiet while he considered his options, none of which seemed attractive at the moment.

'You really want to meet Nagelmann with me?' he asked. 'It doesn't make any sense!'

Coyle produced his grim smile. 'It makes perfect sense, Steve! And if we get to our joint meeting you'll still be alive. If we don't, you'll be dead.'

Henderson seemed to get the point. 'I see,' he muttered, but Coyle tightened his grip until the man winced.

'I can't keep holding on to you when we get there, but if you try to distance yourself from me, I'll kill you right there. These boy soldiers won't have time to stop me.'

33. ZURICH

Nagelmann's residence was a large villa in a demonstratively affluent suburb of Zurich. A discrete brass plate on the wall told Coyle that the man they had come to see was a lawyer by profession and that he held a doctorate – presumably in the field of law.

A pair of steel gates parted smoothly as the vehicle swung into view; and closed behind it with equal efficiency. The people carrier came to a stop in a small courtyard, just big enough to accommodate two other vehicles – one of which was a 7-series BMW – and space for them to turn. The greeter got out and opened the sliding door for them, but no one else appeared. This suited Coyle, and if the greeter thought it odd that his two guests walked so close together he didn't show it.

A solid front door swung open at the hands of a girl wearing a vaguely domestic outfit, and they followed the greeter through a hallway up a set of polished hardwood stairs. Coyle got the impression that Nagelmann had split his house into a residence side and one for doing business, and that they were on their way to the office. This was confirmed as they walked past two respectable looking middle-aged ladies seated behind latest technology workstations. So Nagelmann ran a small legal office from his home, but to finance the opulence of the place the services he provided for his clients had to be important indeed.

Throughout their progression Henderson's stiff movements betrayed his inner turmoil, so Coyle kept him honest by nudging him a couple of times and sending him several menacing glares.

Nagelmann's office seemed taken from a high-end interior design magazine, and the man who rose from behind the enormous glass desk to greet them could have stepped out of a glossy ad for exclusive luxury goods. Tall and strikingly handsome, full silver hair combed back to perfection, suit that cost as much as most people's education, cufflinks and watch to match. This lawyer thought nothing of rubbing in how much he enjoyed overcharging his clients.

'Steve, how good to see you again!' he boomed in excellent English while advancing towards them with his right hand extended. As he became aware of Coyle's respectably attired, but unfamiliar and unexpected presence, his smile stiffened slightly although he carried through and shook Henderson's hand. At that point, the LONA representative's expression revealed that something was wrong, and Coyle took the initiative.

'Very sorry to spring this on you so suddenly Herr Dr Nagelmann,' he said in German. 'But I thought that since Herr Henderson was coming here to complain about me, I should tag along and provide you with a balanced account. My name is Markevich.'

Mechanically Nagelmann shook his hand. 'And are you involved in what happened yesterday in London?' he asked still confused.

Coyle nodded enthusiastically. 'I personally put most of Highgate Security's operatives out of commission. As I'm sure you realise, that leaves Herr Nelson's LONA very vulnerable.'

There was instant recognition in Nagelmann's eyes. He knew exactly what Highgate was to LONA.

Henderson found himself at a disadvantage because of the language, but guessed what was being said and decided he had to do something. He quickly stepped forward past his host, so that Nagelmann ended up between him and *Markevich*.

'Hannes, he caught me at the airport and forced me to bring him here! He threatened to kill me!'

Aware that the greeter was still behind him, Coyle turned so he could see what the man was doing. So far, only confusion on his face, but that would change the second his boss gave him an order.

Unfortunately Nagelmann quickly calculated that it could only be to his advantage to have a gun trained on the interloper, and he gave a graphic nod to the bodyguard. The big young man immediately dug inside his leather jacket, but as he withdrew his Sig Sauer P239 compact automatic pistol he felt a sudden sharp pain in his right elbow and the gun slipped out of his hand.

Coyle stepped back holding the weapon by the top of the barrel rather than the butt to emphasize that he wasn't about to use it on anyone in the room.

'Dr Nagelmann, from my side this is supposed to be a friendly and informative meeting,' he said in English. 'You're in no danger from me, but you'll appreciate that I couldn't allow this boy to point a gun at me.'

Nagelmann sent the hapless greeter a contemptuous look before forcing a smile towards Coyle. 'So we sit and we talk,' he conceded and pointed to a sofa group.

Coyle gestured to the disarmed greeter to take a seat as well. He didn't want him leaving the room. The man was red in the face, but smart enough not to protest.

Henderson looked like he was about to shit himself, so Coyle ignored him and pressed on with Nagelmann. 'The obvious question you want to ask me is "why", so I'll explain. LONA may have a chance to win a snap election if one is called, but the leadership is unfit to govern.'

The lawyer glanced briefly at Henderson before asking almost as if he already agreed, 'Why do you say that?'

Picking up on the tone, Coyle pointed at Nelson's envoy. 'Because they're all useless shitheads, like Steve here! Even Nelson himself is nothing more than a bullying buffoon with a bit of cunning and a lot more ambition than what's good for him. If they get into power, they'll make a mess of it, so it's my job to stop them before they get that far.'

'And you started by taking out their enforcers!'

'Exactly! As you know, they've used your L&O money to bribe a lot of useful people, and the enforcers to keep these traitors in line.'

Nagelmann bristled at the direct description but didn't contradict. 'And who do you represent, Mr Markevich? Who pays you to do all this *dangerous* work?'

'I could ask you the same question, Dr Nagelmann.' Sensing that he had come up against a brick wall, he pushed on. 'My principals want the same thing as yours. L&O minded governments in as many European countries as possible. But solid, well functioning governments! Not embarrassing incompetents like the Longbows!'

Henderson started to blurt out a protest, but stopped in mid-breath as Coyle delivered a rapid blow to his shoulder area. Gasping in pain, he bent forward on the sofa.

'I broke his collarbone,' Coyle explained. 'It'll tech him not to interrupt the grownups.'

Nagelmann looked uneasy, so he made an effort to reassure him. 'As I said earlier, you're in no danger from me,' he said. 'I've come for a friendly and constructive discussion.'

'But you want something from me, right?'

Coyle considered switching back to German, but decided that that Henderson ought to hear everything.

'I want you to cut off all ties to LONA and instead throw your support behind the Rightful Tories. They're already *in* government, as you know.'

'Only as a junior partner. And not for long either!'

'Together we must persuade them not to pull out of the government. This is not the right time to force a decisive election!'

An incensed gurgle escaped from Henderson's mouth right before Coyle grasped him by the neck and slammed his face against the coffee table.

Nagelmann appeared unruffled by the scene. 'Let me think about it,' he said neutrally, once again speaking German. 'Call me on this number at 10am my time the day after tomorrow.' He handed Coyle a neatly printed business card.

34. ZURICH

His departure was a charade of correctness. Keeping the bashful greeter's Sig Sauer in his pocket as insurance, Coyle walked out of the villa accompanied by Nagelmann himself. The lawyer raised no objection to lending him the people carrier for a few hours, and in return Coyle promised to leave it in a public place, locked and with the keys under the front seat.

That public place was the *Hauptbahnhof*, the main railway station, where he bought himself a first class ticket to Munich. The train left three quarters of an hour later, so he used the time to buy toiletries, spare shirts and underwear plus an elegant leather carry-on to hold them.

It seemed prudent not to fly back to London from Zurich. Although Nagelmann had professed not to hold a grudge and was unlikely to attempt an intercept, the possibility could not be ruled out. Fortunately the train connection to Munich was excellent, and there were frequent enough flights available from there to London. He would lose some time, but gain a valuable opportunity for rest, plus peaceful surroundings in which to think the situation through.

The moment before he got into the people carrier he had looked Nagelmann straight in the eye and said: 'I'll phone as agreed. It'll be interesting to hear what Mesmer wants to do.'

Unfortunately the Swiss lawyer was very good. He said nothing, merely raised his hand in a dismissive wave. Had there been just the slightest hint of a reaction? In all honesty, Coyle wasn't sure. But Mesmer was as close to an educated guess as he had been able to get. If not Mesmer, then who?

He finished off a light meal before sending Joanne a text message to let her know that they were on schedule. He also sent a text to Sir Hugh, not to report but to ask for another favour. Two hours before they were due in Munich he reclined his seat and fell asleep in minutes.

35. LONDON

Before Coyle's train pulled into the Munich station, Steve Henderson's private jet was already making its London approach. Once they were rid of Markevich, a short phone call to Rita Ridgewood – Nelson himself happened to be unavailable – made it clear that a totally unexpected situation has arisen, and Hannes Nagelmann offered to arrange a one-way charter flight immediately. The LONA leadership had to meet in person; anything else was unthinkable from a security point of view.

Nelson's own Jaguar met him at the airport and deposited him at Party HQ on the outskirts of Belgravia. Moments later he was back in the conference room where they had met the previous night. Whitmore was not there of course, but all the others. Nelson himself, Bill Utley, Barry Vickerton and the two contrasting ladies, Bonnie Stevens and Rita Ridgewood. There was a collective gasp as he entered.

'You look like a fucking crime victim,' Nelson observed. 'Did Rita get it right, Markevich was there waiting for you?'

Frequently touching his still very painful and probably fractured nose, Henderson gave a condensed account of what had happened. He got several snide comments about letting an unarmed man hijack him, and Nelson seemed ready to burst with anger and contempt, but he persisted and finished his tale.

'How did he know you'd be on that specific flight?' queried Rita. 'For that matter, how did he know you were going to be there at all?'

'He guessed we'd have to reach out to L&O after what he'd done to us in London. Then he hacked my reservation using Whitmore's computer.'

'Too much fucking incompetence!' barked Nelson. 'Can we change the way we manage travel?'

Rita wasn't sure whether she was included in the incompetence. 'Of course, but for the time being any travel abroad will have to be by private plane only,' she responded. 'Wait a minute! Steve, did he actually mention Hannes Nagelmann's name to you when he grabbed you at Zurich Airport?'

'Not sure, love. He spoke mostly German.'

The condescending endearment made Rita take a stronger line than she had intended. 'Well Nagelmann sounds the same in any language. Did he, or didn't he know the name or *did he learn it from you?*'

'What are you getting at, Rita?' asked Nelson.

'I'm thinking that Markevich took a big risk just to speak with Hannes if he already knew about him. But if he didn't, and this was a fishing expedition to discover the identity of our L&O contact, then he succeeded brilliantly don't you think!'

'He also made us look weak and stupid in front of Nagelmann,' observed Bonnie.

After another furious look in Henderson's direction Nelson commented. 'To be precise, he made *Steve* look weak and stupid, but I guess it reflects badly on all of us in a way. But what will Hannes do? What did he say he would do?'

Henderson swallowed hard before replying. 'He said we had a real problem with Markevich and whoever's behind him, but that he's sure we can handle it.'

'Which translates into *handle it or else!*' Nelson surmised. 'People, we're in a serious situation here! We *have to* find Markevich and deal with him! There's simply no alternative!'

But Bonnie disagreed. 'Maybe there is something else we can do,' she ventured excitedly. 'What if Markevich is exactly what he says he is, someone who wants the Twits in power instead of us?'

'He did push the Twits thing hard with Hannes,' offered Henderson.

Nelson was interested. 'So what do you suggest, Bonnie?'

Once again the sweetest looking person in the room had the most ruthless thought. 'Could we speed up rather than slow down? We bring down the government and force an election before Markevich and his people can do anything about it. Once the election is announced, it'll be too late to build up the Twits. Especially if you make a deal with Brian!'

The party leader looked at his Chief Whip with a mix of admiration, lust and maybe even love. 'Go and see him!' he commanded.

36. LONDON

Joanne had spent the evening trawling through Whitmore's computer, which Coyle had left in her care. The man in charge of keeping discipline amongst the corrupted officials on LONA's secret payroll obviously had to know the identities of these people. With horror she realised there were 1894 personal files under the seemingly innocent heading *Assets*. A staggering amount of time and money must have been spent building up this network of traitors, and she was horrified to discover that she recognised many more names than she had expected.

She had fallen asleep quickly, but suddenly found herself awake and oddly conscious of Coyle's empty bed next to hers. It seemed an eternity since she had last shared a bedroom with a man. Tom had been her regular boyfriend for nearly four years; two of those even after she had figured out that he was an immature, self-centred prick who used her for convenient backup sex when he couldn't score elsewhere. She blamed herself for postponing the inevitable breakup, but blamed him *more* for stringing her along so long with fuzzy promises of some kind of future together.

Well, she wished him well in his life of fast-food management and predatory bar-hopping. No, actually she didn't. She would rather he drowned in his own puke or got smashed by a cement truck while staggering to take a piss on the curb.

Coyle's text message had come just before she went to bed. *Thought you'd like to know all went well today. Back tomorrow.*

Hardly a declaration of affection, but he could have made it shorter still. She did get a sense that he wanted to treat her fairly, but whether out of general fairness or because he liked her, she couldn't tell. Who *was* Coyle? Hell, *what* was he? Her dad hadn't exactly been helpful when she tried to quiz him about her strange new acquaintance.

He's got to have a vulnerable spot, she thought. Everyone has one. For sure, she herself had more weaknesses than she liked to admit, such as joining the police mainly because her dad categorically refused to let her follow him into the army. She had sailed through the Academy and actually quite enjoyed her first year in uniform, but once she was given more and more desk bound duties she felt frustrated and trapped. Making CID, and most lately DS, only made it worse. It seemed she was struggling for her reports to meet formalistic expectations, and filling out nonsensical forms, rather that *doing something* about the deteriorating crime situation she saw all around her.

Coyle certainly made things happen. Maybe that was why she had taken to him in a way she couldn't quite explain. It wasn't lust and it certainly wasn't love, but the man was – well, different. Deep down she had always wanted to be where there was real action. She wanted to do what it took to get results. But of course it seemed crazy to think that the two of them could take on such a well-funded and connected enemy as LONA.

Well, we've made a hell of a start! She contemplated.

37. LONDON

Bonnie and Rita shared a cab back to the Chelsea Harbour building where they both owned high floor apartments.

'Up for a nightcap?' asked the older woman as they stepped into the lift.

Bonnie thought about it for a second. 'It'll have to be my place,' she decided. 'I need to get into a robe! What a day!'

'I'll be down in five,' Rita told her as the lift stopped on Bonnie's floor.

It turned out more like a quarter of an hour until Rita rang the bell, but used her own key to enter. Bonnie had turned on her decorative gas fire and arranged two crystal glasses and an ice bucket containing an uncorked bottle of Chablis on the coffee table. She wore a fluffy turquoise bathrobe and had her legs curled up on the L-shaped sofa that dominated the living room.

Rita had changed into a deep plum coloured sweat suit and black embroidered slippers. She sank contentedly into the sea of soft cushions her hostess kept piled high on the sofa.

'How are you going to play Atkins?' she asked while Bonnie poured a generous measure into each glass.

'Well, luckily I didn't get hold of him today. I was supposed to put pressure on him, remember?'

'But now the message is a bit different. How far do you think Neil is prepared to go to get the Twits onboard? Only the other day he wanted to destroy them before the election!'

'Here's to men changing their minds.' Bonnie smiled and raised her glass. Then struck a serious note. 'We'll have to offer Brian a senior cabinet position however well or poorly they do in the election. Anyway, with the Twits committed to us, we're bound to come out with a majority. Without them I wouldn't be so sure actually.'

Bonnie had come to Rita's attention several years earlier as a bright media expert connected to UKIP, but unable to persuade that party to offer her a winnable seat in Parliament. It had been an easy recruitment process, greatly helped by the fact that Nelson's eyes had filled with desire the moment he met her.

It amused Rita to pretend towards their Leader that she was unaware of what went on right here in her own building. In fact, the affair – if you could call it that – was just one of the many holds she had on Nelson. What else would you expect from a career intelligence officer, with fifteen years in the clandestine service of MI6 to her credit before branching out into party politics!

As head of security and intelligence, she was effectively the spider in a great web of ruthless power, of which Nelson thought himself the undisputed master. And then there was the matter of Vernon Cox!

Bonnie and Vernon had already split up when she jointed LONA, but the divorce kept dragging out for a multitude of reasons, and Nelson quite irrationally lost his patience and had Bill Utley arrange for what he joked about as the *widow option*.

Cox was a freelance journalist who specialised in feeding controversial items to the tabloids. He moved in many murky parts of society, and it had not been hard to arrange for a fatal accident while the idiot was mile-high on cocaine. Bonnie had been well and truly over him by then and in fact shrugged off his death with a *Serves him right*, but Rita had no doubt that if she ever found out the truth, she would turn against Nelson with venom.

For a while longer they discussed the timetable for the next couple of days. Then Bonnie leaned forward and put down her empty glass. 'I think that's enough for me,' she said.

Stretching for the table made her robe open slightly and expose her right breast. Rita looked at it and then into Bonnie's eyes. They held each other's glance for several seconds. Then Rita edged herself close and kissed her lightly on the mouth while she carefully teased the exposed nipple with her fingertips. It hardened immediately and she felt Bonnie's tongue push into her mouth.

Moving to the bedroom would have broken the mood. Besides, this was about relieving tension rather than luxurious lovemaking. She knew exactly what to do.

Bonnie's robe came undone as she leaned back into the cushions. As usual, she wore a pair of expensive lace-trimmed knickers. Ah, another secret outside the Leader's grasp!

With a swift movement Rita pulled off her top and dropped the bottom part of her sweat suit enough to reveal that she wasn't wearing anything underneath. Then she leaned into Bonnie, left hand caressing her head, mouth finding the other nipple and right hand exploring the front of those exquisite knickers.

Sooner than she had expected, Bonnie's hands came down to her waist and pulled down on the elastic. The knickers came off, revealing what was of course not new to her – however delightful the sight – but still a symbol of the special bond between them. She was allowed to see it, but no one else, especially power and sex addicted Neil Nelson – the scar!

Bonnie had been seventeen and in pregnancy denial for so long that an abortion was too hard to contemplate. She had given birth to a baby girl, but signed her over for adoption well before the birth. Three days before she was due, the bleeding started, and the pain! Rushed to hospital, she had endured hours of agony until the staff finally opted for a caesarean section. And there it was, the scar that indisputably revealed that she was technically a mother!

This is why women who aren't really lesbians enjoy having sex with women; we know our way around and we don't rush it, Rita thought as she gave Bonnie the full benefit of her right hand. Index and middle fingers first probed, then gradually entered her vagina, moving rhythmically but not too hard - constantly sensing her body's mood. The thumb gently circled her clitoris – barely touching but finding the same rhythm. Finally, when Bonnie was close to climaxing, the little finger bored its way into her anus.

The stress of the past days erupted from Bonnie in a high orgasmic squeal, and she thrashed about longer than Rita had seen her do before. Those magnificent breasts heaved and jiggled, and her lovely thighs closed on Rita's hand and squeezed it in appreciation.

'I needed that!' she gasped.

Rita pulled herself up and wiggled out of the sweat suit bottom. 'Shall we see what the Chief Whip can do,' she purred.

38. ALBANIA

Unbeknownst to Steve Henderson, Hannes Nagelmann has chartered not one, but two business jets. An hour after the first plane had taken off towards London with the bruised LONA man onboard, another sleek machine roared into the evening sky bound for Albania's capital Tirana.

Some three hours later, Nagelmann walked a short distance from where the plane had parked to a waiting helicopter, which took off as soon as he had strapped himself into his seat. Despite its shabby outward appearance – he assumed it was intentional – this helicopter was a special VIP version of the American Sikorsky S-76 with extra sound insulation, comfortable leather seats plus state-of-the-art avionics that made flying at night unproblematic.

The flight took him over rough mountain terrain, but of course he saw nothing of it, except the occasional fleck of light. After less than an hour the pilot made a practiced landing on what looked like a football pitch lit only by the headlights of a Mercedes Geländewagen. Nagelmann made his way towards the car, knowing that he had a short but bumpy ride ahead of him before reaching his destination.

Shortly after midnight he arrived at the compound and was driven directly to Mesmer's residence. Architecturally more concrete bunker than hunting lodge, the structure was large and not at all uncomfortable. The mountain air had a cold bite to it, but the inside temperature was pleasant and he noticed the appealing smell of burning logs.

Mesmer was waiting for him in the library, a large dimly lit room with wood-panelled walls and a magnificent fireplace, from which the flames cast a dramatic light on a collection of antique hunting and military rifles that covered more wall space than the bookcases. The host was proud of his fire. It had required clever technology to disperse the smoke in such a way that it could not be spotted outside.

Mesmer could stop a drunken bar brawl by just clearing his throat. Entirely bald, his enormous head sat squarely – seemingly without the need for a neck – on top of massive shoulders and a matching chest. Even neckless, he towered over most men. His face might at some point have been described as handsome, but countless incidents of armed and unarmed combat had left marks that could only be described as gruesome. It seemed a miracle that he retained the use of both eyes, although the left one was nearly blocked by overhanging scar tissue. The nose was an unshapely mess of twisted flesh and cartilage, but against all odds air still flowed through it.

Only his teeth gleamed impeccably straight and white. But then they were fake of course. Reconstructed from scratch at great expense by the best orthodontic surgeons money could by. Many wondered why Mesmer hadn't extended the reconstructive approach to his face, but of course no one ever asked him.

They exchanged greetings and a stunningly beautiful girl placed a tray with cold cuts and bread on a low table before gliding out of the room. Mesmer poured vodka into two glasses.

'So what's the problem we can't talk about by phone?' he asked in accented German. His nationality wasn't known to Nagelmann, who assumed that the shadowy power behind L&O was not a native of Albania, but found it a convenient to base himself there.

'I know we pay to have secure connections, but in a situation like this – I couldn't risk it,' began Nagelmann. 'Did you read about what happened in London?'

'Of course. Very strange! But should we really be worried?'

'The man who launched the attack – he calls himself Markevich – he came to see me in Zurich.'

'He came to *see* you!'

'Nelson sent Henderson to brief me, and Markevich jumped on him just as my people picked him up at the airport. He was unarmed, but told Henderson he'd break his neck unless he pretended they had planned on seeing me together.'

'And your men suspected nothing?'

'He spoke to them separately in German and made it all sound plausible. If Henderson was okay with it, so were they.'

'What a cowardly idiot! Now *I* would happily break his damned neck!'

Nagelmann had a quick mental vision of Mesmer doing just that, but then gave a meticulously accurate description of the strange encounter he'd had with Markevich.

After he had finished, Mesmer reached for his glass and took a substantial gulp of vodka. 'He actually mentioned my name!' he exclaimed. 'How on Earth is that possible?'

'I got the impression he is a very serious operator, and I think we should assume that he has serious people behind him as well. It was clever of him to bring up your name only when Henderson couldn't overhear. That showed sensitivity to our interests.'

Mesmer silently swerved his drink in deep thought. 'Perhaps,' he conceded. 'What do you propose we do about him?'

The lawyer had anticipated and spent most of the journey thinking about that question. 'He may very well be right about the LONA leadership. And it could be in our interest to cooperate in Great Britain. Whoever is behind him doesn't seem to be concerned with any other part of Europe.'

'Wouldn't the obvious solution be to arrange a meeting and eliminate Markevich and anyone coming along with him?'

The thought had occurred to Nagelmann. 'There should be a meeting, but I think we should use it to find out more and build up trust,' he ventured. 'From what I've seen of Markevich, he'll be very cautious. If we set up an ambush and he gets wind of it, we could have an unnecessary war on our hands. Why not first get to know these people who claim they want to be our allies, and fight them only if becomes necessary. Besides...'

'Yes, what are you thinking?'

Nagelmann knew he had to thread carefully indeed. Although he was the face towards all the L&O parties and Mesmer a nameless mysterious entity in the background, only Mesmer knew from where their orders and the funds ultimately came.

'Isn't it possible that Markevich is on a parallel mission to ours, and sent by more or less the same principals?'

To his surprise, Mesmer didn't react angrily. Instead he sipped his drink, put down the glass and produced what resembled a smile. 'A dangerous thought my dear Nagelmann, but one we can't afford to ignore. Let's get closer to Markevich before we decide anything final.'

Having spoken, Mesmer indicated that their nightly chat was over. There would be time to work out the details in the morning. Nagelmann picked up his small overnight bag, said goodnight and left his employer to digest their discussion.

39. ALBANIA

Nagelmann always had the same guestroom on the lower level. An opulently, if not tastefully, decorated bedroom with an almost equally large bathroom inspired by Roman villas of antiquity but transgressing well into the tasteless.

He had been so caught up in the events of the day and so tired from his travel that he had forgotten about the girls. As he spotted the two of them, both very pretty and wearing the outfits his host knew he enjoyed, his first thought was to send them away. But that would have been discourteous to Mesmer, who enjoyed offering his stable of girls to those guests who – like himself – appreciated being able to push sex beyond the *normal and legal*. Besides, perhaps the exercise would help him sleep.

Motioning to them to get ready, he undressed and washed up before wrapping himself in one of the provided robes. When he returned to the bedroom both girls were standing up waiting for him. It took him a few seconds to decide which one he would allow to touch him. In the end he picked the smaller and more delicate looking.

He steered the other girl to the wingback chair in the corner and made her bend forward over the backrest. The riding crop was where it always was, on top of the dresser, so he picked it up and used it to lift the girl's skirt.

The Albanian idea of an English schoolgirl's uniform was perhaps not entirely accurate, but it worked for him. He happily noted that the girl wore proper knickers, not one of those diminutive thongs prostitutes and porn producers seemed to think men found exciting.

Once he had carefully taken down the knickers to expose the girl's buttocks he swung the crop just hard enough to make a small red mark. Then again, a little harder this time. The girl gave a small whimper and he felt himself stiffen. He waved the other girl over and made her take off her top and bra before kneeling in front of him.

It took longer and was harder work than he had expected. When he finally ejaculated into the kneeling girl's mouth, the other one's entire bottom was crimson red and his arm so tired that he was quite relieved to let go of the crop.

40. LONDON

The early morning flight from Munich landed on schedule and Coyle was relieved, though not surprised, to slip unnoticed back into the country. Despite the ease by which David Baker's passport passed U.K. Immigration scrutiny, he decided to drop this identity very soon and at the same time alter his appearance.

He found the Kawasaki unmolested, and quickly pulled the leather gear over his business suit. Minutes later he was on the M25 heading for a north London encounter he considered important enough to squeeze in before he returned to Joanne and their hotel in Earls Court.

Osman Khan was a special kind of crook. Although his main activity was distributing opium-based drugs from his native Afghanistan, he had also found it advantageous to support the radicalised Islamic community. Young men with more or less jihadist views made excellent foot soldiers when violence was called for. They were uninterested in drugs themselves, but more than happy for westerners to corrupt their own bodies. It seemed a logical part of the global struggle against the infidel.

As his influence amongst the radicalised fringe of British Moslems grew, Osman Khan came to the attention of MI5. At Thames House he was first seen as a potential informer, but he deftly deflected their overtures in another direction. Would he not be of greater use to his adopted country if he became a voice of tolerance and moderation? He had the contacts and he had the standing of a respected leader in the Moslem community!

This line happened to fit nicely with a *strategy* being pushed at the time, and his inclusion was quickly blessed by senior levels and reported to their political masters as another success in the fight for British Moslems' hearts and minds.

Rita Ridgewood picked up on this, and after some further study of Osman Khan's background and operation, suggested that Bill Utley pay him a visit equipped with a million pounds in cash and half a dozen Highgate enforcers as backup in case there was a misunderstanding.

In the end Grant Whitmore joined the recruiting expedition in person, and together with Utley found Khan not only willing but positively delighted to take LONA money for instigating and funding domestic terrorism if and when it suited his new friends. This had been the beginning of a carefully measured terror campaign that greatly contributed to Nelson's own growing popularity and enabled LONA to evolve in the mind of many voters into a real alternative to the inept politicians ruining the country.

Coyle doubted that Osman Khan was on Bogdan Konev's Christmas card list, but even if the Bulgarian had conveyed his warning, Khan would almost certainly ignore it. That, plus the fact that with the east-European criminals unlikely to play ball anymore, Khan was Bill Utley's most valuable ally made Coyle's decision a simple one. Intimidating Khan would not be enough. An accurately placed bullet would.

41. LONDON

The Victorian house was large enough to accommodate many members of Osman Khan's extended family. According to Whitmore's *contingency plan* notes, Khan relied on his assorted cousins and nephews for the delicate task of mixing security with the important routines of daily business. Trust was everything to Khan. With so many temptations around, only those connected to him by blood could be relied on not to steal, or worse – betray him to outsiders.

Khan did have an proper office of course, but Coyle had got the impression from Highgate Security's research that his target was more likely to be at his home at this time – late morning. This seemed confirmed when he parked the bike a block and a half away and observed the house for fifteen minutes. There was just too much activity in evidence and too many vehicles in the drive for the lord and master to be away at his office. No, Khan was clearly holding court at home.

Coyle rode up to the gate, but left the bike outside with the engine idling. He wanted the quickest possible getaway. The gate was only semi-closed, but two sturdy young men made their presence known as he approached while keeping the MP7 hidden inside the overnight bag.

'As-salamu Alaykum,' Coyle greeted them in Arabic. *Peace be with you*!

The response was pure Lancashire. 'What've you got, mate?'

'I have an urgent message for Khan from the Council of Elders,' Coyle persisted, still in Arabic. When it was clear that neither man understood a word, he repeated the statement in heavily Middle East accented English while speaking as someone used to giving orders.

It took several seconds while the two sentries processed his apparent transition from motorcycle courier to envoy of a likeminded authority, but they finally relented and led him to the back of the house. It seemed that Osman Khan conducted business in a backroom.

They passed through a large plant-filled conservatory and entered a short corridor. At the end was a black door and one of the young men knocked respectfully. Shortly afterwards someone unlocked it from the inside and opened it a few inches.

Rather than leave the outcome open to debate, Coyle knocked the closer of the young guards unconscious with a single blow to the head. Then he kicked the door wide open and entered the room pushing the other guard ahead of him.

The man who had unlocked the door had to take a couple of steps back. He was a bit older than his outside colleagues and slightly more capable. He had been holding a pistol – casually as part of his job description. Now he brought it up and made a good effort to aim it at the intruder.

Coyle had by now let the overnighter drop to the floor while holding on to the MP7. Rather than shoot the man with the pistol he swung the MP7 at his wrist, then followed up with a left elbow to his chest with enough force to put him out of action for a minute or two.

With his usual talent for rapid situational awareness Coyle noted that Osman Khan sat in a group of five men around a table that held a similar number of teacups. Three of the men appeared to be either Middle Eastern or Pakistani, but the last man was a westerner. And a familiar face!

He ought to have factored in the possibility that Bill Utley would be here. It made perfect sense, since Khan was undoubtedly a logical person to see after Highgate's destruction and Konev & Co's presumed uncooperativeness. Whether Nelson wanted a terrorist incident to rail against or replacements for his battered enforcers, Osman Khan was the obvious conduit!

He was an obese man with an expressive face that could switch from obsequious to haughty at will. Right now scared shitless seemed the correct description to Coyle. He fired a single bullet into Khan's forehead and knew instantly from the size of the exit wound that a second shot would not be required.

'No martyrdom operations in this country by the Council of Elders' order!' he shouted in Arabic. Two of the men seemed to understand. The other two just stated at him terrified.

The fact that Coyle was still wearing his helmet saved Utley's life. Not being able to identify the gunman, he could be useful as a messenger, and Coyle wanted Nelson to know exactly what had happened.

He repeated the message in his Middle Eastern English and saw sudden comprehension in Utley's cunning eyes.

'Look, we're just talking here!' he shouted. 'Nothing's been decided!'

Almost casually Coyle shot him in both shoulders, then added a bullet into the right knee. This made the others attempt to scramble out of their seats, but it was of course entirely futile.

Having spared Utley, he decided that Khan would be the only lethal casualty and quickly dealt with the three men. The PM7 fires a special small caliber high velocity bullet that does extensive damage to all human tissue hit. Khan's guests would remember his visit for a long time as they recuperated!

The sound suppressor kept the shots muffled, but far from silent. The general commotion with shouts, screams and furniture overturning was enough to alert others in the house, and an armed man barged into the room followed by another. Coyle immediately registered that these two weren't part of Khan's crew, so he assumed they had been brought by Utley and were probably drawn from what remained of the enforcers.

It is one thing to precision-wound an opponent who can't return fire, but altogether another when he is pointing a gun at you. As much as Coyle wanted to avoid killing anyone except Khan, he couldn't afford to become a target himself.

He managed to aim and fire at the first man's gun hand. The bullet tore through the wrist, the effect of the bullet both instantaneous and devastating. But his partner used the moment to squeeze off a round of his own and a loud bang filled the room. The bullet missed Coyle, but not by much. He dove to his right in an effort to make the shooter readjust his aim. Before touching the floor he fired at an upward angle and caught the enforcer in the lower abdomen. The man shuddered in shock and left himself open to another round, this time very well aimed. Coyle shot him through the right shoulder joint and made the mental note that although the first wound would require serious hospital treatment, it was unlikely to be fatal.

Unfortunately the unsilenced shot sent an alarm signal through the whole house. Coyle heard excited shouting and decided to exit the way he had came in. After a final look at Khan to verify that he was definitely dead, he ran back through the corridor into the conservatory.

A woman in her mid forties came running in the opposite direction. She was unarmed, and rather than shoot her Coyle fended her off with his left arm and decided to use her for disinformation.

'Khan betrayed us!' he shouted in Arabic as he pushed past her.

Then he was in the driveway and moments later back in the street by the bike. The engine was still humming so he jumped into the saddle and kicked off. He accelerated rapidly and a quick glance in the mirror confirmed that he was out of pistol range.

Any pursuit by the cars in the drive would be futile. He had not taken the time to shoot out tyres, but within a minute the great speed and agility of the bike put him well beyond the point where giving chase made sense. The only thing he had to worry about now was attracting the attention of the public or ultimately the police.

A narrow lane caught his eye and he braked suddenly so he could manoeuvre the bike into the opening. He rode a short distance into the lane, then stopped and dismounted. In less than two minutes he changed the number plates and stowed the MP7 out of sight. Then he set off again, followed the lane until it connected with a bigger road, and drove at legal speed towards his hotel in Earls Court.

42. LONDON

Alerted by a text message to her phone, Joanne was waiting for him in the room. She surprised herself with the intensity of the hug she gave him as he stepped through the door. A moment of awkwardness followed, but then Coyle sprang into his brisk business mode.

'Did you manage to get all the shopping done?' he asked. 'We'll need to check out of this hotel before too long.'

Slightly taken aback by the mundane subject, Joanne walked over to the bed and turned two large shopping bags upside down. The most eye-catching item was a black leather outfit, complete with boots and helmet.

'Will this do?' she asked with a hint of an edge to her voice.

'Looks perfect!' he responded happily. 'Too bad you don't actually ride bikes, but you'll make a fine passenger in that gear.'

'I'm not sure I'm looking forward to it,' she admitted. 'It looks dangerous.'

'If you don't know what you're doing it's *very* dangerous, but fortunately I do. The bike is the safest and quickest way we can move about. It's an operational edge that we need.'

'So where are we staying? I need to present myself at Scotland Yard at two o'clock.'

Earlier that morning she had phoned her boss DCI Wainwright to tell him she would be ready to come back on duty the next day. He had immediately, and somewhat petulantly told her that she was to report for special duty at the Metropolitan Police instead. A DCS Clara Miller was expecting her call.

'I've booked us into a B&B in Ruislip,' Coyle informed her. 'It looks better if we check in together, so when you're through with your meeting we can drive there in the van. Good of Sir Hugh so arrange things so quickly, but that means you'll have one more piece of shopping to do.'

'Not another disguise I hope!'

'Not as such. You need to get yourself a pay-as-you-go phone so you can give a contact number to your nominal boss at the Met. The phone I gave you has to be off limits and I made you leave your own phone back at your dad's place.'

Joanne saw his point. DCS Miller would definitely insist on a contact number. 'No problem, it shouldn't take me long,' she agreed. 'What will you be doing meanwhile?'

Coyle was rummaging through the rest of her shopping. He pulled out several cartons of hair dye and a set of electric hair clippers.

'I thought I'd give myself a new hairdo before seeing the Minister for Transport,' he replied.

43. LONDON

The lunch meeting at one of London's oldest and most traditional clubs had a clear objective: to determine whether the Rightful Tory Party's above board – meaning non-LONA – financial supporters and influential backers supported further participation in the coalition, or preferred an act of defiance that would bring down the government and pave the way for an early general election.

Brian Atkins explained that although he held the cabinet position of Minister for Transport, he had been compelled by the party's platform to trespass extensively on the Home Secretary's turf. This had caused great friction within the coalition, and Atkins by now felt so frustrated and ostracised by his cabinet colleagues that he was ready to concede that his government gamble had failed. If they couldn't advance their agenda within the ruling coalition, surely it was better to let their principles lead them into opposition. Who knows, an early election might even give them an enhanced powerbase from which to negotiate and barter.

To his surprise however, he found that a slim majority of the party sponsors held the opposing view and they had found an unlikely ally in his deputy leader, Caroline Steele. Damnation! He had hand-picked plump and plain Caroline for the position precisely because he could not imagine her ever standing up to him. That and the air of solid respectability she brought to his renegade party as mother of two and wife of a university professor.

It was too early to force an election, she argued. There was still much to be done by working within the Government, so why should they risk an undesired election result? If some polls were to be believed, LONA might emerge from a general election as the largest party, possibly even acquiring a majority.

These words played well with the prudent men and women in the room, who generally took a more detached and objective view than Atkins, the front line political fighter. As they were financial donors to the party, he couldn't really try to sway them with LONA money, the way he controlled some of his more difficult MPs.

His private secretary appeared behind him and whispered that Dr Barnes was waiting to see him. Interrupting a lunch meeting wasn't exactly exceptional – he had taken a couple of important phone calls already – but the way this appointment had been made was unusual. An old contact at MI6 had phoned his private number and insisted that he should see a Dr Barnes the same day.

With a mumbled excuse, he left the table and followed his secretary down a set of stairs and into a billiard room, unused and unlit at this early hour.

'Thank you! You can leave us alone.' The voice was polite but firm and full of authority. The secretary tactfully withdrew and closed the door behind her.

'Dr Barnes?' Atkins half asked, half stated. He was off balance and on the point of getting annoyed.

'Neither name nor title are actual, but when you consider how the appointment was made it shouldn't surprise you.'

'Then who are you? And what can I do for you?'

'First of all, the person who asked you to meet with me doesn't know who I am either, but is acting in good faith. It's important that we talk.'

Dr Barnes kept approaching and as he passed from shadow into daylight seeping in between curtains by a window, Atkins had a chance to appraise him. He carried himself with the confident grace of an athlete, but wore a conservative and clearly expensive business suit. Blond, very short cropped hair. Sharp blue eyes dominated a face that was strong, but in truth neither pleasant nor unpleasant to look at.

Atkins himself had been listed by a prominent ladies' magazine as one of the six best looking men in British politics, something which had done his career no harm at all. His photogenic smile and trademark high fashion haircut made him a familiar figure throughout the nation. Still, the visitor – whoever he was – had an intimidating effect on him.

Deciding he would give the mystery man a chance to explain himself, Atkins said, 'Well I'm listening, but I can't give you much time.'

Coyle nodded sympathetically. 'Not a problem! What I have to say is simple. I'm the instrument of those who want to ensure that the country is not taken over by LONA and turned into a dictatorship. You can help.'

'How? The Longbows are a rival party. We work against them as a matter of course!'

'If you pull your party out of the coalition you might as well hand Nelson the keys to Number Ten! Not that he'll stop there!'

'Nonsense! The British voters. . .'

'Will be overwhelmed by the immense election campaign LONA will put together with billions in undeclared financial support from Law & Order! They've already used this money to buy over eighteen-hundred influential people in the civil service, police, military, intelligence community and even the media.'

Atkins was unconvinced. 'How can you possible claim to know that?' he argued.

'A very sensitive computer fell into my hands.'

'What does that mean?'

'Nelson was using a security company called Highgate as his private army to intimidate those he'd paid off and make sure they stayed loyal. The other day I eliminated that army as a threat. But that was only the beginning of our battle to stop LONA.'

The Rightful Tories leader took a deep breath as he made the connection. 'I was briefed on the Highgate attack,' he said quietly. 'It was *you* who did it?'

Coyle let a couple of seconds pass before he responded. 'It is possible that Nelson will offer you an alliance, or something else to entice you to help him get the election he wants. Whatever he suggests, you mustn't accept! It won't be in your interest!'

'Because?'

'LONA *will* be discredited and finished as a political force whether there's an election or not. That I guarantee! Anyone who goes to bat for Nelson will be dealt with as well.'

As a man who considered himself both important and influential, Atkins bristled at being given what amounted to an order.

'You're threatening me!' he said coldly, but Coyle's look stopped him from continuing.

'Mr Atkins, I'm not in the habit of making threats, but I *have* given you a warning not to play into the hands of Nelson. The best thing you can do for your country right now is to deny LONA an early election. Whatever short-term advantage you imagine you can grab for your party, forget it! The survival of British democracy is at stake and you need to think like a statesman rather than a politician!'

The words appeared to be sinking in, but Coyle knew there wasn't time for a debate. Atkins had received the message and would now have to make his choices. He certainly had the option of calling out to his protection officers to try and have him arrested.

'Thank you for your time! I'll let you get back to your meeting.' He grabbed Atkins's hand and squeezed it firmly enough to leave little doubt that he could crush it if he wanted to. The distraction unsettled the RTP leader and by the time he regained his composure, Coyle had retreated into the shadows. Seconds later a door closed and Atkins found himself alone, shaken and very confused. The strange encounter had given him plenty to think about in advance of his agreed *quick chat* with Bonnie Stevens later that afternoon.

44. LONDON

After leaving the club, Coyle took precautions against being followed. It was just possible that Atkins could have sent someone after him.

Once he was satisfied that he did not have a tail, he walked about slowly in St James's Park and gathered his thoughts. Then he called Sir Hugh Canderton, who answered on the second ring.

'Meeting go okay?'

Coyle spoke rapidly. 'Yes, but I think it was a mistake. My error. I expected a more definite reaction. Not sure what he'll do now, but we need to plan for the worst case scenario.'

'What can I do to help?'

'You should disappear for a while. Up to a week. You have a *just-in-case* stash of course?'

'I'm not without resources. Where do you want me to go?'

'Anywhere you can get to easily by commuter train. Hide out in a high volume hotel. Don't bring your normal phone or computer. Only devices that can't be traced.'

Sir Hugh was not quite convinced. 'You're sure we're not overreacting here?'

'Even if he doesn't start tracing us back from your friend who set up the meeting, the game is about to become extremely dangerous.'

'What about the others?'

'Can you pass word to our financial friend that this would be a good time to make a business trip out of the country. I'll handle the Sergeant and the girl.'

Even as Coyle spoke he had a premonition that *handling* Stack might be anything but straightforward. As soon as he had finished talking to Sir Hugh, he made another call to the former Staff Sergeant, but when he suggested that the man should leave his home and lie low for a week in some obscure B&B, the response was a solid *Fuck off mate!*

45. LONDON

She waited for him on a street corner and quickly jumped into the innocuous white van. The introductory meeting with DCS Clara Miller had been cordial but somewhat tense as the question of *why* hung over them. Senior officers don't like the idea of something important going on right below them that they are excluded from.

'So now I'm officially part of a task force on human trafficking,' she explained.

'Not a bad cover,' Coyle agreed.

'Good thing you told me to get a phone! She did insist on having a number where they can reach me.'

Coyle drove west towards Ruislip and used the time to brief Joanne on his meeting with Atkins.

'In the end I was left with an uneasy feeling,' he concluded. 'I may have made a serious mistake going to see him.'

'But what can he do even if he decides to turn you in, so to speak?'

'One of Sir Hugh's high-up contacts arranged the meeting. That means I've left a trail.'

'Atkins calls in the police or MI5 and they put pressure on the contact and he gives them Sir Hugh?'

'Precisely! And at some point or in some way, Sir Hugh can lead them to Henry Elliott and to me. I've asked both of them to drop out of sight for a few days.'

'And we're shifting our base to Ruislip.'

Coyle drove half a block in silence. 'You may want to reconsider staying with me,' he finally said, and received a sharp glare.

'What do you mean? Aren't we way past the point of no return?'

There was a blockage ahead and Coyle had to break sharply to avoid contact with a delivery lorry.

'I'm sorry Joanne, but you know you weren't part of my original plan. When you showed up at your dad's place you forced me to think quickly, and getting you involved seemed a good way to stop you from trying to arrest me. You've been very valuable, that goes without saying, but we could be getting into really dangerous territory from here on. I don't think I have the right to risk your life.'

The van started moving again. Joanne looked out of the side window while they gathered speed.

'Can we talk about it later tonight please? I can't concentrate here and I don't want to say the wrong thing.'

He nodded with evident relief, and they continued the drive through London in silence. Less than hour later they arrived at their B&B and registered innocuously as Mr and Mrs Paul Davis.

46. HAMPSHIRE

The two women arrived from London by chartered helicopter. Neil Nelson watched it land on the vast front lawn that separated his minor Georgian mansion from the country road. With Bill Utley in hospital and Steve Henderson still stunned by his Zurich encounter with Markevich, the ladies were taking on even more of the crucial work at LONA.

There was still Barry Vickerton of course, but outside his core expertise of finance and money laundering, the Chancellor of the Exchequer in waiting did not have a lot to offer. At the moment he was savouring one of his host's vintage ports while telling Henderson his nose would probably need reconstructive surgery.

As Rita and Bonnie entered the library, Nelson rose with uncharacteristic courtesy and directed them to an enormous leather chesterfield by the equally monstrous fireplace.

'How did it go?' The question was aimed at Bonnie, who smiled excitedly.

'Can you believe that Markevich actually came to see Brian at lunchtime today! Well, he called himself Dr Barnes and looked quite different, but from what Brian told me it had to be him!'

'Different from how Whitmore described him?' asked Rita sharply, and everyone turned to look at her.

'Yes, but nothing that couldn't be done with makeup, hair dye and contact lenses,' Bonnie countered. 'Markevich is dark haired and brown eyed, Dr Barnes blond with sharp – Brian used the word *penetrating* - eyes. But they both walk the walk and talk the talk.'

'Let's hear the rest of it,' Nelson urged her. 'What'll Brian do?'

'Apparently Markevich warned him not to pull out of the coalition. He said that could lead to a LONA majority in Parliament.'

'Spot on, but what's his game?' Nelson looked pleased that his ascent to power was predicted by their enemy.

'He told Brian that he'd already crippled Highgate and stolen Whitmore's computer. Now he intends to destroy us, and wants the Twits to stay out of his way. Or I guess he'll take them on as well.'

The good-natured expression left Nelson's face. 'Does Brian telling you all this mean that he'll do what we've told him to do?'

Bonnie beamed at him. 'Of course Neil! He doesn't like being threatened by some shadowy character with a gun! Naturally I pointed out that we're not exactly defenceless despite the Highgate debacle.' She glanced at Rita, who gave her a knowing nod of the head.

Nelson wasn't quite convinced. 'When are the Twits pulling out?' he insisted.

'Brian claims he has the MPs behind him already. He'll arrange a vote of their party board as soon as I confirm that you accept his terms.'

'He can't have Number Eleven and he can't have the Home Office! Every other cabinet post is negotiable.'

'He doesn't want a cabinet post,' Bonnie stated.

'Then what the fuck *does* he want?'

Then answer was simple but also utterly revealing. 'He want to get out of politics with plenty of money in his pocket.'

This made Vickerton pay attention. 'What sort of money, Bonnie dear? We've already given him over ten million!'

'A big part of that was to the party rather than Brian personally. He wants two hundred million. Split between four different offshore accounts. No record, no strings.'

Bonnie's words made Vickerton's fleshy face wobble in disbelief. 'The nerve of the man! You know we don't have that kind of money available!'

Nelson was less rattled. 'Don't be silly Barry,' he gruffed. 'Maybe we don't have it lying around, but we can get it from Hannes. It's not a bad price for this country of ours if you see what I mean. Especially when you consider how much we've spent already.'

Vickerton did not like the thought of giving that amount of money to a political opportunist, but he saw the logic behind Nelson's reasoning. 'So which one of us goes hat in hand to Nagelmann?'

Nelson threw a contemptuous glance at Henderson, who squirmed in his seat. 'You should go Barry. I don't think Hannes wants another visit from red-nosed Steve here.'

'But no commercial flight this time!' Rita Ridgewood stressed. 'I'll arrange a private charter for early tomorrow morning.'

The Leader acknowledged her astuteness. 'Now let's have your news Rita! You've been busy, right?'

'And productive, I hope!' she added. 'First of all, I had to do something about our security. We lost two more Highgate operatives with Bill, so we're actually down to just seven men. And that includes Craig and Johnny.'

Craig Baines and Johnny Gordon were both team leaders. They normally reported to Whitmore, but Rita had placed them directly under her own command.

'The east-European gangs have turned uncooperative as if *someone's* sent them a message, and with Bill in hospital I think we can write off the Islamists as well.'

'Are we sure it was Markevich who killed Khan and wounded Bill?'

'Not totally sure, but it seems likely. He tried to make Khan's people think he was from a rival terrorist organisation, but the timing and the method are just too similar to be a coincidence.'

'But he spoke fucking *Arabic*!' barked Nelson. 'Who the hell *is* this cunt?'

'He's someone we need a lot more firepower to stop. I've lined up fourteen quality men. By tomorrow they'll be operational in two teams, one led by Craig, the other by Johnny.'

Nelson was impressed. 'That was quick! Where did you find them?'

'Old contacts of mine. These chaps have all done contract work for MI6. The *deniable* kind. They're at least as competent as the Highgate squad, probably better since they're used to dealing with people who fight back.'

Bonnie was thinking of the broader picture. 'They may be able to take care of Markevich, but what about whoever sent him?' she asked. 'If he's their chosen instrument, we must assume they're very powerful.'

Nelson looked uncomfortable, but Rita pushed on. 'Unless Markevich turns out to have much less backing than he wants to make us believe.'

'Any reason to believe that's the case?' There was an almost pleading undertone to Nelson's voice.

'Joanne Stack.'

'Who the fuck's she when she's at home?'

Rita placed her tablet on the coffee table. The screen showed the inside of a clothing store.

'I got his from MI5. They collected security camera footage from the whole area at my request. Watch the grey-haired woman! See what she's doing between the aisles where she doesn't think anyone can see her!'

'She's changing her wig!' exclaimed Nelson.

'And reversing her jacket. A standard surveillance trick! This is while Carpenter and our team are right in the vicinity, following Henry Elliott around!'

'How do you know her name?'

'MI5 used facial recognition software to identify her. Fortunately she was on file as DS Joanne Stack of Cardiff CID.'

Nelson was unconvinced. 'Couldn't that mean she was doing normal police work?'

'It's possible, but at the time she was on compassionate leave because of a sick father, who by the way happens to be a retired SAS staff sergeant. Then earlier today she was suddenly assigned to the Metropolitan Police as part of a task force on human trafficking.'

'That doesn't prove she's working with Markevich,' Bonnie challenged.

'No, but she was *exactly* where you'd expect her to be at *exactly* the right time. Then there's Henry Elliott.'

The Leader looked bewildered. 'What about fucking Elliott?'

'The reason I sent Carpenter on the mission was to find out about that deep cover agent hidden away in Bhutan,' Rita reminded him. 'When Elliott responded to a coded message, we hoped he'd lead us to this agent. Instead Markevich snatched Carpenter and you know the rest.'

'Spell it out, damn it!'

'If Markevich is in fact the Bhutan agent, and Elliott helped him set up Carpenter, everything points to this being a very small organisation. Not nearly as powerful as he's implying. Why else use an obscure policewoman on leave as his field support?'

'Isn't that a circular argument?' Bonnie objected. 'She's with him because he doesn't have anyone else, and we say he doesn't have anyone else because she's the one he's using!'

Rita shrugged. 'Perhaps, but my instincts tell me they're working together. It fits with everything we've seen so far.'

She received Nelson's support. 'I agree with Rita. There are three things we must do. Pick up this DS Stack, go and talk to her sergeant dad, and finally someone please work out how we can get to Henry fucking Elliott!'

47. LONDON

At Coyle's suggestion they gave the take-away food option a pass and instead explored the Ruislip restaurant scene until settling on an Italian place that seemed refreshingly genuine. There was sufficient space between the tables for privacy and enough diners to make it easy to blend in and not be remembered.

Joanne wanted to know more about the connection between LONA and the L&O movement. 'Who's behind it all?' she asked.

Coyle twirled his linguini for several seconds before responding. 'L&O is supposedly just a convenient label for the anti-crime and anti-immigration parties in various parts of Europe. There is no joint structure at the top – again supposedly. That may even be true, but I'm convinced that the funding comes from a single source. *Someone* is promoting the L&O agenda by channelling enormous amounts of money to parties that meet certain criteria.'

'And who could that be?'

'It's all conjecture at this point, but this is my own best guess. I think the purpose of L&O is to replace democratic governments all over Europe with authoritarian regimes. Therefore the parties seen as potential power-takers get the support.'

'And some political advice along the way?'

'I'd think so yes. But there doesn't seem to be real *management* of the process. Maybe because it's early days still.'

'What about Hungary? L&O sponsored government, right?'

Coyle thought about it. 'The only one so far, but I'm not seeing Hungary behaving like somebody's puppet state.'

'Maybe L&O are taking care not to show themselves too much.'

'That's what I think. In the end it's always a question of who benefits. Who would like to see Europe run by dictators?'

'Who do you think?'

'Let's not speculate too much. Right now the priority is getting to the money distributor.'

'You mean Nagelmann?'

Coyle took a sip of Chianti followed by double the amount of Pellegrino. 'No, Nagelmann is merely the front. The respectable face of L&O, so to speak. But even he keeps a low profile. That's why I had to smoke him out with Henderson's help.'

'Then who?'

'This is just a theory, so don't assume too much. For years now I've been aware of an almost mythical character called Mesmer. He seems to have evolved from mercenary to destabilisation expert.'

'Meaning you call him if you want something destabilised?'

'Like a company, an organisation or even a country, yes. He does it both externally, using normal mercenary methods, but also internally, through manipulative financial operations.'

Joanne saw the logic at once. 'And that's what L&O has been doing! Changing the political power structure through big money contributions!'

Coyle nodded encouragingly.

'But how did you narrow it down to Mesmer?' she pressed him.

'Basically because I think he's the only non-government operator who could pull off something of this magnitude. But I admit I can't prove it – yet.'

'If this were a police investigation, I'd say you've got a weak case.'

'Well I'm hoping Nagelmann will make it stronger when I talk to him tomorrow. I mentioned Mesmer's name to him just before I left, and he said – nothing.'

'Non-denial being close to affirmation?'

Coyle laughed softly at the police language. 'We'll know tomorrow,' he said.

Undeterred, Joanne wanted more. 'What if you're right about Mesmer? Then what?'

'I'll have to figure out how to eliminate him.'

48. LONDON

Throughout dinner they avoided the touchy subject of Joanne's continued involvement, but once they were back at the B&B, Coyle reintroduced it.

'From all I've told you, I'm sure you can see that I have no right to put you at even more risk. I shouldn't even be *discussing* it with you!'

Her response caught him off guard. Rather than get angry or annoyed, she stepped close to him – well within his personal space – and looked him in the eyes.

'Coyle, if those people have picked up your scent, sooner or later they'll track me down too. And to be honest, I'd feel a lot safer with *you* than hiding somewhere on my own!'

'Your confidence in me may be misplaced.'

Stepping even closer, she put both her hands against his chest and looked up at him. 'I feel safe when I'm with you,' she said softly, giving him only two options – kissing her or pulling away. He kissed her.

Soon afterwards they were on one of the twin beds, the tacit point of no return well behind them. Joanne was surprised by how delicately Coyle made love to her. Despite his immense strength, he had the martial arts expert's total control of his body and seemed almost weightless against her. He gave her pleasure, but somehow didn't seem to take as much back. This was something else than the passionate start of romance. More a recognition of mutual attraction – even respect.

Even so she felt happy as she lay beside him, her head against his shoulder. Now that there was *something* between them he couldn't exclude her from what was to come! And yes, she did feel safe.

'How did you do it?' she asked. 'Back at my dad's place.'

'You mean with the gun?'

'Of course I mean the gun! I shot you in the hand for God's sake! What's the trick?'

'It's no trick Joanne. Nothing special really. I just held you in such a way that I could feel the muscles in your right arm. No one fires a gun without a slight tensioning of the arm muscles.'

'You mean you felt it when I squeezed the trigger and pulled you hand out of the bullet's way?'

'When you were *about* to squeeze the trigger. Once you've fired it's too late. I can't move faster than a bullet.'

She thought about it for a moment. 'Happily you're good at slow movements too.'

49. ZURICH

Nagelmann had a feeling that the meeting with his suddenly announced and slightly unwelcome guest would drag out, so he received him in a small conference room rather than his main office. Barry Vickerton's bulk overfilled the smallish chair and the man looked distinctly uncomfortable. Once he had explained the latest developments his expression was that of a large fat dog expecting a biscuit.

'Two-hundred million Sterling sounds too high a price for one politician,' observed the lawyer, pushing Vickerton to justify himself.

'Atkins is a greedy sod for sure, but we do get instant results. An early election and almost certainly a majority in Parliament! Neil thinks it's a reasonable price for power.'

'Neil's power, but my money Barry!'

Assuming this was all a bit of banter for show, Vickerton attempted a relaxed little laugh.

'Nothing compared to what you've already contributed, Hannes. You know you'll recover it all with interest eventually.'

'Perhaps, but Markevich seems to be a game-changer. Look at all the trouble he's already caused, and now you're asking for two hundred million because of him!'

'Well, it's our opinion that it's worth it to get past the situation we're in.'

Nagelmann glanced at his watch and rose to his feet. 'Sorry, but I have to take a prearranged call in my office. But think about this. What if Markevich won't go away just because you pay Atkins and get your election? What if he stops you getting elected?'

Deep down Vickerton knew that the point had merit, but before he could think of a sensible response the lawyer had left the room.

As expected, the phone rang mere seconds past the hour and Nagelmann immediately recognized the voice.

'Does *he* agree to cooperate with us?' asked Coyle, forcing the lawyer to make a decision. Pretend not to have heard of Mesmer, or tacitly agree that Markevich knew the L&O leader's identity. It seemed foolish to underestimate the man, so he went with the honest option.

'Maybe. He wants to meet with you.'

A short pause. 'That would be good. When and where?'

'Tomorrow in Budapest. I'll be there as well of course.'

Coyle's reaction was swift and negative. 'Too much home territory for your side! The best way to steer clear of *security concerns* is to meet in the transit area of a major airport.'

That sounded reasonable to Nagelmann. 'Which airport do you suggest?' he asked.

'To avoid suspicion of foul play, I'll let you decide. Any major airport in Western Europe is acceptable. Let's say 3pm local time tomorrow.'

Nagelmann thought quickly. As a frequent traveller across Europe he knew several suitable airports. 'Do you know Copenhagen?' he asked.

'No, but go on.'

'There is a secluded steakhouse restaurant in the old part of the transit area. You go upstairs from the main shopping and eating level. At that time it won't be busy.'

'Then it's agreed. I'll meet you there.'

Nagelmann wanted to ask if anyone else would attend the meeting, but Coyle had hung up. All in all, not a bad result. They would get a feel for Markevich and then decide how to deal with him.

'That was quick,' remarked Vickerton as his host re-entered the conference room. 'Can we get back to the matter at hand?'

There was an espresso maker on a sideboard and Nagelmann carefully selected his beverage before answering. 'Actually I think we're done here, Barry. Let me get back to you in a couple of days when I've had time to discuss it properly at our end.'

The big dog looked like it had lost a bone. 'But there isn't time. . .' he began, only for Nagelmann to interrupt.

'I'm afraid you'll have to tell Neil to *make* time. This is not a decision we're going to rush.'

50. LONDON

It took Rita Ridgewood all morning to discover Joanne's contact number, the one she had given to DCS Miller. There might have been a quicker way, but alerting Miller that outsiders were looking for her secret operative was out of the question. The request had to come from a legitimate police authority and one that had a logical connection to DS Stack.

In the end, their second most senior asset at the Metropolitan Police managed to convince a Cardiff based administrator to ask for the number under the guise of needing clarification on a report linked to a pending court case. Clara Miller thought it a bit odd that Joanne hadn't told her own department how to contact her while she was away, but did send the number to the administrator's email address.

Rita had secluded herself at Party Office with her intelligence team and, for extra reinforcement, Craig Baines and Johnny Gordon. It was the less-than-gentle giant Gordon who slapped the desk in delight with his enormous hand and asked the obvious question. 'So do we call the number and have her come where we can grab her?'

Remembering that Nelson wanted DS Stack *picked up,* Rita deliberated for a while in silence. Getting hold of Stack would be useful, but tracking her phone might also lead them to Markevich and give them a shot at him with the element of surprise on their side for a change.

'No, I want MI5 to start tracking the phone and patch the data to us in real-time. Once we have a fix on the location, we decide what to do next.'

'She won't have it turned on long enough!' Baines objected. Nearly a foot shorter than Gordon, he was even wider in build and looked like he could smash through a brick wall without breaking his stride.

'We'll soon find out,' said Rita. 'For the number to be any good to DCS Miller it's got to be active most of the time. Let's assume we'll end up somewhere in Greater London, and start getting the teams ready.'

'What about the sergeant in Wales?' Baines interjected. 'Do we move in on him as well or hold off for a while?'

Rita gave him an irritated look. 'Please do exactly as we agreed earlier. Four men drive to Wales, find the place, wait until dark and then take old Stack by surprise. Alive of course - he's no good to us dead!'

51. LONDON

Buying the gear had been fun, and when she looked at herself in the full-length bathroom mirror she was amazed by the sexy effect. *I look part Catwoman, part Mistress Zelda*, she thought, remembering a lurid vice case she had done some work on earlier in the year. To actually get on the bike, precariously poised on a small seat with her arms wrapped around Coyle's waist, was another matter altogether. But he had insisted that they practice riding the Kawasaki together.

'You have to have complete faith in my driving,' he explained. 'Don't try to fight it when we lean into the bends. Fast driving is only possible if we work together, so if you can't do it we'd better know now and not when someone is chasing us with guns blazing.'

The first few minutes were easy. Coyle drove at low speed though the residential areas around the B&B, but once they merged into heavier traffic on the A4 the pace changed. Exceeding the speed limit in brief bursts the powerful bike weaved its way past vehicle after vehicle. Each weave meant a violent swing from upright to what to Joanne seemed nearly horizontal – and back up again. Then smoothly into the same manoeuvre, but in the other direction.

Several irate drivers protested by sounding their horns, but were quickly outdistanced by the Kawasaki. Once they hit the M40, Coyle suddenly accelerated to a speed that was definitely beyond legal, although she could only guess how fast they were going. After maybe twenty seconds she felt herself pressed into Coyle's back as he braked sharply. Well, he had said he was going to test the bike's balance with the two of them onboard and get her used to the various ways they might ride it together. As long as she didn't throw up, she would be all right. Vomit inside a motorcycle helmet wasn't something she wanted to contemplate.

After Beaconsfield, they left the M40 and drove south along various smaller roads. Whenever traffic allowed, Coyle would take bends at what seemed like impossible speed, but each time the bike straightened back up with the grace of a ballet dancer equipped with explosive power. Despite her stomach's protestations Joanne was beginning to enjoy herself in an exhilarating, light-hearted, way. It was a bit like dancing, she thought. You had to rely on and trust your partner every step of the way. Especially in the dips!

They were driving down Marlow High Street and getting close to the Thames, when Coyle abruptly turned into a wooded park and let the bike come to a stop. Turning off the engine, he signalled for his passenger to dismount, and she managed to do so despite unsteady legs. After they had both freed themselves from their helmets, she even smiled at him.

'I could get used to this – I think.'

'You did well! A bit stiff in the beginning, but that's normal. After a while I could sense you were relaxing and going with the bike.'

She smiled at him and was about to say something funny or cute or both when she saw him suddenly go tense. His eyes were sweeping the sky and settled on a helicopter that appeared to be circling the town.

'We may have a problem!'

He spoke in a calm professional voice. 'I've been seeing too much of that helicopter.'

'Maybe your driving has attracted attention.'

'No, the police wouldn't waste that much resource on a traffic offender. It's got to be LONA connected. And there'll be land vehicles involved as well. The chopper's their command post.'

This didn't make sense to Joanne. 'How could they possibly spot us?'

'Did you bring your new phone? The one for DCS Miller?'

'Sure. It's in the inside pocket of my jacket.'

'Turned on?'

She nodded and Coyle's face turned even graver. 'Damn, they know who you are!' he cursed.

'I don't see how they could!' she protested, but without real conviction. How could she be certain of anything in this strange game?

Coyle preferred to think ahead rather than analyse the past. 'It doesn't matter how! Somehow they *did* get your phone number from Miller and they've been tracking it. Probably not for very long or they'd have closed in on the B&B, but if they decide to review the phone's movements over the last 24 hours, they'll get a pretty good fix on our base.'

By now Joanne had dug out the offending phone. 'Turn it off and remove the battery?' she suggested, but Coyle rejected the idea.

'That would just encourage them to track back to Ruislip. It would be *inconvenient* if they found the van and the rest of our equipment. Not a risk I want to take.'

'But if we dash back there, they might catch us. The helicopter is much faster – even the way you ride!'

Coyle took the phone from her. 'I'll see if we can't lay a false scent for them to follow. Let's get moving again.'

A few seconds later the Kawasaki's roared back into life and they headed towards the bridge. Once on the south side of the river, Coyle followed the road and used every opportunity to overtake the cars in front of them until he found what he was looking for – a large pickup truck with an open-top cargo bed. Joanne saw that it belonged to a garden centre, but the letters were so worn and mud-stained that she couldn't make out the name.

As they pulled alongside the pickup, Coyle eased off slightly on the throttle and tossed the phone in amongst an assortment of spades, rakes, shears and other gardening tools. Then the Kawasaki roared ahead, leaving the driver impotently flicking his headlights at what seemed to him just another careless asshole on a motorbike.

52. SLOUGH

Their next home was to be a business hotel between central Slough and the M4. Once again, the van was inconspicuous and there was ample parking. Unfortunately Coyle felt he had to assume that the Paul Davis identity was no longer safe to use. If the Longbows persisted in their search they would sooner or later discover the Ruislip B&B. Therefore David Baker had to re-emerge.

Coyle spent most of the afternoon preparing for his meeting with Mesmer and Nagelmann. He decided to leave the same evening by train to Brussels and continue from there, still by train, through Germany to Denmark. He would arrive in Copenhagen as a train passenger and proceed to the airport in plenty of time to catch his evening flight to Brussels. That way, if anyone tried to track him down based on the flight connection, there wouldn't be one. Hundreds of people flew from Copenhagen to Brussels every day, so he would not stand out.

Of all the equipment that might have been lost in Ruislip, had they not gotten to the B&B ahead of the Longbows, Coyle was especially relieved to have his trawler phone back safely. Joanne thought it looked like any mobile phone, but he explained it to her.

'It's not actually a phone. Well it is, but you can't use it to make calls. I've modified it to interrogate nearby phones and find out their details.'

'And then?'

Was that a hint of pride she saw in his eyes? 'If I can determine which number is Mesmer's, which ought to be possible, then I can lock on his phone and use another device of mine to home in on him. As long as he's connected to a mobile phone network anywhere in the world, my gadget will track him!'

'When will you be back then?'

'Late tomorrow night. I'll take the train from Brussels into London. But you'll get texts from me before then.'

The prospect of being cooped up in a hotel room for so long didn't appeal to Joanne. 'Isn't there anything I should be doing while you're away?' she persisted.

The look he gave her was one of serious concern. 'Now that we have reason to think they have your name, you're in real danger until this is all over,' he said. 'That means as little exposure as possible. If I need you to do something, I'll let you know, but let's hope it won't be necessary.'

She knew he had a point, but it wasn't what she wanted to hear. 'I'll go crazy just sitting in the room watching daytime soaps and game shows!'

With a glance at his watch he got to his feet. He reached out for her and she came to him. They stood close and he stroked her cheek with unexpected gentleness.

'Look Joanne, I need you in this,' he said. 'I need you safe and I need you alive!'

They kissed briefly and then he was out of the door and she was alone. Thinking about his parting words made her felt better, but only a bit.

53. GWENT

They came at night just as he had expected, but not a couple of hours before dawn like real professionals. The road alarm went off twenty-three past midnight. If things had been normal he might still have been reading or listening to the radio. Even enjoying an old movie. But he was forewarned about a possible attack and had taken precautions. The cottage was dark and empty as the men approached it.

As soon as Coyle alerted him – even preposterously suggested he leave his home and run – Mike Stack had bivouacked in the woods about two hundred yards from his stone cottage. No one would catch him out in his bed!

Erecting a cleverly camouflaged shelter that would keep him dry and reasonably warm was a task quickly accomplished. Compared to most spots in which he had slept in the field during his army years, it was positively luxurious.

Tactical advantage is all about knowing the enemy's movements before he knows yours. Mike placed eight motion sensors in the surrounding terrain; each wirelessly connected to a small receiver he kept in his pocket. The furthest sensor would alert him to an approaching vehicle when it was still a mile away on the rough but passable vehicle track that lead from the nearest semi-public road, which in turn wound its way through the remote countryside for eight miles before reaching a road that actually had a number.

It was extremely unlikely that the uninvited guests would drive so close to the cottage that their engine noise might reveal their presence. Instead they would come on foot, and probably spread out shortly before they reached the perimeter of his little homestead. At that point he would ambush them.

From Coyle's cellar arsenal he had selected what he felt would best serve his purpose, then *secured* the concealed entrance. The Heckler & Koch MP7 was one of Coyle's favourite weapons and there were several to pick from. He decided against a silenced version. There was no major advantage in suppressing the noise in this remote part of Wales, and he felt that the basic version had better balance and was easier to handle in tight quarters.

In case he needed a handgun at some point, he strapped a shoulder holster containing a Sig Sauer 45 cal P227 pistol over his upper body armour. If it came down to a shootout at close range, he wanted the stopping power of the 45 ACP cartridge, and the P227 in its special SAS version had been his handgun of choice when he was on active duty.

He also made sure his NV goggles were in good working order, took several spare battery packs, and finally stuffed four flash-bang stun grenades in his jacket pockets.

He heard them before he saw them, which told him they were confident although not necessarily incompetent. Three of them, moving in tandem like a normal army patrol anywhere in the world. All of them wearing NV goggles and each man carrying an FN Herstal P90 compact automatic rifle – an expensive, exclusive and highly effective weapons.

As the intruders approached his hiding place they did exactly as he had predicted. The leader pointed towards the cottage, the outlines of which were now visible against the night sky. Then he indicated the path each man should take to converge on their target from different directions. Mike heard instructions given and acknowledged, but the men kept their voices so low he couldn't distinguish the words. Time to act!

In a smooth movement he tossed a flash-bang in a high arc towards to group. It landed on the track just ahead of them and Mike momentarily covered his NV goggles with his left arm and looked straight down into the ground to keep his own vision intact.

The next moment he raised the MP7 and out of a sense of fairness towards men who like himself had served in uniform, shouted a three word warning, 'Drop your weapons!'

He didn't expect them to obey, and they didn't. The leader fired first and in the right general direction, leaving Mike no option. A short burst from the MP7 took the man in the chest and sent him tumbling backwards a couple of steps before he collapsed.

Number Two had his P90 switched to full auto, but the burst was cut short when Mike fired into his face. That left Number Three, who had enough tactical awareness to drop to the ground and make himself a smaller target. Like the combat veteran he probably was, he rolled quickly sideways hoping to find himself a firing position.

Taking him alive was a tempting option, but the angle made it almost impossible to hit him with required precision. When he opened fire and the second bullet hit a tree only yards away, the former SAS sergeant squeezed off a three round burst. All bullets struck home, the second one penetrating Number Three's torso from neck to lower abdomen. The body shuddered and lay still.

Mike knew he had to control the adrenalin in his body. Only Coyle could kill men and not suffer the body's chemical reaction. Adrenalin helped you overcome fear and fatigue and it gave you strength, but it also clouded your judgement and made you less observant. First priority! Were they as dead as they seemed?

Making his way through the undergrowth he saw no sign of life. The bodies lay still in the oddly unnatural way dead men lie. All three P90s were visible on the ground. Still, something bothered him.

The NV goggles didn't provide much peripheral vision, and he sensed rather than saw movement to his left. There was a fourth intruder!

Mike Stack's combat instinct kicked in and he did three things at once. He turned his head, dropped to the ground and fired a sweeping burst of 4.6mm high-velocity bullets. Before his arms made contact with the road surface he felt the violent impact of a round hitting him in the chest. Unable to hold on to the MP7, he felt it slip out of his grip and bounce out of immediate reach.

But the target had taken a hit as well. The man had fallen only twenty yards away, and was struggling to get his weapon back into a firing position. He displayed the same hard and battle-tested demeanour as his dead comrades and Mike knew he had to react instantly.

The Sig Sauer was where he expected it to be. He ripped the familiar weapon from its holster and aimed it one-handed at Number Four's head. Knowing he would not get a second chance, he took an extra half-second to steady his hand, and the trigger squeeze was as sweet and controlled as he had ever managed under combat conditions.

The 45 ACP bullet smashed into Number Four's face and ended the fight with a massive exit wound in the back of his skull. Mike shifted his priority the moment he recognised a deadly headshot. Were there any more attackers?

As he tried to turn his head for a better view, the pain welled up within him and told him that getting to his feet was out of the question. He had felt the hit, but hoped the body armour would stop the slug. It clearly hadn't. Like his MP7, those P90s fired more potent rounds than ordinary submachine guns. At least one round had penetrated.

Letting go of the Sig Sauer he thrust his right hand inside the chest armour. He didn't have to probe long before the truth became apparent to him.

54. SLOUGH

Sleep had come slowly and uneasily to Joanne, but once she finally dropped off exhaustion took control and she slept soundly until a piercing beep woke her up. In the fleeting seconds of sleep-filled grogginess she had the sudden panicky thought that she was completely alone.

The special phone, her link to Coyle, was ringing. She snatched it from the nightstand and pressed the answer button. 'You woke me up!' she said with fake seriousness, but the voice at the other wasn't Coyle's.

'Sorry Jo. It's – important!'

Jo? Only her dad called her that. 'Dad?'

Nothing! No, she heard breathing. Then his familiar, yet suddenly very different, voice.

'Tell our friend the stockroom is sealed secure. He'll know what to do. Important!'

'Dad, what's going on?'

Another pause of strained breathing.

'He was right Jo! They came for me. But I was ready for them. All dead! Not amateurs, but not top drawer either. Tell him that.'

Suddenly she understood. 'My God, you're hurt!' she screamed.

'I clocked – the fourth one too late. He got me with a lucky shot. Then I – finished him.'

'Stay calm Dad! I'll call for an ambulance – no, a helicopter!'

The response was something between a cough and a gurgle.

'Dad! Stay with me!'

'Sorry Jo, I can't. A minute or two, then I'm gone. I know what I'm talking about.'

'I'll get to you!'

'No you stay were you are! That's – an order! Don't raise hell. Let *him* deal with it!'

She was sobbing with frustration and helplessness. 'Please Dad!'

'You stay focused – on your mission! Don't mind me – I'm happy!'

She was crying and trying to find words, but nothing made sense at that moment.

Her dad spoke again, with even more urgency. 'No better way for an old soldier to die, Jo! In battle for his country – and king!'

She understood then and stopped sobbing. This was his moment and she could not spoil it. 'I'll miss you, Dad,' she said gently, and added 'I love you so!'

His voice was fading, but she heard 'love', 'shoot' and something that sounded like 'bastards'. Then the connection broke and she pictured him smiling to himself before death claimed him.

She knew he had fired a final bullet into the phone so the Longbow bastards would not learn anything if they found it before Coyle.

55. LONDON

DCS Clara Miller was heading back to her office from a briefing, when she spotted Joanne in the waiting area.

'Come to see me, DS Stack?' she asked in evident surprise at the unannounced visit.

'Sorry to barge in like this, Ma'am. I was hoping you could help me stay under the radar, so to speak.'

Miller shrugged and indicated that the door to her office was open. A moment later they were facing each other across the Detective Chief Superintendant's desk.

Clara Miller was three inches taller and twenty years older than Joanne. She was very thin, which made her look even taller. Short dark hair with a substantial amount of grey framed a face that had once been pretty, but now appeared tired and worn. Well, running a task force on human trafficking would do that to you, Joanne thought. Everything about organised crime seemed to have expanded beyond recognition in the past few years.

But all she wanted from Miller was an unmarked police car. One not signed to her by name, so it couldn't be traced to her.

She had hardly slept after the terrible call from her dad. By six in the morning she was desperate to do something, so she tackled Whitmore's computer again – more specifically the list of traitors.

Coyle had attacked Highgate to neutralise LONA's offensive capability, but it occurred to her that he must have accomplished something else as a by-product. Surely the same enforcers who intimidated or even eliminated those who tried to break with LONA, would also be handing out the rewards. Senior figures like Carpenter probably had secret bank accounts abroad, but there had to be many among the nearly two thousand on the list who didn't. They had to be paid in cash, and if the enforcers had been handling this function it meant the system was badly disrupted at the moment. That might make some people open to persuasion.

She spent most of the day going through the list of names trying to identify those who might be sufficiently low level to get rattled when challenged. The Home Office seemed the best target, and in the end she had settled on three names and decided to visit them after working hours. She had their home addresses – all she needed was a suitable vehicle. Driving around in Coyle's van was too risky, and without a fake identity she would be easy to track if she rented a car.

She explained her need for an anonymous vehicle to Clara Miller, who grasped the request at once but was obviously concerned.

'So you want a car that's undercover even inside the Met,' she established with a thin smile. 'I can only assume you're working on something internal.'

The conversation was taking a turn Joanne was keen to avoid, but she had to say something. 'Yes there's an internal aspect. How critical I'm not sure.'

'Oh, did your colleagues in Cardiff get hold of you? They didn't have a valid contact number for you so I let them have the one you'd given me.'

That explained the helicopter chase, and it had to look suspicious to Miller that an officer assigned to her would appear to be hiding from her own unit. Joanne hoped that the little laugh she produced didn't sound too contrived.

'Yes, they did. But I've had bad luck with phones lately. I keep losing them. Even the one I had when I was last here to see you. I bought a new pay-as-you-go this morning. Let me look up the number for you.'

She quickly opened her handbag, but as her eyes fell on the two phones – the other being her link to Coyle – she heard a sudden commotion outside the office.

She shouldn't have come here, where she had to sign in under her own name! If LONA had someone monitoring Scotland Yard's system, her presence would be flagged.

But this quickly? She had been in the building less than twenty minutes!

With her right hand she placed her newly acquired phone on Miller's desk, drawing the DCS's glance. With her left hand she dropped the other phone onto her right foot so that the impact was silent. Just as the door to the office started to swing open, she kicked the compromising phone under the desk.

In stormed a middle-aged man with a healthy looking body but flabby face. He was followed by three uniformed officers, all of whom held pistols at the ready. And there were several more uniforms outside the office.

'Sorry about the intrusion Clara, but I have to borrow DS Stack for a bit of questioning if you don't mind,' he announced in a voice that signalled he was not inviting a debate on the matter.

Clara Miller looked startled, but perhaps not entirely surprised. As if she had sensed all along that something was not quite right.

'Go ahead Clive,' she said with a slight shrug. 'Anything I should know about?'

Ignoring her, he turned to Joanne. 'I'm Commander Reid, SO15. We need you to come along with us please.'

SO15 was counter terrorism, which explained why Miller did not even make a token effort on her behalf. Joanne felt herself taken by both arms and swiftly bundled out of the office and towards the lifts at the end of the corridor.

Commander Reid stayed behind for a moment. 'What's she been doing for you?' he asked Miller.

'Nothing at all. I was just asked to provide her with a temporary London base.'

'Asked by whom?' asked Reid eagerly.

There was no reason to lie. 'Sir Hugh Canderton at MoD.'

'Why?'

'No idea, Clive. He didn't say, and he is not the kind of person you ask a lot of questions.'

56. LONDON

A quick call established that Sir Hugh wasn't at his MoD office. She had a mobile number for him, but it switched to voice mail right away and she didn't want to leave a message. He had however given her an email address, and once she had retrieved it from her files she wrote to him using her own private email.

Please call me as soon as possible. Clara Miller.

It didn't take him long – barely ten minutes, and she immediately felt the tension in his voice.

'Is this about DS Stack?' he asked.

'She's just been taken out of my office for questioning by SO15. You tell *me* if that's cause for concern, Sir Hugh!'

'Most unfortunate, but you've got nothing to worry about. You're not connected to the operation. Who grabbed her, by the way?'

'Commander Clive Reid himself. And he turned up with a whole squad. Are you sure I don't need to know more?'

There was a moment's silence while Sir Hugh checked his list of LONA collaborators. It came as no surprise that Reid was on it.

'No Clara, you're better off not dragged any deeper into this, and there's not a lot you can do anyway. I'll have to think of a way to help DS Stack, but it looks like it could be tricky. If you happen to hear anything, I'd of course appreciate if you could let me know.'

She promised she would, but didn't expect to be told anything useful by her SO15 colleagues.

57. COPENHAGEN – KASTRUP AIRPORT

As the main Scandinavian aviation hub, Kastrup was forever expanding and transforming itself. Coyle recced the inter-connected terminals with great care and vigilance. He wanted to know exactly what his options were if things went pear-shaped and he had to make his escape. Local police and airport security staff would complicate his situation, but that applied to the opposition as well. That was why he had insisted on meeting Mesmer in a rigidly enforced weapons-free zone.

If he could spot at least Nagelmann in advance, it would be a bonus, but it was equally important that he himself was not clocked by the other side. He didn't think it much of a risk since Nagelmann had last seen him with black hair and dark eyes, but all the same he moved cautiously and stayed close to other travellers whenever he could.

He was worried about Joanne, but forced it to the back of his mind. There was nothing he could do for her right now, and Mike was beyond help. She had called him while he was on the train. Their conversation had been short and surprisingly professional – Joanne had not forgotten the need to minimise communications that might be intercepted – but also charged with emotion. In essence, he had told her that he would be there for her, and she had said he could depend on her not to break down in her grief.

The restaurant was called the Modern American Steak House, or MASH for short. He found it without difficulty, but decided against going inside. It would have been too easy for Mesmer to place somebody there to identify him.

There was no sign of Nagelmann anywhere in the airport, but that didn't mean he had not arrived. There were plenty of airline lounges to which Coyle didn't have access, and barging in would only have attracted attention. Once he felt there was nothing left to do except blend in, he spent an hour in the largest tax-free shopping area, from where he emerged with two plastic carrier bags emblazed with the Kastrup logo. Unless he would be forced to ditch them later, Joanne would have a year's supply of cosmetics and the two of them could feast on Danish delicacies for days.

At exactly 3pm he activated the trawler device in his pocket and ascended the wooden steps that led from the internal shopping avenue to the restaurant. MASH was a symphony in glass and red leather, with an open style kitchen along the only wall that didn't have a panoramic view. Both his nose and a quick look at the beef on display told him that the steaks were probably excellent.

Nagelmann was sitting at a booth at the opposite end, with a view of parked aircraft – but also the entrance. Next to him sat a massive bald man with a face that at first glance just looked deformed, but on closer inspection revealed both intelligence and mutilated handsomeness. At a table just out of earshot of normal conversation sat a couple of hard looking men, who seemed so out of place that they had to be backup muscle.

Coyle waved away an approaching waiter and explained that he was joining his *colleagues*. Then he approached the table, from where another waiter was clearing away a set of plates. It seemed his hosts had passed the time by eating. Nagelmann looked up and after a brief moment of disorientation recognised him.

'You're a man of many faces, it seems,' he observed, 'but at least you're punctual.'

Coyle took the extended hand, but looked at the other man. 'Pleased to meet you Mesmer.'

The giant fixed him with cold calculating eyes, and the hand he offered was as rough as it was enormous. 'And what other name might you have than Markevich?' he asked in a deep monotone voice.

Coyle slid into the booth at the opposite side of the table. He did not acknowledge the two bodyguards, or in any way indicate that he was aware of their presence.

'I could give you several, but what's the point? You and I both work in the background and don't appreciate publicity.'

Mesmer's face twisted into a semblance of a smile, but his eyes remained cold. 'Wouldn't Dr Barnes's practice benefit from some publicity?' he suggested. 'To attract more patients?'

This was a piece of bad news up front! Atkins had revealed where his loyalty lay, and it was not with British democracy. So be it. But what did using the information so soon in the meeting reveal about Mesmer? Maybe that he was prone to overconfidence.

'Dr Barnes has all the patients he can handle at the moment,' said Coyle lightly, but didn't follow up. He let a few seconds of silence develop. Would Mesmer or Nagelmann break it?

It was Mesmer of course. L&O was his show.

'We do seem to have a problem, my friend. You've been telling Nagelmann here you want our help to put the Rightful Tories in power, and that we should stop supporting LONA. But now the leader of these so called Twits tells us you personally warned him not to pull out of the government because LONA would win an election.'

Coyle kept his face and voice neutral. 'Why is that a problem? I already admitted to Dr Nagelmann that LONA could win an election. Our concern is not that Nelson can't win power, it's that he can't *govern*! That's why we take the longer view and support Atkins.'

Mesmer chuckled with something close to genuine amusement. 'What if I told you your carefully selected leader, Mr Atkins, offered to arrange the election and then retire from politics? For two hundred million pounds paid into four separate offshore accounts?'

So that was it. Brian Atkins was an even lower form of weasel than he had been able to anticipate. And speaking to him *had* been a mistake.

'What do you *really* want, Mr Markevich?' asked Nagelmann, who thought it safe to weight in.

Coyle wondered if he could finesse his way through and continue the bluff. But no, the bluff had been called – he was never going to infiltrate L&O. That meant his best course of action was honesty – and the device in his pocket.

He said, 'Fair enough. I'll tell you exactly what we want. We want *you* to get the hell out of British politics! You pull the plug on Nelson's gang as of now! And stay away from all other parties as well!'

Mesmer exhaled a burst of air in a show of superior derision. 'You don't see, do you? It's much bigger than the UK! This is the future of Europe!'

Yes Coyle knew that, but for now he had to pretend he didn't care.

'Then leave us out of it!' he demanded. 'We're telling you, politely for now, to stay out of our country's affairs.'

'And what if we don't? What will you do? Shoot every British politician you believe works for us?'

From Nagelmann's perspective it looked like his two table companions became locked in a visual power game. When *Markevich* finally spoke, his voice was flat and ice cold.

'No, I won't be shooting British politicians, but I'll certainly eliminate *you* and anyone obviously on your team.'

He shifted his glace to Nagelmann to make the point sink in, but it was of course Mesmer who responded.

'Then we have nothing more to discuss. Nagelmann and I will leave. You will stay at least until four o'clock. Have a steak or stew in your own juices, I don't care. But if you try to leave earlier, the two gentlemen over there will do what they can to detain you.'

Seeing Coyle's contemptuous look at the bodyguards, Mesmer explained his thinking. 'We need the time to make sure you can't track us. Perhaps you can deal with my men, but hardly without drawing attention to yourself from the Danish police. For those two,' he made a vague gesture in their direction, 'a Danish jail would be like a heath club. For you on the other hand – *inconvenient?*'

Coyle instantly realised that an airport brawl was not in his interest. 'Have a nice flight then,' he said evenly. 'I'm very happy to stay behind and enjoy my meal.'

58. LONDON

Questioning! No one had asked her a single question yet! Instead she had been frisked, relieved of her weapon as well as personal effects, and unceremoniously locked in a holding cell. She was furious, but most of all with herself. It had been a huge mistake to assume she could breeze into New Scotland Yard and not attract the kind of attention she was trying to avoid! There *had* to be some kind of discrete alert out on her, and the head of SO15, whose unit had great latitude when it came to handling suspects, was the ideal man to apprehend her.

She recalled with chilling clarity that Commander Reid was on LONA's list. Of course he was! What better ally for Nelson, who used terrorists to stir up anxiety among the public, than the man leading the Met's fight against terrorism!

It certainly explained why she was kept in the cell for so long. Not being interrogated, but not able to do anything about her situation either. No doubt there were frantic discussions going on between Reid and his paymasters about how to get her transferred into LONA hands.

Would that transfer involve only persons loyal to LONA or would Reid have to allow non-initiated proper police into the process? If so, she might be able to say a few words to them – make them question what was going on.

She clung to the thought for a short while, until she had to admit it wasn't much of a plan. What policeman or woman would take her word against the head of Counter Terrorism Command?

Until now she had fought off the fear, but as the hopelessness of her position truly dawned on her, the shock and grief from losing her dad overwhelmed her and suddenly she noticed she was cold, miserable and trembling with emotion. Despite telling herself not to succumb to crying, she broke down in bitter forlorn sobs.

59. COPENHAGEN – KASTRUP AIRPORT

The fillet steak was as delicious as he had anticipated, and would in truth have demanded a glass of full-bodied red wine, but he couldn't risk anything that reduced his awareness.

Once he had finished eating, he casually pulled out the gadget that looked like a smart phone and looked at the results of his fishing expedition.

At first there were hundreds of numbers registered in the time he had been in the restaurant, but the device allowed him to filter them by proximity to rule out all that were not in his immediate vicinity. Most began with 45, the national code for Denmark. A couple of 46s for Sweden, a 49 for Germany, and even a 32 - meaning Belgium. Then things got interesting. There was a 41 – obviously Nagelmann – and finally three numbers beginning with 35. No, make that 355. Two were still there, the third no longer close by, but had left its imprint behind. A quick check revealed that 355 was the international dialling code for Albania. Short of a printed invitation card, Mesmer could not have given him a better clue on how to find him again.

A slight vibration in his jacket pocket alerted him to his actual phone, so he switched the two devices around. An encrypted message had just come in from Sir Hugh – the only other person who had the same encryption key.

We have a situation. Please fly back immediately. Do not contact the young lady! Ask for me (as M) at R's main residence. Uncle.

A glance at his watch told him there was only seven minutes until the two Albanian hoods were supposed to let him leave unhindered. That gave him time to re-book his flight. He decided on a British Airways flight to Heathrow that would get him into central London by about 9pm.

After writing a short confirmation to Sir Hugh and settling the bill, he got up and walked over to the two Albanian goons.

'My compliments,' he said as he dropped the two tax-free shopping bags by their table. 'Have to travel light, you see.'

It was worth it to see the bewilderment on their faces. They would spend quite a long time making sure that there was no tracking device or other sinister content in the bags, and that would enable him to disappear into the airport crowd without fear of being followed.

Besides, he could hardly show up at Buckingham Palace loaded with tax-free purchases.

60. LONDON

First the light went out in the cell, leaving Joanne in what seemed like total darkness for several minutes. Then things happened in rapid succession. The door flew open and a powerful light beam blinded her so she only perceived dark outlines of the men coming at her. She felt her arms grabbed hard and pulled behind her back. Then came the metallic click of handcuffs. Someone reached across her face from behind to apply a piece of sticky tape across her mouth. The light quickly dimmed as some kind of hood was pulled over her head, and she felt herself more lifted than dragged out of the cell by her elbows.

They allowed her no time to compose herself, let alone resist. The air around her changed and then she heard car doors opened. Professional hands bundled her into what seemed like a van, and she felt a strong unyielding body on each side of her.

Little was said. Only brief commands and acknowledgements. Every voice was male. As the vehicle drove off and accelerated into traffic she felt like the package she had become.

61. WORCESTERSHIRE

Nobody had told her anything! The tape had come off in the car, but every time she asked a question, it was met either by silence or a clipped response along the lines of 'can't talk about that, ma'am.' She had been efficiently conveyed from the car into a building and then into the room she now occupied. The handcuffs and the hood had been removed and she had been told to get some rest. The room was surprisingly comfortable, like a budget hotel room, but with higher quality furniture – all securely bolted to either the floor or a wall.

At least there was a proper bathroom with a shower stall in stainless steel and an assortment of harmless plastic toiletries. She was contemplating a shower when she heard to door to the room opening.

A woman of indeterminable age and no-nonsense demeanour walked in holding a food tray. Joanne glanced through the open door and saw two even more no-nonsense men outside.

'Brought you something to eat,' said the woman in a voice devoid of any emotion. Then she looked Joanne over. 'What are you – an eight?'

'Beg your pardon?'

'Clothes size. An eight?'

Joanne nodded in agreement. Eight was probably right – most of the time at least.

'I'll bring you some clothes when I collect the tray. Since you'll be staying a while.'

The last sentence sounded vaguely less mechanical, but before Joanne could think of a worthwhile question to ask, the woman was gone and the door closed with the firmness of a bank vault.

62. LONDON

'Hope it's not a formal dinner, mate.'

When you hail a London taxi at the airport and give Buckingham Palace as your destination, you have to expect a bit of levity from the driver. Coyle conceded that his comfortable travel attire would not be appropriate for tea at the Ritz, let alone a royal banquet.

'Just picking up my knighthood,' he joked back and handed over the fare in cash. 'They're very informal these days.'

Palace security was anything but informal however, and it required a call to someone in authority to establish that there was indeed a Mr Metcalfe on the premises, and that he was expecting a visitor.

The screening was thorough nevertheless, and Coyle was grateful that he did not carry any weapon. Once the formalities were out of the way, he was kept waiting until a plainclothes policeman from the Royal Protection Command appeared and silently conducted him through several hallways and corridors into a surprisingly austere office.

The plainclothes man knocked on an adjoining door and responded to a voice from the other side by withdrawing from the room. Then the door opened and Coyle found himself facing the King.

'Happy to finally meet you Mr Coyle,' was the royal greeting.

'One might say we move in different circles, Your Majesty.'

'But we do have some friends in common. One of them is waiting for us. Let's wait to talk until we are in a secure place.'

The King motioned for Coyle to follow him and they descended silently together into the deeper regions of the palace.

The final obstacle was a sturdy metal door that required a code, a retinal scan and a royal handprint to open. Sir Hugh greeted them inside the King's private communications chamber.

'You made good time, my boy! We've been rather busy here as well as you can imagine.'

'What's the situation you mentioned?' Coyle wanted to know.

'Joanne went to see DCS Miller – for some reason we don't know. While she was at Scotland Yard, SO15 grabbed her. Their commander is blasted Clive Reid and he is on the list, as you know.'

'What can we do about it?' snapped Coyle impatiently.

'Thanks to His Majesty, we've got her out of there.'

'Fortunately the Commissioner himself is *not* on the list, and he is a reasonable man,' the King explained. 'I persuaded him to allow DS Stack to be taken into Special Unit custody.'

'Well done! I mean, which unit would that be, Sir?'

The King hesitated, so Sir Hugh supplied the answer. 'Over the last years we've created some ultra low profile units around the SAS Regiment. They draw on Regiment personnel – mostly – but are set up to operate independently, especially in the area of counter-terrorism.'

'A very good old friend of mine commands Unit Gamma, which is essentially an extra secure safe house in Worcestershire,' explained the King. 'The sort of place one could hold a secret conference between world leaders or hide away especially dangerous spies or terrorists. But the Gamma team also specialises in certain covert operations.'

'She'll be more than safe there,' added Sir Hugh. 'Though maybe not as comfortable as she might like.'

'What are you saying?' Coyle inquired, and made the King clear his throat before responding.

'The Commissioner acted in good faith, as does Major Harcourt, Gamma's CO. As far as they know, DS Stack is a potentially dangerous suspect and she'll be treated accordingly.'

'But of course no one will try to interrogate her,' Sir Hugh assured him. 'She'll be strictly guarded, but not mistreated in any way.'

Coyle saw the point, but had some misgivings. 'How long before she can be released?'

The King gave him a penetrating look. 'When it's over, Mr Coyle! And since this is your operation, you're really the only one who knows the end game.' He left the sentence hanging in their air, expecting a response.

'How about you take us through everything that has happened up to this point,' suggested Sir Hugh, and Coyle gave a weary nod.

'I'll be happy to,' he said.

63. LONDON

The King and Sir Hugh interrupted Coyle's narrative several times with questions to ensure they got the full picture, but it was clear that the audacity of his approach impressed them. Both men were stunned by the sheer magnitude of the L&O plot and by Brian Atkins's cynical betrayal of British democracy.

'They'll pay him of course,' the King fumed. 'Now that they're sure you're working against them.'

Coyle agreed. 'They'll pay, but we may still have a couple of days. Atkins won't commit himself until he has verified that the funds are where he wants them and he has full control of the accounts.'

'So you want to hit Mesmer?' Sir Hugh assumed.

'That's why I set up the meeting! If I can have a bit of time on the equipment I see over there,' he pointed at the King's impressive stack of IT hardware, 'I should be able to locate his base.'

Royal permission instantly granted, Coyle quickly connected his own device – with its phone tracking software – to the King's secure web interface. He typed in the three Albanian numbers and set his programme to hunt them down. The search played out in graphic detail on a map of Europe.

'Each of these coloured dots indicates more than an hour's contact with a local relay tower,' he explained. 'The red colour is for Mesmer himself. Blue and green represent his two goons. See how more and more dots appear until we get a pattern?'

As the dot clusters became denser, he zoomed the map to concentrate on the key area in south-eastern Europe.

'All three have made frequent trips to, Milan, Belgrade, Budapest and Vienna. Mesmer also seems to be going a lot to Zurich, Berlin, Paris and Warsaw. He moves about a bit in Albania, but most of the time he's right here.'

He pointed at a large cluster in the southern part of Albania.

'That seems to hold for Blue and Green as well,' noted Sir Hugh.

'It has to be their base of operations,' agreed the King. 'How close can you get with this map?'

'It's hooked into Google, so quite close.'

He kept zooming, and when the dots filled the whole screen he switched them off to reveal – nothing. It looked like forest terrain surrounded by rough mountain slopes.

'This is the centre of the dot cluster,' Coyle confirmed.

'Unless these bastards live in caves, we've got nothing!' Sir Hugh lamented, but the King was more resourceful.

'If you write down the exact map coordinates, perhaps we can try something different,' he suggested and proceeded to boot up one of his own computers. 'Don't watch this,' he muttered with an undertone of irony as he passed through a sequence of screens, all with elaborate security protocols.

In the end he called them over and pointed to a very sharp aerial picture of the terrain immediately around Coyle's coordinates. Unfortunately there was still nothing even remotely resembling a human dwelling.

'Very strange,' mumbled Coyle and rechecked his own readings. Then a thought struck him. 'Sir, can you please zoom out a bit?'

'How much do you want? The distance across the screen is 100 metres right now.'

'Let's make it 1500 metres – no wait! How close can you get to this spot here?'

He pointed to a grey fleck that seemed a little too angular to be a natural feature. The King managed to get very close indeed, and despite a slight edge blur it was obvious that something made of metal had caught Coyle's attention.

'I bet it's a relay mast!' he exclaimed. 'Mesmer is a clever bastard, but of course we knew that already.'

'How is he doing it?' enquired Sir Hugh.

'His HQ will be outside the coverage of normal cell towers, but he'll have his own *private* cell so all his phones can work through it. That cell will be connected by cable or some kind of microwave link to the contraption we're looking at. That relay mast makes contact with the nearest official tower, which then treats all Mesmer's signals as coming from right there.'

No stranger to tactical navigation, the King quickly zoomed out to 20 kilometres across and put his finger on Coyle's coordinates.

'In which direction from here would he be most likely to build this secret base?' he asked, and Coyle immediately pointed northeast where the terrain became even less accessible. 'Then we'll do a bit of systematic grid searching.'

He zoomed closer again and began carefully scanning the wilderness in small segments, making sure that he kept moving in the direction Coyle had indicated. Soon they were dizzy from scrutinising what seemed like an endless sequence of trees, shrubs and rocks.

'This could take all night!' lamented Sir Hugh, but the King was undaunted. 'Nothing beats good reconnaissance!' he assured them. 'We know what we're looking for, and we'll find it if we keep trying!'

'That looks man-made!' Coyle observed and pointed to a rectangular field. A closer zoom revealed a camouflaged shed and a distinct track that had clearly been used by some kind of vehicle.

'Could be a landing strip,' suggested Sir Hugh.

'Too small for fixed-wing aircraft, but looks perfect for helicopters,' the King contributed. 'I'll follow the track, shall I?'

Exploring the crude road in 30 metre parts as it traversed the undulating mountain terrain was a painstaking effort, but it paid off in the end. Suddenly they were looking at angles and shadows that could only mean buildings. Very professionally concealed in the middle of a forest, but impossible to hide completely from someone who knew exactly where to look – and had the right equipment.

Coyle indicated what might be steam rising from some sort of pipes. 'That would be the heating and ventilation system,' he surmised. 'Judging by the outlines of the buildings we can see, I'd say the built up part of the compound is well over an acre. And there are probably several levels.'

'So quite a substantial base!' Sir Hugh agreed. 'How do you propose to tackle it, my boy?'

Making some further mental calculations, Coyle felt his initial elation at finding Mesmer's lair fade. You did not build that kind of fortress and leave it under-manned. Mesmer was bound to have a detachment of highly capable mercenaries around him, and the buildings and grounds were no doubt saturated with hi-tech security equipment.

'It doesn't look feasible even for a man of your exceptional talents,' said the King, and Sir Hugh added his own conclusion, 'Pure suicide!'

Coyle kept looking at the secret base. 'There has to be a way!' he insisted.

'Maybe there is,' said the King. 'Major Harcourt's Gamma Unit – the men have from time to time volunteered for completely off-the-book missions.'

'Then let's ask them to volunteer!'

'They'll do whatever Andy – Major Harcourt – asks of them. But I'd need to convince him in person first. This isn't something I can do by phone – however secure the line.'

Sir Hugh sighed in frustration. 'You can hardly pop in on him without attracting attention!' he groaned, but Coyle was having none of the pessimism.

'I can get you there, Sir!' he said with a confident smile.

64. IN TRANSIT

The tree of them left within minutes of each other. Coyle by taxi to his hotel in Slough, Sir Hugh on foot towards Victoria for a train to Horsham where he had based himself at a nice old country style hotel, and the King by royal car and minimal escort to Windsor Castle.

Shortly before midnight Coyle drove his van slowly down Eton High Street towards the river. As he approached the pedestrian bridge that connects Eton with Windsor he tried to pick out the King somewhere in the shadows. Nothing. The area looked completely deserted.

Stopping was not a good option. Instead he drove up to the corner as slowly as he dared, made a right turn and increased his speed again. He navigated through the narrow streets and eventually arrived back on High Street where it became one-way towards the Thames. He was back at the rendezvous point in just under four minutes, but still no King.

This was not good. Sooner or later a van circling Eton's centre, this close to one of the royal residences, was bound to be noticed. Still, he really did not have a choice at this point.

The fourth pass was successful. A running figure dressed in a hooded jacket emerged from the other side of the bridge and closed the distance with surprising speed. Coyle pulled onto the curb and waited. Moments later the King pulled open the left door and heaved himself into the passenger seat.

'Sorry I'm late!' he puffed. 'Getting away unnoticed was harder than I thought.' Then he produced a guilty grin. 'My security chaps are very good actually. I don't like having to give them the slip.'

It was only a ten-minute drive to Coyle's hotel, and they used the time to discuss their destination and the best route to take. Once they were in the hotel parking lot, the King pulled on Coyle's spare biker's overalls.

'Not a bad fit,' he admitted. 'Let's see about the helmet.'

This might have been a problem, but fortunately the helmet was slightly too large, which was a lot better than too small. The mirror finish visor hid the royal features completely. What better way for any monarch to travel incognito than outfitted like this on a fast moving motorbike!

After some discussion they decided to use only one of the bikes. The King was tempted by the sleek Kawasaki, but had to admit to himself that it was an unfamiliar vehicle for him and that this was not the best time to practice.

The agility by which Coyle negotiated the bends in town and the mighty acceleration the Kawasaki produced once he opened up the throttle for motorway driving made the passenger's ride an exhilarating experience. They roared through the night, and taking advantage of the low traffic density, left every other vehicle in their wake.

Coyle's SatNav told him the distance was just over 140 miles. He aimed to cover it in two hours or less. The King considered tapping him on the shoulder to suggest he might slow down a bit, but decided against it. Coyle clearly knew how to handle his bike and the shorter time a king went AWOL, the better.

65. WORCESTERSHIRE

At first glance Major Andrew Harcourt seemed an unlikely friend of a reigning monarch. There was a roughness about him that spoke of humble beginnings and a youth spent as far away from elite schools as one could get. You sensed he was a grand fellow to have at your side in a pub brawl, but who might struggle to fit in at Royal Ascot.

His powerful build rather than his height intimidated would-be opponents, as did his hard grey eyes and predatory smile when provoked. Those under his command knew that he hid a keen sense of humour behind the gruff exterior, and that he had forsaken the temptation of higher rank in order to remain in the SAS into his 40's. A soldier's soldier, he led from the front and received unswerving loyalty in return.

Roused abruptly from his bed by news of the unannounced visitors, he stormed into the reception area and was pleased to see that his security protocol was adhered to perfectly. The three-man guard team was spread out so one man would always be able to fire his weapon if the others were attacked.

Fixing his glance on the tall red-blond stranger with penetrating blue eyes, he didn't strike the most welcoming of notes. 'I'm the CO. What the hell is going on? Better not be a joke!'

The King spoke from within his helmet. 'No joke, Andy! I'm going to remove my helmet, so please don't anyone get trigger-happy!'

On recognising his head of state, the major had one further decision to make. Accept the situation at face value or assume foul play – like a hostage situation. The King understood.

'Mr Coyle is unarmed and he is very much on our side,' he assured his friend.

'Stand down, men!' the major commanded, and came to attention himself. 'Welcome to the Unit, Sir!'

The King took a couple of steps and shook the Harcourt's hand. 'We need to talk in private, Andy.'

Within minutes they were seated around a conference table in the Gamma Unit's situation room. Both the King and Coyle had removed their motorcycle outfits and received military sweaters to warm themselves from the trip.

The King conducted most of the briefing, calling on Coyle to fill in some of the details. In the end Major Harcourt had only one question. 'How can I help?'

'Can you send some men over to Mike Stack's place?' said Coyle. 'I'll give you the exact coordinates. The bodies should be removed, and also – well – the *ordnance*. If you could have it brought here it would be a great help.'

'This would be your stash of weapons and explosives?'

'And some other sensitive items. By the way, the basement vault is booby-trapped. I'll write down the instructions how to deactivate the devices. It's not complicated if you know what to do.'

'I'll have to take your word for that. What about DS Stack?'

The King looked up. 'Is she a problem for you, Andy?'

'No Sir, but in view of what you've just told me, I don't feel right about keeping her prisoner. On the other hand, releasing her might be both problematic and dangerous – for *her* I mean.'

'Why don't you upgrade her to house guest for the time being?' suggested Coyle. 'I'll talk to her and make sure she understands.'

'Okay, that makes sense. But what do we do about Mesmer? That's what you really want us for, right?'

Coyle exchanged a glance with the King and got a Royal nod to proceed.

'I want to put together an assault team to hit Mesmer's base as soon as possible,' he explained. 'If we can take him and his setup out, L&O will be severely crippled.

Nagelmann can be dealt with separately. Nelson's bunch too. Without L&O, they'll be exposed and vulnerable.'

'How big an assault team? It seems a formidable stronghold from what you've told me.'

'A dozen of you best men should do. Especially if we bring along enough explosives to permanently damage the place.'

'Would your men sign up for this?' asked the King. 'Nothing could be less official!'

'Sir, I guarantee that if given the chance every single one will volunteer! I'll have to think carefully about what would be the optimum team composition. Getting the skill balance right.'

Coyle had not expected any other response. He had worked enough with Special Force's soldiers to understand their total commitment.

'Can we leave tomorrow?' he asked, but this time Harcourt was less confident.

'The men can be ready, but how do we get them to Albania?' he asked. 'Even off-the-books operations get authorisation from *somewhere* when it comes to the use of military aircraft. I don't have the clout to requisition a plane on my own. How about the Royal Flight?'

The King shook his head. 'I'd love to, but it wouldn't work,' he sighed. 'Too much red tape involved! We'll have to think of another way.'

'Henry Elliott!' suggested Coyle. 'He is already involved, and he's got a decent size plane. Unfortunately I don't know where he is at the moment.'

'How do we find out?' demanded the King.

'I'll get his private mobile number from Sir Hugh, but we need something more secure if we want to go into details.'

Harcourt understood. 'If you can get hold of him we can set up a reasonably secure computer connection from here.'

Coyle sent en email to Sir Hugh's *Metcalfe* iPad. The response was once more incredibly quick. A mobile number with the prefix 49 – for Germany. Probably a phone registered to an Elliott subsidiary there.

The businessman answered on the sixth ring and groaned something like *yeah-what*. Coyle spoke quickly. 'I know you recognise my voice. I'll text you an instruction when we're finished. How to sign in on a website where we can talk to each other. You okay with that?'

'No problem, son! Give me ten minutes and I'll be with you.'

66. MADRID

Having heeded Sir Hugh's warning to leave the country for a while, Henry Elliott found himself aching for something to do. He had flow to Frankfurt for some interesting, but non-essential meetings, and continued onwards to Madrid where he had called an ad hoc get-together with his local managers. Once that session was over however, there was not a lot he could do without revealing his whereabouts to a large number of people. And he did not feel like becoming a tourist!

The hotel suite was registered in the name of a Spanish company and booked for entertainment and hospitality use. He avoided paying with his credit cards and did not go to any of the better-known restaurants. This was not exactly deep cover, but it would take a serious effort to find him. Besides, he would be moving on soon.

When he signed in to the website Coyle had pointed him to, he was asked to download an operative software package. The process took close to ten minutes and he had to resist the temptation to bite his nails or pour himself a drink.

Once the connection was established, it was excellent. A voice with almost metallic clarity greeted him.

'This is the Unit CO. We have an encrypted voice link in place. It is considered secure, but I urge all of you to be economical with names and specific pieces of information.'

'Understood,' said Elliott. 'Can I please speak with the person whose voice I know?'

'That would be me,' responded Coyle. 'There is a second person here you should recognise, but not the one you may expect.'

Elliott wondered who other than Sir Hugh might have gotten involved, but said only 'go ahead.'

The King spoke. 'I'm not sure if my voice is all that familiar really, but I certainly appreciate any assistance you can give us.'

Henry Elliott wished he *had* opted for a drink. This was beyond incredible!

'I *do* know your voice and I'm at your service,' he said.

Coyle took over. 'The people causing all the mischief have a secret base in Albania. I'm hitting it with a volunteer team from the Unit. Unfortunately we don't have an aircraft. Can you arrange something? For tomorrow if possible!'

Elliott didn't hesitate. 'Of course! My plane can carry up to eighteen. That enough for you?'

'Sure. It leaves capacity for *useful cargo*.'

'To which airport should I send it? I guess Brize Norton is out.'

Coyle deferred to the major, who made up his mind quickly. 'Wolverhampton,' he decided.

'Got it. I'll have it there by noon tomorrow. You can discuss destination with the pilots. No, wait a minute! It's not enough, is it?'

'What do you mean?'

'My plane will get you to the region, but how do you get from an airport to your target? Don't you think you'll attract a lot of attention if you line up at the local Hertz office?'

'We'll sort something out,' Coyle reassured him. 'That's the next step now that we know we have a plane.'

'You need a helicopter! And not a small one either!'

Major Harcourt agreed. 'I can't see another way if we're to do this quickly.'

'You wouldn't have one, would you?' asked Coyle.

'No, but I think I know where I can get one for you. In the right part of the world as well! A friend of mine – fellow football enthusiast really – has got a rather big private yacht in the Mediterranean. And it's got a nice big helicopter!'

'Would he let us have it?' The King sounded sceptical.

'I should think so. Last year I did him a big favour. He isn't – well, *British* – you see, and some of his enemies tried to put him out of business. Suddenly he faced a serious liquidity crisis, and if I hadn't helped him out he would have gone bankrupt.'

'Fantastic!' exclaimed Coyle. 'That's how we do it then. We start thinking in terms of an airport in southeast Italy or northern Greece, where we can switch from fixed-wing to rotary.'

'Unfortunately I don't know how long it'll take me to get hold of this chap, but I'll get on it right away. How do I contact you again?'

'Just sign on to this website again,' said Major Harcourt. 'We'll be monitoring it at our end.'

67. WORCESTERSHIRE

The bed was comfortable, but she slept badly and awoke early – her mind invaded by details of all that had gone wrong. Her dad killed, herself getting caught at Scotland Yard by that creep Reid, then hauled to some mysterious off-the-map location. The horrible essence of it all was that she had become untraceable and therefore deniable.

Incongruously there was a knock on the door before it opened. Her nose sensed bacon and toast and coffee before her eyes recognised the figure in the doorway. Coyle – holding a breakfast tray!

'That was an unacceptable risk you took,' he said rather matter-of-factly. 'You knew there were LONA collaborators at Scotland Yard.'

She sat up and pulled the cover to her chest. Not out of modesty – she hadn't undressed for bed – but instinctively to create a protective barrier.

'How did you find me? Where am I?'

He walked calmly into the room and put the tray on the only table. 'This is a Special Unit that is more or less connected to the SAS. You have four people to thank for being here rather in the clutches of the Longbows. None of them me, by the way!'

'Then who?'

'First of all DCS Miller had the good sense to inform Sir Hugh. He then turned to someone who was in a position to ask the Police Commissioner for a favour. To discretely hand you over to the Special Unit, where you'd be safe from harm.'

So Clara Miller hadn't been intimidated by Reid's show of force. She certainly owed her more than a thank-you card. But who had the authority to spring her from a SO15 cell?

'Not the King!' she gasped.

'Afraid so. Your adventure brought you to the attention of your Monarch, and he intervened very personally on your behalf. He is here by the way.'

'Oh my God!' She started thinking about what would be a thoroughly embarrassing meeting and wished she didn't look such a mess, but Coyle wasn't finished.

'We've persuaded Major Harcourt, the Unit CO, that you're not to be regarded as a prisoner while you're here. In fact, I need you to keep working on the LONA material while I'm away.'

'Where are you going?' she asked reflexively, but then remembered the plan. 'Did you find out something in Copenhagen?'

Coyle indicated that she might as well enjoy her breakfast. 'Give you twenty minutes to eat and freshen up. Then we talk properly and you can meet the others.'

He started to leave, but she grabbed his sleeve. 'Just tell me where you're off to!'

'With a bit of luck, I'll be in Albania tonight. We've managed to pin down Mesmer's location. He is holed up in a kind of mountain fortress, so I'm bringing along some of Harcourt's useful chaps.'

'What about me? Can I come too?'

A straight putdown would have been so easy, and she expected it. Instead Coyle dropped his casual demeanour and took hold of her hands.

'It wouldn't be appropriate, Joanne. For several reasons, the King being one. He's gone out on a limb for you already.'

'Yes, I see,' she agreed, though disappointed.

'Besides – there is another field mission I think you'll want to join.'

'What's that?'

'Harcourt is sending some men to clean up your dad's place. You'll want to be there to pay your respects and make sure everything is done properly, right?'

She nodded quietly, and he turned to leave. Holding on to his left sleeve, she made him look back at her.

'Thanks for arranging it,' she said.

68. WORCESTERSHIRE

When Henry Elliott came back on the computer link they interrupted their other conversations and gathered in the conference room. The King, the major, Coyle and Joanne.

Elliott was full of energy and enthusiasm.

'My jet is on its way to Wolverhampton,' he informed them. 'And I managed to speak to my friend with the mega yacht. He is happy to lend us his helicopter – an AW139 from Agustawestland, so it's big enough – but it's not onboard the yacht at the moment. It's being serviced at the manufacturer's facility in Frosione - about an hour's drive southeast of Rome.'

'Could we pick it up there?' asked Major Harcourt.

'Unfortunately Frosione doesn't have a runway. It is strictly for helicopters and run by the Italian military. And it's quite a long way from your destination anyway.'

'What do you suggest?' asked Coyle, sensing that the businessman had worked out a plan.

'I just got confirmation that the service work is finished, so we've asked the company if they can have the chopper flown over to the airport at Brindisi. That'd put you about 250 kilometres from your target.'

Coyle was delighted. 'That would be excellent! If they agree, the timing is perfect. We'll switch aircraft at Brindisi tonight.'

'Oh they've agreed – that wasn't a problem. But there is something else.'

'Serious?'

'I don't know. You see, the company pilot will bring the machine over, but then he is going back. We can't ask him to do the mission for us! And the regular pilot – who works for my friend – isn't suitable, it seems. Besides, he is off on holiday somewhere in America at the moment.'

'We couldn't use a civilian for this anyway,' the major pointed out.

'But we definitely have the helicopter?' Coyle insisted. 'And it will fly to Brindisi?'

'You can bank on it! It's pity that the yacht is nowhere near the area – it's doing some retrofitting in Germany. I thought you might want to use it as a backup landing platform. After you're through with the job that is.'

'That would have been *very* useful,' agreed Coyle.

Elliott emitted a soft chuckle. 'My friend called me back. He'd had a thought and checked with one of his – friends – who also has a big yacht. As it happens, it's lying off Corfu at the moment. If we say the word, the owner will send it north into the Adriatic.'

'What about its own chopper?' enquired Coyle.

'Too small for our purposes, and it's not onboard anyway. But the landing platform is big enough for the AW139. I checked.'

'I say we take him up on his kind offer,' Coyle suggested.

The Major hesitated. 'We still don't have a pilot. I don't have anyone in the Unit who can fly a helicopter, and going to the outside for this would be. . .'

There was a pregnant pause. Then the King spoke.

'*I'm* a helicopter pilot,' he said.

69. GWENT

It seemed a lifetime ago she had driven up the track towards her dad's cottage as a surprise, only to find him with the illegal guns – and Coyle. She was in an extended wheelbase Land Rover with four of Major Harcourt's men. They went by first names. Frank was the sergeant in command, although none of them wore uniform. He was in his mid thirties, broad shouldered and bald as a billiard ball. Tony and Ted were identical twins. Fair haired, compact, tough and superbly competent. Bernard was the smallest of the team, but probably the brightest, she thought. He did the driving as well as most of the talking.

They paused briefly at an abandoned Toyota SUV.

'How far to your dad's place from here?' asked Fred.

'I'd say a mile and a half,' she replied, but Bernard was more precise.

'The GSM says one point eight four miles,' he announced. 'Smart of them to walk that far.'

It didn't take long to give the SUV a quick check, but they didn't learn anything new so they piled back into the Land Rover and drove on.

Joanne didn't spot the bodies right away. Instead her old Golf caught her eye where it stood out of the way under a tree. But then she became aware of human shapes on the ground between the Land Rover and the cottage. Five of them. And one was unmistakably her dad.

'Pull over!' ordered Frank. 'We'll take care of the bodies first.'

They had brought several military body bags with them, and the twins started unloading them as soon as the vehicle was stationary. Bernard had the highest medical qualifications – field medic of course – so the cursory post mortems fell to him. Bending over the first body he called out.

'Seems consistent with the time you gave us, Joanne. Dead about thirty six hours.'

She didn't respond as she slowly approached the remains of her dad. The ground around him was dark with dried blood – as expected. And she had been right about the phone. The device lay a few feet away, its innards well and truly scrambled by the staff sergeant's last bullet.

Frank was standing next to her. 'He put up a hell of a fight, your dad! Only like you said, he must've seen the forth man too late.'

Joanne liked the tone of professional respect. She turned to give Frank a quiet smile, but in that moment his head exploded. The crack of the shot reached her ears but didn't penetrate her consciousness until half a second later. It seemed like Frank's head erupted in silence, but that his body fell with a hellish roar.

'Get down!' screamed Ted, and she became aware that a fierce barrage followed the first shot.

As she dived in the general direction of the Land Rover, she saw Bernard take a round in the abdomen and heard him emit a sickening groan as he collapsed.

Ted returned fire – he and Tony were the designated point men and carried their weapons at the ready – but was sent flying like a ragdoll by a bullet to the chest.

Tony had managed to take up position behind the vehicle and motioned for her to come closer. 'Crawl over!' he yelled. 'I'll cover you!'

He eased himself slightly above the bonnet in order to open fire, but one of the attackers had a clear view of him and caught him with a shot through the throat. He buckled and fell with a helpless gurgle and blood gushing over the Land Rover. The fight was over.

Lying flat on the ground was no good – they knew she was there. But there was no escape either. She was too far from anything that could provide real cover. And those bastards didn't know she wasn't about to shoot back at them. Only one thing to do!

'I'm unarmed!' she shouted and rolled over on her back so she could show them both her hands in the air.

'Stay where you are!' came the reply. Cold and professional. Two men approached. She sensed a third in another direction before she heard his footsteps. He must have been the one who shot Tony. And he seemed to be in command.

'DS Stack!' confirmed Craig Baines. 'Luck smiles on us at last! Great idea to stake out this place, wasn't it!'

He implied that it had been his idea, but of course the instruction had come from Rita Ridgewood, who considered the mission important enough to commit one of her two lead operatives.

Joanne stared at the disproportionately broad figure standing over her, a satisfied smirk on his face. Like something out of a violent video game, she thought. An Ork or similar. Maybe not the brightest, but shrewd enough to keep the ambush team's vehicle a long distance away from the cottage. The Gamma Unit men never had the slightest warning!

They pulled her to her feet and quickly frisked her to confirm she was indeed unarmed. There was no point in talking, so she kept her mouth shut. Finally the Ork spoke.

'Markevich!'

He was about an inch shorter than her so she looked slightly downwards into his eyes as she responded. 'Joanne Stack, but of course you know that already Mr Markevich.'

The blow was open-handed and looked like a casual slap, but it hit her with such force it would have dropped her to the ground if the men behind her hadn't caught her first. The left side of her head felt crushed and she briefly wondered if her jaw was dislocated. The pain made her disoriented and she never saw the follow up blow to her midriff. Suddenly the Ork's gigantic fist connected, and for what seemed far too long for a human being to survive, she couldn't breathe. Even bending over wasn't possible as the Ork's men held her upright.

First she coughed, then she vomited – the puke soiling her jacket front – and then finally managed to draw breath. Her tormentor allowed her about a minute to recover before he spoke to her again. Then he leaned in close to her ear.

'Me and the chaps – we're not boy scouts, luv. You tell us where we can find your friend Markevich or we'll go to work on you proper!'

'You won't like it!' one of the men holding her added with the implied subtext that he *would* enjoy their side of it.

Clear thinking is hard when you're in intense pain and struggling to breathe, but to her horror Joanne realised that she knew too much. If they broke her – as no doubt they would in the end – she would reveal that Markevich was on his way by private jet to Brindisi in Italy, where he and his commando team would switch to a helicopter for the final flight to Mesmer's – the L&O movement's leader's – headquarters in Albania. Coyle would walk into an ambush as bad as the one she had just witnessed. She had to find a way to divert them.

She nodded her head. 'Need air!' she croaked. 'I'll tell you what I know! But must breathe!'

The Ork gave a sign and the others let go of her. She dropped to her knees, which made breathing easier but it took a couple of minutes. When her captors showed signs of getting impatient, she pointed towards the cottage.

'My dad let him have his UK base here,' she said while struggling to form the words with her face still throbbing. 'He doesn't tell me where he goes, but he keeps everything down here. His weapons, his files, his computers. There must be a way to track him down if you look through the stuff.'

'Where is it?' asked the Ork.

'See the barn to the right of the cottage? There's a hidden basement.'

'Show us!'

She was yanked to her feet and forced to walk between the two foot soldiers. For a second she reflected on how sad the cottage now looked and how she would never again sit in the little-bit-of-everything room with her dad. Then she forced herself to think ahead.

Once inside the barn, she indicated the bales of hay that concealed the basement entrance. The Ork shifted them like they were weightless, and carefully inspected the solid looking steel lid in the concrete floor.

'How does it open?' he wanted to know, and she saw no advantage in further attempts to delay. She pointed to a fuse box on the wall.

'There is a keypad underneath,' she explained. 'You punch in the code and the cellar door unlocks.'

The Ork confirmed that the keypad was indeed where she claimed. 'Code!' he barked.

She hesitated just long enough for effect. When she felt the grip on her arms tighten, she let out a long sigh, followed by 'ef1alte5x'.

Keying in the digits was a challenge for thick Ork fingers, but he managed it, although he had to make her repeat the sequence twice. There was an audible click as the lock disengaged.

One of the men released his grip on her arm and bent down over the lid door. It opened on well-lubricated hinges, and automatically switched on the basement lighting. The man peered down into the space and whistled.

'Well fuck me!' he blurted. 'All that for one guy! Looks like a bloody arsenal down there!'

'Let's have a look then!' The Ork pushed him aside. As the careful professional he was, he examined the steps for traps, but finding nothing untoward he sent his subordinate down.

'I don't believe all this stuff!' the man shouted back at him.

'Hold on to her!' he ordered the other minion and descended the steps himself.

Joanne had been counting seconds. She was up to seventy-two and experiencing pure terrifying fear inside. The charges would go off in eighteen seconds!

The trick was simple. The correct code unlocked the door, but an extra digit punched in immediately after the first eight activated an electronic ninety-second fuse. The x was her weapon!

Fortunately the goon gripping her arm was too interested in what was happening in the basement to be fully alert to what she was doing. With desperate strength she swung to the right and drove her free elbow as close to his kidney area as she could reach. He grunted and let go of her left arm. This allowed her to complete her turn and bring her left knee hard up against his groin. He bent over instinctively, the pain yet to come, and she pulled him forward towards the basement opening. Off balance, he couldn't fight the momentum and landed with the upper part of his body over the steps.

Her count interrupted, there was only one thing she could do – run for it! She made her legs propel her away from the hole in the floor and saw the barn door draw closer with dreamlike slowness. She felt a flicker of hope as she reached the outside and noticed gravel rather than concrete under her feet.

How many seconds? If she could throw herself to the ground at the right moment she stood a chance. But first she had to get far enough to avoid the imminent blast effects. How far was far enough, she wondered. Then something happened and her world went completely black.

70. BRINDISI

They worked hard during the flight and when Henry Elliott's Gulfstream G500 touched down at Brindisi, they had agreed on a fairly detailed tactical plan for the assault on Mesmer's hideout. It did bother them that they were thin on local intelligence, but the satellite photos the King had accessed yielded a surprising amount of information on close study.

Everyone was still a bit stunned by their Monarch's decision to join the mission, but he had made his case very convincingly. He was an experienced helicopter pilot, he was on the spot and he was the one who had set everything in motion to begin with. If Coyle and the Gamma Unit men were risking their lives on an unauthorized mission, he could hardly ask less of himself. When Coyle quietly pointed out that he was risking his throne as well as his life, his response was subdued but unwavering.

'Whatever happens, I won't become the figurehead of a LONA dictatorship! That would demean everything I stand for.'

'I respect that Sir,' said Coyle, his face thoughtful. He was weighing up the combat risks awaiting them, and considering how he could keep their royal team member as safe as possible, but the King read something else into his expression.

'I'd like to ask you a deeply personal question,' he began. Coyle nodded encouragingly.

'Why are *you* putting your life on the line to save British democracy as well as my throne?'

For the first time there was an utter lack of comprehension in Coyle's eyes. 'Because I've been trained and prepared for something like this. That was always my mission.'

'Yes, Sir Hugh filled me in on your background, but the sense of loyalty required of you in this is – immense!'

'Why wouldn't I have an immense sense of loyalty?'

'Your parents. They were Irish republican terrorists, right? British troops killed them. Some might call it murder.'

Coyle saw where this was heading. 'So what's a son of Irish terrorists doing fighting the King of England's battles?'

'Something like that, yes.' The King looked ill at ease, but Coyle produced an easy smile.

'They weren't my parents,' he revealed. 'Of course everybody thought they were, and acted accordingly. But in fact I was not their biological child.'

'You were adopted and no one knew about it!'

Coyle's smile turned ironic. 'Not adopted, no. Abducted! As a baby. Before my conscious memory became active. I don't know who my real parents were and I've never bothered looking for them. It didn't seem consistent with my mission.'

'But at least one of them must have been rather extraordinary!'

'All the more reason not to dig up the past. There might be unpleasant surprises!'

The King was intrigued. 'And even Sir Hugh doesn't know this?'

'No, and I'd rather it stayed that way. It's really nobody's business but mine. I only mentioned it to explain my lack of disloyalty.'

'Sorry, I never meant to insinuate – only understand.'

Coyle shrugged. 'It was a reasonable line of enquiry,' he conceded.

'Just one more question if I may. How come you know this? I mean, how did you find out? And when?'

'I listened to my – *parents*. They often argued about it. Apparently *Father* wasn't happy about having me around.'

The King looked incredulous. 'But you were, what – two years old! How could you understand and how could you remember?'

Coyle shrugged. 'I suppose it's part of the way I am.'

71. BRINDISI

The transition from business jet to helicopter might have been tricky, but turned out routine - perhaps because Coyle did all the talking in fluent Italian. No one questioned their cover story of heading out to the private yacht *Dunyana* for an exclusive Adriatic cruise. An adventure cruise with plenty of mountain trekking and hunting on the programme, as he described it to explain an all-male group toting canvas bags and fibreglass containers rather than designer labelled leather luggage.

The King being recognised was a real worry, especially since he had to take charge of the AW139 from the Agustawestland pilot. Fortunately the Italian was in hurry to get back to Rome and eagerly rushed through the pilot-to-pilot briefing. He didn't give much thought to why his counterpart wore sunglasses at 9pm and kept his sports cap on the whole time. Pilots have their idiosyncrasies!

As soon as he was gone, Harcourt's team set about removing most of the AW139's VIP interior. Plush leather seats were too bulky for their kind of mission. Twelve men in serious combat gear had to fit where six passengers normally lounged in great comfort.

'Anything we should worry about?' asked Coyle as he opened the cockpit door. The King was busily punching information into the flight computer.

'I can certainly fly her,' he said. 'But some of the avionics look a bit unfamiliar in this configuration. I'll need a bit of time on them before we take off. But my biggest concern is the payload fuel balance. To carry every man and all the equipment I'll have to reduce fuel to 800 kilo – that's just under half our tank capacity.'

'How much range does that give us?'

'Theoretically the distance to our target is 223 kilometres. Taking into account that we'll be lighter on the way back, we should have enough to get us to the yacht, but returning straight to Brindisi would be a stretch.'

'So we'll *have to* find the Dunyana!'

'And land safely on her small platform! The weather report isn't all that encouraging. Winds up to 11 metres per second. The sea could get choppy.'

Major Harcourt had overheard the last part of their conversation. 'We could leave a couple of men here,' he suggested, but Coyle shook his head.

'I don't want to do that. Every man plays a vital part in the plan. Either we go as we are, or we abort.'

'Guess it's up to you, Sir,' said the major to the King.

After a couple of pensive seconds they got his decision. 'It looks to me like we're already committed. If we abort now, the game's over. Let's go in forty-five minutes.'

72. ALBANIA

Coyle sat in the co-pilot's seat as they traversed the Adriatic Sea. Major Harcourt had preferred to be in the back with his men. He had been quite right about them of course. Every man offered the chance to volunteer for the King's mission had done so.

The King pointed to the main navigation screen. 'That's the positional beacon onboard the Dunyana. She's made excellent progress. We'll be passing very close to her on our route.'

'How close?' Coyle wanted to know.

'About six kilometres. We could swing right past her without losing significant fuel.'

'Then let's do so! It'll be useful to see what she looks like and gauge how hard the landing will be.'

It took eighteen minutes to reach the yacht, and Coyle used the time to make an adjustment to their plan.

'What do you think, Sir?' he asked as they passed the nicely lit up luxury craft.

'Piece of cake, actually!' said the King. 'I expected a much smaller helipad. And look how well she rides the waves. Must have brilliant stabilisers!'

That settled it for Coyle. He twisted around and indicated to Harcourt that he should turn on his headset.

'That our carrier we just flew over?' asked the Major.

'Yes, and our *pilot* says he's happy with her. Better than expected. I'm thinking of changing the plan slightly. How about the chopper heading to Dunyana right after dropping us, rather than hang around on the ground? Then come pick us up when we've done the rough stuff.'

'If the *pilot* is okay with it, I think it's a much better plan. The less time our bird spends sitting on the ground in enemy territory the better.'

The King broke into the conversation. 'The pilot is totally okay with it, Andy!'

'Great! Then I say we do it that way. Maybe with one small modification.'

Coyle looked surprised. 'What's that?'

'One of my men goes back to the yacht, and when the chopper comes back to get us he acts as airborne machine gunner.'

Coyle thought about it. 'Won't it leave you short on suppressive fire?'

'A little, but if that becomes crucial we'll be in serious trouble anyway. It everything goes shit-shaped I'd rather have a machine gunner in the air than on the ground. Could make all the difference when we extract.'

Glancing over at the King, Coyle got a nod of approval. 'All right, that's what we'll do. Pick out the man you're sending back.'

'It'll have to be Ned. He's such a fat bastard he'd probably get shot on the ground.'

The two men on the flight deck both laughed. *Fat* was an extremely relative term when applied to Gamma Unit men. But that was scarce comfort to Ned, who would much rather join his peers in combat than shuttle back and forth across the Adriatic with a crowned head of state at the controls.

He turned to the Major. 'Andy, what about the radio mast?'

'What about it?'

'Wouldn't it be worth blowing up? You could see from the satellite shots there's a lot more to it than mobile phone relay. If we take it out, the bastards will be completely cut off – communications wise I mean.'

'Go on! What are you thinking?'

'How about you drop me at the mast on the way to the landing zone? I set the charges and the chopper picks me up on the way back to the ship. From then on I'm just the gunner.'

This was the sort of tactical creativeness Gamma expected from its members, and Harcourt gave Ned a sign of appreciation.

'Let me run it by the flight deck,' he said.

He did so on the open channel so Ned could hear the decision. The King made the obvious objection. 'There is nowhere to land around the mast. He'd have to drop by rope.'

'Not a problem for me Sir,' Ned assured him.

'But how do you get back up? There'll be no one onboard to operate the winch! I'll have my hands full just hovering on the spot!'

That seemed to kill the idea, but Ned was tenacious. 'What if I climb to the top of the mast? It's higher than the trees around it. You dangle a short rope for me. Don't worry about the rest – I'll climb onboard by myself!'

'Your call Andy! Can he do it?' asked the King.

'Yes Sir! For a fat bastard, Ned is pretty good at climbing up ropes.'

73. GWENT

The fog in Joanne's head began to make way for pulsating pain. Gradually she became aware of two major facts: She was lying face down and there was mud in her mouth. As she slowly lifted her immensely heavy head off the ground, a third piece of information penetrated her mind – she had survived the explosion!

Spitting and retching to clear her mouth of debris, she briefly panicked when she could not see. Her eyes appeared cemented by the mixture of sand, mud and rainwater she had been thrown into by the blast. She gingerly probed her eyelids, but stopped when even more coarse matter came in contact with her eyeballs. Rinsing them in water became a high priority, but could she move?

Her whole body felt bruised, wet and cold – very cold! Of course – she had been unconscious for hours! Now that she was fully conscious she began to shiver uncontrollably.

The property was familiar to her, but not to the degree that she could find her way around blindly. Rather than attempt to stand up – without eyesight she would not have enough sense of balance to walk – she started crawling in the general direction of the cottage. After an agonising few minutes, she figured she was heading in the wrong direction and reversed back about halfway before adjusting to her left.

The cold was really getting to her now, and she realised that she had little time before she drifted into hypothermia and eventually died. The cottage couldn't be far away by now, but in what direction?

She felt a small surge of elation as her fingers found a stone surface that had to be the cottage wall. With renewed determination she dragged herself to a standing position with both hands against the wall. Then shuffled sideways while probing for the door.

First she passed a window and rejected the notion of breaking it. Climbing in that way would be dangerous and probably beyond her anyway. She had to find the door! And the key! Dad would not have left it unlocked! She knew he kept a spare key under a loose slate nearby, but finding it would not be easy either.

The door's smooth wooden surface felt delicious to her touch, and she grabbed hold of the iron handle for reassurance. The door wobbled slightly and a touch of her fingers around the edge confirmed that it wasn't locked. Or rather – the doorframe had been forced and broken.

Of course! The LONA men would have broken in when they first arrived on the scene, before they hid themselves and waited to spring their ambush.

Once inside, finding the kitchen sink was easy. She turned on both taps and let the water first clean her battered hands. Then she set about carefully washing her face, the area around the eyes and finally the eyes themselves. As soon as she could see, she turned on the lights and took a quick look around the cottage. Yes, the intruders had been there, but it had been a cursory search and the mess looked manageable. Almost like the men had known they would not find anything.

She always kept some spare clothes in the guest bedroom closet. On her way there, she flipped the bathroom light switch and leaned in far enough to turn on the electric shower. By the time she had stripped off her wet and muddy rags, the water was hot and the shower stall invitingly steamy. She remained there until she stopped shivering, and most of the abrasive matter had washed out of her eyes. Afterwards she dried herself vigorously, and quickly put on the warmest odd combination of clothes she had available.

It was obvious what had happened. Once the men her dad had killed failed to report back, someone at LONA had become concerned and sent in a backup team. These men had taken in what had gone down and rightly assumed that sooner or later she or Coyle would show up on the scene. All they had to do was stay concealed and wait.

There was always plenty of food in her dad's freezer. She picked out a shepherd's pie and heated it for ten minutes in the microwave. Nourishment was essential when you were in a weakened state. Once she had eaten and downed several glasses of milk, she knew she had to venture outside.

There was a flashlight near the front door, so she grabbed it and let the beam wander over what had been the barn. The structure was no longer recognisable, with only parts of the walls standing. There was no point trying to get into the basement, as the pile of debris would take hours to shift. Days if she tried it on her own.

Her Golf had stood near the barn and she needed no expert opinion to know that it was a write-off. At least she was able to reach in and remove her service weapon from the glove compartment. It was time to consider what to do next.

As far as she knew, she was still officially a terrorist suspect in custody. That ruled out making contact with the police, with the possible exception of Clara Miller. But calling DCS Miller would be putting her in an impossible position. She would feel under pressure to act against her professional code. Not fair on her, and what could she do for Joanne anyway?

Staying at the cottage was hardly an option either. Sooner or later Longbows or Government agents were bound to show up. Coyle might come before than, but probably not. He would have his hands full in Albania.

There really was only one course of action open to her, and that was to find her way back to Gamma. For a moment she thought she might call – one of the men must have a phone with a pre-programmed number – but with Major Harcourt away there was no one she knew to ask for by name, and she feared it could become a complicated and risky conversation. Especially if intercepted!

No, she had to get there in person. That decided, she made her way to the scene of the battle and forced herself to regard her dad's corpse as just another dead body. The paying of respect and formal mourning would have to wait. Maybe a long time!

Bernard had left the keys in the Land Rover, and she felt embarrassingly relieved not having to go through his pockets for them. The engine started with a reassuring rumble, but after that she had to struggle with the heavy steering and stiff pedals of the utilitarian vehicle. It took her a long time to make a three point turn – continuing up to the cottage was out of the question because of the bodies – and when she finally drove off, the bumpy track and the stiff suspension conspired to throw her around.

Too fast! Slow down!

The Land Rover could take terrain many times worse than this, but at a sensible pace. She stopped and shifted into first gear. Got going again and kept it at a crawl. It took a long time, but eventually she reached the point where her dad's track met a narrow country lane. Here she stopped and concentrated on the SatNav. Her own version of it had a simple *Go Home* function, but this device was military issue. It took her agonisingly long before she found the word *Base* in a pull-down menu and clicked on it.

To her relief, a route rapidly materialised on the screen, and she saw that she had 61.7 miles to cover. Still struggling with the unfamiliar gearbox, she turned in the direction indicated by the display and finally took some comfort in being alive against all odds.

74. ALBANIA

By the time Ned unceremoniously descended from the helicopter along a rope, everybody had donned NV gear.

Andy Harcourt watched his man drop smoothly to the ground, a lighter green shape in a dark green world. 'He's down – let's go!' he informed the flight deck, and the King broke off the hover and flew the AW139 at not much more than treetop level towards the LZ.

The dash was scary but only took a couple of minutes. Coyle wondered to himself whether Mesmer would have a sentry posted at the field. Probably not, but there might well be a motion sensitive security camera, in which case their element of surprise would evaporate.

Coyle and the King exchanged a handshake, and when the former climbed to the ground he found the full team already assembled. Impressive, he thought, considering the helicopter had been hastily adapted from VIP transport to assault troop carrier.

'Three point two kilometres,' Harcourt confirmed as he looked at the miniature SatNav on his wrist. 'We're slightly ahead of schedule, so shouldn't be a problem getting everyone to their stations on time.'

One of the men handed Coyle his equipment bag and he slung it on his back after first removing the MP7 – still his weapon of choice, but this time without silencer. The situation would go noisy at an early stage, although two of the men carried silenced weapons in order to deal unobtrusively with visible guards.

The plan called for them to avoid the forest road. There might be trip wires or sensors. Instead they spread out in the surrounding terrain and headed towards their objective as a procession of ominous dark figures. They had to keep climbing upwards, since Mesmer's base unsurprisingly nested higher up than the LZ. If they were spotted, they would have conceded higher ground advantage to the enemy, but it was an unavoidable risk.

Without incident they arrived at a slightly more open point in the forest, from where they could look at Mesmer's compound. They heard it the moment they saw it. There was a low hum that could only mean a large diesel somewhere in a basement. Sound proofed and muffled, but still audible in the quiet of the night.

'So that's his game,' Harcourt muttered. 'Blacked out completely. That's not easy to do, you know.'

He was right. The entire base was devoid of artificial light. No lamps, no fires, no glow from an unshuttered window. The low, bunker-like buildings formed a ragged crescent in the terrain, each structure surrounded by tall trees. Only immediately in front was there a clearing where vehicles could park and turn. There were tracks leading into what had to be a subterranean garage.

The forest setting made the base harder to spot but trickier to defend, thought Coyle. Except for the front entrance, there were no clear fields of fire. He therefore had to assume that intruder detection was handled electronically. There had to be numerous sensors concealed around the periphery. Maybe infrared, maybe vibration or pressure sensitive. Even simple tripwires could make things difficult.

Fortunately the kind of missions the Gamma Unit normally performed required the men to be experts at detecting and defeating security measures. With the exception of one man, whose task was to provide covering fire across the open area, and Major Harcourt himself, the whole team spent an hour methodically exploring the near vicinity of the buildings. It became clear early on that there were no sentries, and as the men came across and dealt with detection devices, they muttered quiet reports and confirmations into their secure battlefield radios. After a while there were no more sensors found, and Harcourt spoke quietly to Coyle.

'Simon found a couple of satellite dishes on the roof and put them out of order. Do we go to phase two?'

Coyle checked his watch. 'Ned's charges will go off in one minute twenty seconds,' he noted. 'Let's wait for that before we start.'

Because of the wind in the trees, the explosion was barely audible. Certainly no one inside the buildings could have heard it.

On Andy Harcourt's signal the first demolition team of two men – known as Don and Potter – made their way to the building thought to contain the compound's heating, ventilation and plumbing centre.

Potter was a wizard with locks – hence his nickname – and made easy work of the entrance door. 'We're in,' came his calm voice in Coyle's earpiece. 'It all looks modern and high quality here. But don't worry, we'll soon have it malfunctioning nicely!'

'Cover team in position,' reported the man for some reason known as Wilson, although it was neither his Christian nor surname. He and Nigel were the designated silent killers and equipped with appropriate sound-suppressed H&K MP5 submachine guns. Since there had been no sentries to take out, it meant that Wilson and Nigel could go straight into their phase two role, which was securing initial tactical advantage through stealthy fire.

It wasn't obvious to those on the outside what exactly had been tampered with, but they heard a screeching sound followed by a long hiss. Less than five minutes later a door opened at the opposite end of the compound and two men appeared carrying flashlights. One of them lit a cigarette while they walked across the crescent. He sucked greedily at it, and threw it away with great reluctance once his colleague made it clear that he was not about to hang around waiting for him to finish. With a grunt he followed the other man into the service building where both were to meet with quietly effective violence at the hands of Potter and Don.

Harcourt waited another five minutes, and when no one else appeared he told Potter to ratchet up the sabotage a notch. Moments later, a loud clang could be heard, followed by an ominous metallic rattle. The diesel hum stopped.

He noticed Coyle scrutinising the buildings in front of them through magnifying NV gear.

'There are six floodlights as far as I can see. Once they figure out they're under attack they'll probably turn them on.'

'Even with the power down? I think Potter just cut off their juice supply.'

'Mesmer will have a backup generator, or at least enough battery power to keep going for a while,' said Coyle. 'I'd feel better if those lights were shot out before the fun starts.'

Once told about the lights, Wilson and Nigel obliterated them with suppressed precision shots in less than two minutes.

'Okay, here they come!' one of the team members announced over the radio.

Seconds later Coyle saw them as well. A group of about ten – heading out of what seemed to be the staff barracks. Most of them had flashlights, but only half carried visible weapons. The group drifted towards the service building with the kind of exasperated annoyance people display when things they don't fully understand go wrong.

There was no need for Harcourt to micromanage his team. Each man could be trusted to use his judgement as the situation evolved.

'Couple of chaps dropping in on you Potter,' informed Wilson.

'Thanks mate – we're ready for them,' came the reply.

Two more figures appeared in the yard. One of them moved with the authority of someone in charge, and he was shouting something at his people. Probably telling them to be quick about whatever they had to do. Nigel took careful aim and dropped him with a single shot to the head.

Wilson quickly followed his example and fired two rapid rounds into the other newcomer. There was a brief moment of confusion as the main group wondered what had become of their leader. The silent killers used the time to switch their attention to the figures closest to them and furthest to the bodies. In methodical single shot mode they dispatched four of the men. That left three, as the other three had entered the service building.

Two of them were armed and one of these had enough situational astuteness to realise they were under attack. He swung his compact Russian made PP-2000 submachine gun in the direction where he sensed the enemy and squeezed the trigger. The burst went nowhere near Nigel and Wilson, but it did alter the battle status. The element of surprise was gone, although the intruders still maintained tactical advantage.

With no reason to avoid making noise, the Gamma team did not hesitate to cut down the shooter and his two comrades with a brief but brutal barrage. Alerted by the shots, Potter and Don emerged from the service building – the fate of the five Mesmer men who had entered there never in doubt. Both knew what to do next – follow Coyle into the main building, while Harcourt and the rest of the team engaged the bulk of Mesmer's security detail.

Potter found Mesmer's front door a harder challenge than the service building entrance, but he had come well prepared. In under a minute he applied small charges to the lock and hinges and connected them to a single detonator. The explosion seemed to drown in the battle noise as the rest of the team set about taking control of the staff quarters. He got a nod of appreciation from Coyle, and then they were inside Mesmer's lair.

All the main lights were out, but as Coyle had predicted there were dim backup lights – apparently designed to come on whenever the main power supply failed. This made their NV goggles redundant, but also deprived them of the advantage that came with seeing in the dark when your enemy did not.

Carefully, but without losing momentum, Coyle led their eerie progression through a series of empty rooms. The main floor seemed to be mainly for eating and entertaining. Fighting in a building for which you didn't have the floor plan was always a tough task, but it could not be helped.

The library looked like a room of importance. A place where Coyle imagined Mesmer working and conferring with his aides. There was a huge writing desk, but no visible computer.

'The bloke's got himself a nice little collection here,' commented Don with reference to the many antique weapons on the walls.

'Be sure to compliment him on it when you see him,' suggested Potter.

'There's no one on this floor,' said Coyle pensively. 'There was a staircase back by the entrance and I can see another one over there. I'll go down this one and work my way from one end of the building to the other. Potter, follow me and help me out if I need it. Don, I want you to go back to the staircase in the foyer and shoot whoever tries to escape that way.'

Before separating, they set their radios to a new frequency. By flipping back and forth they could still listen in on main battle communications, but it was important that they could talk quietly amongst themselves. Coyle got the impression that Andy Harcourt's force was making good progress. All their radio traffic spoke of calm professionalism. So far no casualties, but that could change in a second.

The stairs behind Mesmer's library were steep and narrow – clearly not intended for general use. This was the route he would take if he wanted to avoid meeting staff – or others. At the bottom was a solid looking wooden door and to its right a full-length mirror built into the wall. Coyle thought it strange. Mesmer's choice of interior was certainly opulent and expensive throughout, but there had not been any large mirrors elsewhere. It seemed reasonable to assume that he didn't care much for his own reflection reminding him of what he had become. So why this mirror?

'In combat, if something doesn't feel right, assume that it isn't,' Mike Stack had hammered into him back in their tutoring days.

Without in any way telegraphing his intentions, he flipped the MP7's to full auto mode and fired a controlled burst across the mirror at midriff height.

Unfazed by the suddenness of Coyle's action, Potter stepped up and aimed at whatever the shattering mirror might reveal. As the glass fragments fell they revealed a man holding a PP-2000. He'd been hit at least once by Coyle's salvo, but there was enough fight left in him to attempt to raise the gun. Potter put a single bullet into his forehead.

The lower floor was laid out like a hotel – a row of doors along a corridor. Three on the left side, six on the right. Despite all the battle noise no one came rushing out of the doors to take them on. Coyle spoke to his two companions over the radio.

'Looks like Mesmer's defensive concept is to stay safe behind locked doors and let the guards deal with intruders.'

Don's response was full of understandable pride. 'In that case he'll have a long wait for the cavalry. Our chaps are kicking their asses over there.'

'Great, but we'll still have to break through one door at a time. Potter get ready!'

The locks were electronic, and although probably not impervious to the wizard's skills, explosives were the quicker option.

'Which one?' asked Potter.

'Middle door on the left. I've got a feeling Mesmer's lurking behind it.'

75. ALBANIA

Andy Harcourt and his seven Gamma Unit men fought a numerically superior but confused and disorganised enemy force. Whoever recommended to Mesmer that the compound rely on camouflage, blackout and sophisticated periphery sensors for security, had not served him well. Once inside the staff building the intruders proceeded methodically but with practised speed from room to room – clearing each with flash-bang grenades and measured shots at anyone holding a weapon.

No doubt Mesmer had done his best to recruit seasoned mercenaries with proven capabilities, but such individuals needed to be constantly trained and tested to stay effective. They also needed a proper command structure, unflinching discipline and a strong sense of purpose. Having guarded the same forest compound for months – or maybe years – these men were no match for Harcourt's professionals.

Some resisted to the end, but most dropped their weapons and raised their arms in surrender when defeat became inevitable. No shame in that, thought Harcourt. Soldiers – even mercenaries – can live to fight another day. Unfortunately the sheer number of prisoners was becoming a problem. Tying them up would take too long, but watching over them with guns required manpower he couldn't spare.

In the end they managed to herd the captives into the compound's canteen, where one man could keep an eye on them. Harcourt quick-guessed their number at about forty. At least twenty had been killed or badly wounded. How many did that leave? Probably not a lot, but not knowing was uncomfortable. They had to press on and clear the rest of the building.

The main floor contained the canteen, a small but very hi-tech movie theatre, several offices – including what seemed to be the security force's command centre – an auditorium, a conference room and a large industrial kitchen. When they descended a level, they found sleeping quarters with adjacent bathrooms and toilets, an extensive fitness gym and an armoury complete with a well equipped gunsmith's workshop.

'Looks like there's another level below,' Wilson announced on the radio. 'Only the door looks very solid. Do we blow it open?'

'Absolutely,' confirmed Harcourt. 'Go to it, but wait for me before heading down!'

Wilson couldn't quite equal Potter's wizardry with explosives, but he did a sound job in about three minutes and the door crumbled. Moments later Harcourt arrived with Simon in tow. They formed a three-man incursion team and started off in the usual way – by tossing a flash-bang down into the basement.

As they ran down the steps they were stunned to hear the screams of women.

'Hold your fire!' Harcourt called out, but just as he entered the large dimly lit room at the end of the stairs he heard a shot. A bullet missed him by inches. Standing in front of them was a tall dark-haired woman of about thirty dressed in an expensive looking black robe. She held a pistol in a two-handed grip, bringing it under control from the recoil of the first shot.

Harcourt shot her once, Wilson twice, and she fell backwards. More screams all around them. Simon rushed forward and picked up the pistol while Harcourt and Wilson did an instant threat assessment.

There were about a dozen young women in the room, all in various night attire. Without exception they were pretty and looked scared out of their wits.

'What the hell *is* this place?' Wilson exclaimed as they took in the strange room full of mirrors, plush seats, glass tables and what looked like a stage.

'Looks like an effing nightclub to me,' suggested Simon, but Harcourt shook his head sadly.

'More like a private brothel, I afraid!' he said.

76. ALBANIA

Coyle went in first. He was not going to let anyone else take on Mesmer man-to-man, despite the respect he had for the Gamma men.

It was clearly the right room – or rather suite. Only Mesmer himself would have this much luxury cramped into every square foot of floor and wall space. Persian carpets, impressionist paintings, furniture straight out of a Sotheby's auction catalogue. Only no ugly bald giant!

The doors leading left and right of the main salon – or whatever Mesmer called it – were done in renaissance palace style. Ornate, but hardly secure. Coyle decided to check out the right one first. 'Cover my back,' he whispered to Potter.

A single kick was enough and with the sound of breaking wood, the door gave way. Something told Coyle not to throw a flash-bang.

'Mesmer!' he called instead. 'We need to talk!'

Nothing. 'In five seconds we'll come in firing, Mesmer! Let me know if you don't want that!'

'Please!' A thin female voice. 'He not here!'

Very carefully Coyle eased himself into the room. Taking out the compound's power had its downside. The backup lights were so dim that getting a good view of anything was difficult, but bright enough to rule out using NV goggles.

Except for the low ceiling this could have been the bedroom of a French king. The girl lay naked on the enormous bed, one hand cuffed to a steel ring in the headboard. The duvets were on the floor, but she was clutching a pillow with her free arm. Mesmer was not in the room.

Prompted by Coyle, Potter quickly unlocked the handcuffs, but the girl only curled into a foetal position. She was young, maybe fifteen or sixteen, and under normal circumstances probably very pretty. Now her face was a mess of tears, spoiled makeup and snot.

'He can't have gone far!' said Don, his frustration showing.

'Pull her to her feet!' Coyle ordered. Potter grabbed her under her arms and dragged her off the bed. Next Coyle put the muzzle of his gun under her chin and spoke with icy detachment in Russian.

'Unless you tell me where Mesmer is, I pull the trigger!'

He saw two things in her terrified eyes. Comprehension – she understood Russian – and a slight flicker towards an ornate wall mirror. Taking a sudden step back he swung around and fired three quick rounds into the lower part of the mirror.

What was it with Mesmer and mirrors? Behind the scattered glass they found a spiral staircase leading down to what appeared to be a sub-basement level.

'He's down there?' he asked the girl, and her terrified look told him everything he needed to know. Dropping his cold demeanour he spoke to her in the kindest voice he could summon up under the circumstances.

'We're going to kill Mesmer, but as long as you stay here you'll be safe. Understand?'

She gave the faintest of nods. Coyle picked up the duvets and put them back on Mesmer's bed.

'Stay warm!' he said and forced an awkward smile.

77. ALBANIA

The girls were a handful. Initially terrified by the shoots and the death of the woman who seemed to have been their leader. But when the intruders did not follow up with more violence, merely seeking to control the situation, the mood changed. The cries turned into angry shouts and the fearfulness gave way to resentment. More girls kept turning up until Harcourt figured there were at least twenty in the room.

Then his men discovered the fuck rooms. There were six, each occupied by a Mesmer goon plus one or two girls. The bed action had obviously ceased some time ago when the shots and explosions started, but the men had thought it wiser to remain below than venture upstairs to join the battle unarmed. They looked a mixture of surly and sheepish as they were led away to join their comrades. The girls did not exactly leap to their clients' defence, but clearly resented having their own business disrupted.

Frustrated, and worried the situation would get out of control; Harcourt fired a shot into the ceiling. Then he grabbed the girl who seemed the most aggressive and pulled her aside.

'Explain all this to me!' he said to her. She glowered contemptuously at him.

'What you are?' she asked in an accent that placed her on the south-eastern fringe of Europe.

Harcourt could hardly say, *well we're a bunch of British Special Forces soldiers on an illegal mission at the personal request of our King*, so he tightened his grip on her arm and pulled it behind her back until she winced in pain.

'I have to make a decision,' he whispered into her ear. 'Do I let you live or don't I let you live? It's up to you!'

'What you want?' She was still surly, but street-smart enough not to take him on.

'Your operation here. How does it work?'

She gave him a contemptuous look and a condescending smile. 'You not know how work?'

'No I don't. Please tell me!'

A disbelieving shake of the head – like when confronted by a stupid child.

'We are whores!'

Harcourt's heart sank. This was going to take longer than he had time for. But he really had no choice; he needed to find out if these *whores* were being held against their will or not.

In the end sheer persistence prevailed and he was able to form a picture of the *arrangement* Mesmer had with the girls. They came from several of the countries in the region, as did of course the men they serviced. A stint in the basement brothel lasted up to three months, never more, and no one was allowed to return. The girls arrived and departed blindfolded and were never allowed out of the basement during their entire stay. There only exception might be a call to *special duties* in the residence, when Mesmer or his guests wanted a diversion. These calls were highly coveted, as Mesmer paid generous bonuses to those selected.

The girl explained that Mesmer maintained a network of contacts to the region's many hubs of organised prostitution and set very high standards for his compound girls. She scoffed at the idea that they had been forced to come here. A stint with Mesmer was considered a plum assignment. Much better money than any of them was used to, and a clientele of mainly young, healthy and relatively well-behaved men.

It sort of made sense, thought Harcourt. This way Mesmer could keep a large number of men in what amounted to extended periods of house arrest in the middle of a mountain forest. By not allowing wives or girlfriends, he avoided turning the compound into a *community* with all its associated tensions, emotions and intrigues. Instead it was a secret male-only place of work, with enough *available females* to keep the workers from getting restless.

'Are you *absolutely* sure than no girl is kept prisoner here?' he pressed her a final time. She started to give him the *haven't-you-been-listening* look but something else seemed to occur to her and she lowered her glance.

'I hear talk. Some girls not like us. In other house. We are good here. But there – maybe very bad.'

78. ALBANIA

Peering down the spiral staircase Coyle decided that flashbangs would not be enough to secure their descent into Mesmer's basement. They had not brought hand grenades, but Potter quickly improvised one from plastic explosives. The detonation shook the floor under their feet.

Coyle slid down first and Potter followed. Two bodies lay crumpled where they had been caught out by the blast. Both wore the dark camouflage paramilitary uniform of Mesmer's guard force. It was obvious from their positions and weaponry that they had lain in ambush and could easily have picked off anyone coming down the staircase.

The space was some kind of storeroom and had only one door. The lock yielded to a burst from Coyle's MP7 followed by a sharp kick. Again they entered a room dimly illuminated by emergency lights, but this time they encountered a vision of pure horror.

Two young women hung from a steel hook at the end of a chain, tied together back to back. Their naked bodies had been craftily trussed with thin white rope into grotesque and excruciatingly painful poses. Both girls were gagged, only emitting muted whimpers as they convulsed in pain. Their torturer had arranged the ropes so that when one girl struggled, her efforts tightened the noose around the other's neck, and vice versa. By struggling against her own torment, each was strangling the other to death.

From the marks on their bodies it was clear that this was not the first time these women had suffered physical abuse in Mesmer's dungeon. A rack against a wall held a neatly arranged assortment of whips and crops as well as even more sinister instruments of torture.

Coyle was taking everything in. There had to be a reason for this. He was *supposed* to stare at the desperate girls. But what *else* was going on?

Something caught his peripheral vision. Yes, at the far end of the room, where the light was even dimmer, an enormous bald head was disappearing through a doorway. No doubt the door would lock when it swung shut, gaining Mesmer more time.

'Cut them down!' he shouted to Potter and traversed the floor in three quick leaps. Then he crashed shoulder-first into the closing door.

It swung open, but the effort made him lose his balance and stumble. Before he could recover he felt a colossal blow to the side of his head and dropped stunned to the floor. Mesmer threw himself on top of him and applied a chokehold from behind.

'I didn't think you made house calls, Dr Barnes.' The voice was scarcely human. Neither angry nor alarmed. Mesmer actually seemed to be enjoying himself!

Pinned down under the giant's weight and feeling his brain rapidly becoming oxygen starved, Coyle realised his only hope of survival was Potter coming to his rescue quickly.

In the torture chamber the girls looked pleadingly at the Gamma man as he approached them. Only slightly curious that he saw only terror and no relief in their eyes, he pulled out his combat knife and reached up as high as he could.

The strangle nooses around the girls' necks had to take priority. Once the wretches could breathe he would figure out how to get them down without further damage.

Both girls were dark brunettes, but one had wavy hair. She seemed to be closer to death than the other, so Potter cut her neck free first. As he did so, her head jerked forward and he caught a glimpse of a grey object suspended in air between the two girls.

He didn't see it fall and he didn't feel the explosion that killed him. Mesmer had rigged a powerful device – more than enough to obliterate everyone in the room. It blasted heat and debris through the door into the room where Mesmer was killing Coyle.

Close to losing consciousness, he felt rather than heard the explosion. His mind knew instantly that the girls had been booby-trapped and that Potter, in his haste to save them, had missed the device.

The next thing he noticed was Mesmer's hold loosening slightly. Then a bit more. He was able to pry a hand under the crushing forearm and push it away – one fraction of an inch at a time.

It was when he put his other hand on the ground to gain leverage that he noticed the blood. He could smell it too. Warm and coppery. A rapidly spreading pond.

Mesmer's breathing became loud and strained as his lungs fought to supply his enormous body with oxygen through a diminishing blood supply. Coyle felt the strength drain from the huge shivering body and gathered his own remaining energy for a decisive push.

Once he was free of the giant's bulk, he could see what had happened. Mesmer's left leg looked nearly severed from his body and it was obvious that he was bleeding out. Victim of his own devious trap.

By now fully conscious, Coyle found his own body essentially intact except for an odd sensation in his ears and a few sore spots. He looked into Mesmer's face as the L&O leader surrendered to falling blood pressure, and the malevolent eyes turned dull and unseeing. Neither of them spoke. There was nothing to say.

79. ALBANIA

Don realised the blast was much more powerful than anything Potter was using, and tried to report it to Harcourt, but the battlefield radios did not reach down to the brothel level. Finally Nigel came down in person and told the Major that there had been an explosion in Mesmer's quarters and that Coyle and Potter were unaccounted for.

With Nigel and Wilson in tow, Harcourt ran over to the residence and found Don waiting for them in the foyer at the top of the main stairs. There seemed to be only one course of action open to them. They had to go looking for the missing men on the lower levels.

At first they appeared to have reached an empty corridor, but one of the doors stood ajar – the one to Mesmer's suite. Inside they found the girl still huddled on the bed, even more petrified by the explosions, but she did point towards the spiral staircase.

They descended carefully and were stunned by the devastation they encountered below. The corpses of the two guards had been rearranged and one almost beheaded by Mesmer's more powerful blast in the next room. The torture chamber itself was a dark and pungent mess of human remains mixed with random debris. Its purpose only became clear when Wilson spotted a few gruesome instruments that could only be useful for inflicting pain.

Consequently they felt little sympathy for Mesmer when they discovered his body. But who else had died in the blast? It was impossible to tell so they pressed on into the next room, which was – surprisingly – an office full of elegant glass-and-steel furniture and cutting edge IT equipment.

'Nigel, place some charges to blow this stuff past its use-by date,' ordered Harcourt. 'But don't go overboard with the stuff, and don't detonate until I've talked to Coyle. He may want to look at the drives first.'

The following room was apparently used as a lounge. Comfortable sofas and armchairs surrounded two slightly scuffed coffee tables. A corner bar and a sophisticated multi-media entertainment setup indicated that those using the room were of high standing in Mesmer's household.

While they were examining the room they heard approaching footsteps and Coyle's voice from the other side.

'Identify!'

'Special and friendly!' replied Harcourt, but still motioned for his men to be on their guard.

A door opened in the far end wall and a tense looking young Chinese man entered, followed by another who looked equally uncomfortable. Then Coyle appeared. He held a third Chinese man – this one looked about 60 – by the arm and eased him through the doorway.

'Gentlemen, let me introduce Clinton Tan and his sidekicks Sherman Wu and Oliver Yeh.'

Tan attempted a show of dignity. 'We work for Red Moon Group – a legitimate business!' he announced.

Coyle shot Harcourt a subtle glance. 'I'm sure we're all happy about that Mr Tan, but unfortunately for you we're in the very illegitimate business of killing people and stealing their money.'

80. ALBANIA

The three men from Red Moon Group could not have been more different from the rest of Mesmer's entourage. After only a brief exchange of words, Coyle had them pegged as accountants with an attitude. When he first discovered them hiding in the back of a storeroom, they had mounted what he thought was a pretty pathetic counterattack, and he had used just enough force to make them reconsider.

He sent Harcourt and his men to roam through the rest of the building – especially what lay behind the untouched doors on the middle level – and positioned the Chinese side by side on a sofa in the lounge. He kept the MP7 visible although not pointed directly at them.

'Tell me about Red Moon,' he began the interrogation. Tan affected irritation that any explanation of his employer was called for.

'Very large industrial business group in China and with many factories also in other Asian countries.'

'Making what products exactly?'

'Most important is textiles – garments – also many other products. Pipes, industrial chemicals, heavy electrical, many many different. But garment side biggest.'

Coyle pretended to think about his next question. 'And what kind of business does Red Moon have with Mesmer and his mercenaries?'

For several seconds the awkwardness hung in the air like an embarrassing smell. Then Tan reverted to 'Red Moon is a legitimate company.'

'Tell you what,' said Coyle reasonably, 'next time you don't respond properly to my question or you lie to me, I'll shoot one of you. Not sure which one, but you have my word. I'll aim this gun at one of you three and pull the trigger.'

It was obvious that in another context, and another place, Clinton Tan was a man of some importance. He was not used to being bullied and threatened with violence. His face became haughty and incensed. 'You have no right!' he blurted, and Coyle shot Wu through the right lower arm with casual ease.

The young man howled in agony and thrashed about so much he seemed about to fall off the sofa. Coyle silenced him with an upward swing of the MP7's butt that caught him on the chin. The brutality was for effect and it worked. The other two looked petrified.

'If you'd like to survive this interview we don't have time for games,' continued Coyle. 'I'll make it easy for you. Just agree or disagree with what I say. Okay?'

A barely perceivable nod from Tan.

'Mesmer is financing some major operations all over Europe. The money is very big. It comes from someone. That someone isn't going to just send billions to Mesmer and trust him with it. He'll want to have a controller safeguard in place. A person he trusts who countersigns every payment Mesmer makes. I suggest that Red Moon is that *someone* and you, Mr Tan, are the controller.'

The gun now pointed directly at him and Tan deflated noticeably. His posture dropped, but his tone remained truculent. 'Yes of course!' he conceded. 'Does it matter?'

'It certainly matters to you, Mr Tan! Because if you help me transfer the money out of the – *business* account – to my own, I'll leave you alive and well. As I mentioned earlier – we're here to rob you of your money.'

Tan glared at him with unbridled venom. 'Impossible!' he spat, but Coyle kept his calm.

'I'd say it's very possible Mr Tan.'

'But Mesmer has the codes and he will never help you!'

Coyle allowed himself a grim smile. 'That's perhaps the first true statement you've made. Mesmer won't help us because he is dead.'

Tan's face registered a mixture of shock and disbelief.
'You killed *Mesmer*?'

'Actually he killed himself – by accident. Rigged an explosion meant for me but forgot to duck.'

'Then we cannot access money!'

'I think we can. You must know where Mesmer kept his codes.'

'No I don't!' Tan did his best to lie convincingly, but a slight flicker of the eyes betrayed him and Coyle shot Sherman Yeh through the throat.

'It would be really helpful if you did know,' he stated as Yeh slid off the sofa while convulsing and choking in his own blood.

Tan was clearly not a man used to violence and brutal death. His mouth moved, but initially no words came. Then he latched on to his last hope.

'If kill me you never get codes!' he blustered unconvincingly, but Coyle merely pointed to the unconscious Oliver Wu.

'Oh, I'm sure your young colleague will be happy to talk to me when we wakes up.'

81. ALBANIA

Harcourt kept his team busy. Each of the remaining eight doors in Mesmer's corridor was blown open. Two were unoccupied guest suites, one had been Tan's private quarters while Wu and Yeh appeared to have shared theirs.

The remaining four suites revealed six men; all Europeans and all in their mid to late thirties. They differed radically from the uniformed paramilitary types. Rather than attempt to fight off the intruders, these men had with one exception attempted to hide in closets, bathrooms and under beds. The exceptional one had initially brandished a gun, but dropped it like a hot potato when Nigel challenged him.

Once all six were rounded up and brought into the largest of the suites, Harcourt made them lie face down on the floor. The mood had to be set, so he prodded them with his carbine and delivered a couple of measured kicks.

'You have one minute to convince me that you shouldn't be shot!' he barked. 'That minute starts now!'

There's always a group leader, he thought, and sure enough one of the men responded in fluent English, but a voice trembling with fear.

'Please! We're analysts!'

'That's no reason to let you live! What exactly do you analyse? Thirty seconds!'

A brief hesitation, then barely audibly, 'politics.'

Harcourt understood at once. 'Ah, you mean you look for the right parties and groups to bring into the L&O movement?'

A surly nod.

'And then you monitor their progress and report back to Mesmer?'

'Of course.'

This makes sense, thought Harcourt. Mesmer and Nagelmann would not be distributing their funds without careful groundwork. Lots of decisions had to be made; what influential people to buy, when to encourage political initiatives or recommend holding back, which opponents to take most seriously.

Suddenly Wilson appeared and seemed agitated.

'Can I speak to you Boss?' His voice had lost its detached operational calm.

'A problem?' Harcourt enquired.

'We found the cell where Mesmer kept the girls he blew up. It was hidden behind the storeroom.'

'What are you telling me, Wilson?'

'There were three more girls. They'd been there for some time. Very ugly marks on them.'

'We'll have to find a way to take them with us.'

Wilson looked at the floor. 'They've all had their necks snapped. Mesmer must have killed them before he rigged the other two as a trap.'

The head analyst squirmed when Harcourt turned to look at him. For a brief moment the Major was tempted by his feeling of outrage, but managed to rise above it. Addressing Wilson and Nigel, he said 'We're not in the business of killing unarmed prisoners, but I don't want these punters doing any more *analysing* until they've gone through a fair bit of orthopaedic surgery.'

82. ALBANIA

Mesmer kept his banking codes on a micro memory card embedded in his watch. Clinton Tan's resistance had crumbled when Coyle made him observe Sherman Yeh's final seconds of life. Almost mechanically he had revealed Mesmer's secret, then opened up his own computer and led his captor through the safeguards.

'You destroy our connections, so I cannot actually sign in to accounts,' he explained, but Coyle was unconcerned. He made Tan wait while he did a quick sweep through the computer room, downloading selectively to his own handheld device. Afterwards he made Tan identify Mesmer's own laptop. It would make for interesting reading later.

While the Gamma team systematically destroyed everything in the compound connected to weaponry or IT, Coyle brought Tan out into the open where he could use his own satellite interface. Hooking it up to Tan's computer was simple, but connecting to the bank site required several minutes.

There were six accounts in all. Two seemed to be for minor operative needs and contained only moderate amounts. The other four held the bulk of Mesmer's capital for conquering Europe.

Coyle left a trifling sum in each of these four accounts, but painstakingly transferred the rest of the money to an offshore account of his own. Once the transactions were completed, he disengaged the satellite link from Tan's computer and plugged it into his own device instead. A few minutes later he had sent the money onwards to another of his accounts, even more untraceable than the first.

Tan had recovered some his composure. 'They will come for you, you know!'

I'm counting on it, thought Coyle, but that wasn't the response he wanted to give.

'Oh I'd have thought anyone with that kind of money must have plenty more,' he quipped instead. 'Risk of the trade, Mr Tan. You make a show of having all this money, and someone like me might come around and steal it. Surely Red Moon can just write it off.'

Tan never delivered his retort, for Harcourt ran over and shouted to Coyle.

'Okay if we leave in three minutes?'

After making a mental check, Coyle nodded. 'I've got everything I want. Our transport on its way?'

'ETA eight minutes from now. We're getting the cars ready.'

They had expected to find vehicles to use for returning to the LZ, and Mesmer's garage did not disappoint. The team had brought up two Mercedes Geländewagen 4x4s and disabled three other cars and a minibus.

Coyle spotted a scratch on the Major's left cheek. 'Are we still okay on the casualties front?' he asked.

Harcourt produced a small but relieved smile. 'Except for poor Potter, nothing serious. A few flesh wounds. Simon did take a round to the stomach but his body armour held.'

Before Coyle could respond, his ears picked up the familiar sound of rotor blades. A helicopter was approaching. His first thought was that the King was early, but why would he fly directly towards the compound?

The same thought had occurred to Harcourt. 'I say we leave at once!' he suggested, and Coyle wholeheartedly agreed. Taking all the material he had collected, he ran to the 4x4s.

83. ALBANIA

The helicopter swept in just as the last Gamma Unit men scrambled into the Geländewagen 4x4s. Coyle had donned his NV goggles and quickly determined that is was not the King's AW139, but a slightly smaller machine. He made it a Sikorsky S-76, but could not make out exactly what version. *At least it's not a gunship*, he thought, but then the machinegun opened up on them.

Harcourt was in the front vehicle and told his driver to step on it. Too late! Bullets tore through the roof material and he heard one of his men cry out. It was Wilson. His left shoulder was suddenly dark with blood, but it was hard to tell how serious the wound was.

Looking up through the side window he saw the chopper swing round and fire a second burst. Fortunately the 4x4s were by now on the move and all bullets missed. *Light machinegun, handheld – not mounted*, the Major thought. It might have been worse, but where had the damn thing come from? Presumably there had been some form of communication they had not closed down, or not dealt with early enough. Someone had alerted Mesmer's people over where the chopper was kept – maybe Tirana, maybe closer by – and it had taken off with a shooter onboard.

In the rear vehicle Coyle decided to return fire. He lowered the passenger-side window and poked his right arm outside holding the MP7 set to full auto. He was well aware that this was beyond even *his* exceptional shooting skills - fast moving target, bumpy road, one-handed firing – but he had to do *something* to distract the men in the helicopter.

His first quick burst must have hit its mark for the Sikorsky veered away immediately. But the pilot now knew what he was up against, and took care to approach from the left side of the road, outside Coyle's line of fire.

Nigel was on the left in the rear seat and did his best to bring his own weapon – an H&K MP5 firing 9mm ammunition – into a firing position. Unfortunately shooting left-handed and unable to support the weapon, it seemed an exercise in futility.

There were two things in their favour; the fact they were moving as fast as the Geländewagen could negotiate the uneven road, and the dense forest around them.

Coyle spoke to Harcourt on the radio. 'Do we dump the vehicles and disperse into the trees? It's not that far to the LZ.'

The Major's reply was instantaneous. 'Negative! I have a man badly hit. Better we drive all the way.'

84. ALBANIA

Suddenly they were within range of the raiding party's battlefield radios. It took the King and Ned only a few seconds to figure out that their people were in vehicles and under attack from another helicopter. Pity they had not known sooner, but minimal radio communications had been agreed. One of Harcourt's men had sent a coded signal that pickup was desired, and the King had sent ETA updates as he covered the distance from their temporary seaborne base.

Landing on the Dunyana had been quite a challenge despite his earlier confidence, but their third attempt had been successful. Except for a short comfort break, he had stayed in the cockpit and let Ned engage with the crew. There were no guests or owners onboard, but nearly a full crew nevertheless. The owner liked being able to use his vessel on short notice, it seemed.

The crew members had been curious, but obviously warned not to intrude or ask questions. And thankfully the yacht carried a plentiful supply of aviation fuel.

The navigation computer in front of him showed less than two minutes to the LZ. He pressed the transmit button on his headset. 'Hunters, this is Songbird approaching. Can we help?'

Coyle's voice came back almost immediately. 'There is an S-76 taking pot shots at us. Single machinegun. Will make pickup tricky unless you deal with it.'

Glancing back to make sure that Ned had understood the massage, the King made his response brief. 'We're on it!'

He sacrificed some precious seconds by climbing. Engaging another aircraft is always easier if you have the advantage of altitude. But where exactly was the enemy chopper?

'Okay, I see him!' cried Ned, who had slid open both side doors and was peering down through his NV goggles. 'Two o'clock,' he added for the royal pilot's benefit.

'Got him! I'll try to give you a decent shot on the first sweep.'

The AW139 tilted onto a shallow dive and approached the S-76 from the left rear. *Shoot*, thought the King and was pleased to hear the bark of Ned's machinegun filling the cabin.

The distance was only about a hundred metres and Ned an excellent gunner, but a helicopter flying through turbulent mountain air is not an ideal firing platform, especially when operating a machinegun without proper support. The first couple of rounds hit their target, but the remainder of the burst went astray. In the Sikorsky the pilot reacted instinctively and banked right. This gave Ned another brief chance, but he was not sure if he had scored any hits.

'Thanks Songbird! He is off our back now!' Coyle sounded incredibly calm, but the King knew that it was now all down to him and Ned. As long as an armed enemy helicopter was circling, the pickup would be impossible. They would have to engage in proper air-to-air combat and shoot the Sikorsky out of the sky.

The S-76 was the smaller and lighter machine and in principle more nimble to manoeuvre, but it did not have the AW139's engine power, and that matters in a chopper fight. The King knew he could out-climb his opponent if he needed to, but more importantly, he could make tighter turns at speed.

When first attacked, the S-76 had been at a near hover trying to hit the 4X4s, but now it dashed about erratically, looking for an opportunity to fire at the AW139. The pilot probably thought he had the faster machine, for the Sikorsky was known for its speed, but in fact the AW139 could more than hold its own and the King became gradually confident that he could stay out of the opponent's reach by concentrating hard and pushing close to the airframe's and rotor blades' limits.

Unfortunately it would play into the enemy's hands the longer the battle dragged on. This kind of intense flying consumed immense amounts of fuel, and the King still had to carry his full complement of men back to the Dunyana. Although he was still a long way from critical on fuel, there was no point in delaying.

Flying straight for fifteen seconds, he could see the S-76 trying to catch up. He let it come to about fifty metres, then suddenly threw the AW139 into a sharp bank to the right, at the same time pulling on the collective control for increased rotor lift. The result was a very sharp 180 degree turn that brought them right behind the Sikorsky. Settling back to level flight and accelerating into the space to the left of the enemy, he provided Ned with a perfect moment to rake the S-76's entire fuselage with high-velocity rounds.

Ned thought he had probably hit everyone onboard. The S-76 immediately lost flight stability and plummeted towards the ground in a tortured spin. The sleek machine tore into the treetops below and seconds later a bright flash announced that it had broken up. Black smoke soon billowed upwards, but the night would make it very difficult for anyone to spot the site once the fire had burnt out.

The King spoke somewhat breathlessly into his microphone. 'The bogey is down. Proceeding to LZ. Good shooting!'

Grinning to himself, but not pressing the transmit button, Ned responded with 'Thank you, Your Majesty!' He would never be allowed to tell the story, but he could enjoy the moment.

85. ALBANIA

The 4x4s had already reached the LZ when the AW139 announced its arrival with a crescendo of engine and rotor noise. After a brief hover, the King took pleasure in landing on firm land and set his machine down with audacious deftness.

Although there was no imminent urgency anymore, the men transferred quickly. Two of them had minor flesh wounds, but were able to walk unaided. That left only Wilson as a serious casualty. Harcourt did not like the look of the wound. The bullet had entered the shoulder at a sharp angle from above and seemed to have penetrated deep into the body. Internal bleeding had to be assumed.

Coyle too had spotted the injured man. 'He'll need proper treatment quickly.'

'We could fly to Greece,' Harcourt suggested, but was clearly troubled by the prospect.

Having overheard the exchange, Ned moved closer. 'There's a doctor, a nurse and a modern operating theatre onboard the yacht,' he informed them. I checked because I thought some of our chaps might need patching up.'

Harcourt brightened. 'Well done, Ned! You've saved the day twice now! Or the night rather.'

This more than made up for Ned's earlier disappointment at not being part of the raid itself. He beamed as he helped his battle weary colleagues settle into the cramped cabin space. Then suddenly sensed that something wasn't right.

'You're short a man!' he shouted.

Don grabbed his sleeve and spoke into his ear. 'Potter got blown to bits. There was nothing left of him to bring back.'

That killed off Ned's momentary euphoria, and he looked into the front where Coyle had settled himself beside the King. They were talking with their gear set for flight deck communication only. Then the engines roared to takeoff power and the AW139 sprang airborne.

Coyle gave the King a condensed but entirely unedited summary of the night's events. The King never interrupted as he listened while handling the chopper, but his expression became grave.

'Well, we seem to hade rid the world of a real bastard!' he finally commented. 'Those poor girls!'

'I don't think they would have been let out of there alive in any case,' said Coyle. 'They were Mesmer's dirty private secret.'

'The others must have known about them!'

'Perhaps. We'll never be sure one way or another. The prostitutes had heard rumours, but rather vague ones.'

'Should we have helped them out of there?'

'Andy spoke with them. It was clear that they were there of their own free will. Apparently a stint at Mesmer's was very lucrative work.'

The King bit into his lower lip. 'It rather says something about where those women come from. Imagine a life that makes Mesmer's place seem a big improvement!'

'Powerful bastards always exploit the vulnerable.'

'What will happen to them now, you think?'

'I think they'll be all right. Whatever is left of Mesmer's organisation will have to clean up the mess we left behind. A lot of people will need hospital treatment, but most of the mercenaries and the girls will go back to their normal line of work.'

'What about the *analysts*?'

'Without Mesmer's backing they'll be harmless – even when they learn to walk again. With unlimited funds they could analyse how to buy maximum influence, but without money L&O is impotent.'

The King gave him a quick sideways glance.

'Let me get this straight. You told the Red Moon people you were stealing their money like some master criminal?'

'Exactly.'

'Why? And how much did you get?'

Coyle composed his words for brevity as well as clarity. This was important for the King to buy into.

'It was always clear that Mesmer's and L&O's money was coming from somewhere. Now we know it came from Red Moon. Because I let Clinton Tan live, he will report back that my operation was all about stealing the funds for personal profit. That's a lot better than Red Moon thinking I was acting for my King and country.'

'Why is it better? Wouldn't it have made sense to send the signal that *we're on to you so keep your paws off our country?*'

'Because it's not just about the UK. Red Moon want all of Europe. And because they won't back off in any case. We have to destroy them, and they'll be more likely to let their guard down if they think I'm a clever but politically irrelevant criminal.'

Now the King turned all the way to look at him. 'You're going after them, but you don't really know who they are!'

'Exactly! Red Moon has to be some kind of front, so we must find out who's behind them. It'll be a fishing expedition and I'll be the bait. A bait they won't be able to resist!'

'Just how much money was in those accounts?'

'It's spread over four currencies, but I did a quick estimate. In pounds sterling terms, about two and a half billion.'

86. BRINDISI

Landing the fully loaded helicopter on the yacht's small platform was tricky, but the King had learnt from his earlier experience and set down firmly on the second pass.

Coyle was delighted to find that Dunyana's Danish captain had realised that something extremely sensitive and important was going on, and decided to be as helpful as he possible could. He was utterly discrete and only asked for Wilson's passport after the ship's doctor confirmed that the man would have to remain onboard for medical attention. Harcourt explained that none of them carried passports with them, but something would be sorted out once the yacht arrived back in Corfu. The captain responded with a laconic *I see* and an understanding smile. It struck both Harcourt and Coyle that he might not be entirely new to clandestine operations.

Once the chopper had been refuelled and surplus equipment discarded overboard, they took off again for the relatively brief flight back to Brindisi. Half an hour later, just after 5am, they landed within short walking distance of the waiting Gulfstream.

One of the pilots was supposed to meet them and bring along their passports in case they were needed for the immigration officials, but instead Coyle recognized the stout presence of Henry Elliott.

'We should probably both talk to him before letting the men off,' Coyle suggested. He then had the strange experience of being formally introduced by the King of England to the benefactor he had spoken to but never met. Elliott had charted a separate plane to take him from Madrid to Brindisi, and spent the night onboard his Gulfstream waiting for the raiding party to return.

'Thought I'd come and check on my plane,' he jested good-naturedly. 'Any bullet holes in my friend's helicopter, by the way?'

'Not as far as we can see,' replied the King. 'It wasn't for lack of trying through,' he added with a glance at Coyle, who agreed.

'They started strafing us from an S-76 with a machine gunner onboard just as we were pulling out of the compound. Fortunately our side had the better pilot and a better gunner.'

Elliott beamed at the King, who showed his hands defensively. 'We certainly had the more powerful chopper,' he said. 'Without the weight of passengers, there's tremendous lift and speed at your fingertips!'

'That may be, but an air-to-air victory is a rare thing these days,' said Elliott firmly. Then he handed over the bundle of passports to Coyle.

'Better get the formalities sorted so we can be off. We can talk more on the plane. My chief pilot is already filing the flight plan.'

'Could you have him make a change?' Coyle interjected.

'You don't want to get back to Wolverhampton?'

'The others do, but I'd really like to be dropped off in Zurich. I've got some unfinished business there. I can explain when we're in the air.'

87. ITALIAN AIRSPACE

The King, Henry Elliott and Coyle huddled together in the front of the cabin during the two-hour flight from Brindisi to Zurich. First Coyle repeated the essence of what he had told the King in the chopper for Elliott's benefit. Then he explained what he intended to do in Geneva, and finally the three of them discussed what would happened after the King returned to the UK.

Fortunately his absence had not yet been picked up by the press, although there must have been some social media chatter about planned appearances for which he had failed show up.

'I did call the head of my security detail before we left and asked him to cover for me,' he explained.

'Was he curious?' asked Elliott with a raised eyebrow.

'Yes, but I never give details about what I'm doing. Making up stories is disrespectful to everyone, don't you think? We have arranged some code words that reassure him that I'm not being held by someone against my will in these situations.'

Coyle listed with a frown.

'All the same, you need to get back as soon as possible. The Gamma Unit could book a helicopter to take you to London directly from Wolverhampton.'

The King thought about it. 'No, better make that the SAS base in Hereford. The Unit can drop me there by car in a low-key way. I'll say hello to the CO and everyone will think it's a courtesy visit because I happened to be in the area. I'd cause too much attention at Wolverhampton.'

Coyle saw his point. 'I'll ask Andy to make the arrangements,' he said and shuffled down the narrow aisle to find the Major.

When he returned, he found the King and Elliott in what looked like conspiratorial conversation. Slight embarrassment showing on his face, the business mogul spoke.

'Coyle, I've just suggested to His Majesty that I should get off at Zurich as well and, shall we say, make things a bit easier for you there. We need to do something about your appearance for starters.'

Like everyone in the raiding party, Coyle had discarded his body armour and other obvious combat related items, but he was still dressed in heavily soiled black fatigues. He had washed the worst blood and dirt off himself while on the yacht, but nevertheless looked like someone the Swiss police would take notice of if he walked down a Zurich street.

'What do you suggest?' he asked in a way that conceded the point.

Elliott grinned with pleasure. 'They know me at the Baur au Lac hotel. I'm sure I can get a suite right away. What I propose is that I head there alone, check in, and then send a hotel car to bring you to over as my lunch guest. That way you won't be registered, but can use the suite to shower and have a few hours sleep. We can get you new and more appropriate clothes from the shops in the area.'

It was an improvement on anything Coyle could think of and he admitted it.

'Then that's what we'll do,' Elliott established. 'The plane will return to Zurich and wait for us at the airport until we're ready to go. Should be early evening, right?'

Coyle nodded. 'That would be perfect, yes. To tell the truth I could use a bit of rest.'

The King looked over his shoulder at the Gamma Unit men. With the exception of Harcourt they had all by now settled into various sleeping positions. Combat soldiers can sleep anywhere, even a private jet with soft reclining leather seats.

'Can I make a suggestion?' he said. 'Things may start to move very quickly once we get back home. We should set up a secret but reliable way to communicate with each other.'

Coyle gave it some thought before answering. 'Could you bring Sir Hugh into the Palace as some kind of temporary senior aide with full access to yourself? If he is there and you always let him know where *you* are, the system should be pretty watertight.'

The King smiled his approval. 'I think that's well within my power,' he said.

'Then as soon as we're on the ground I'll send Sir Hugh a message to present himself at the Palace tonight at 8pm. And you're right about things moving quickly. There was one thing I didn't mention earlier.'

He had both men's attention.

'When I did the money transfers I looked at the most recent transactions. I seems Brian Atkins's 200 million have been paid.'

88. ZURICH

Even the most discerning of third world dictators would have struggled to find fault with the suite Baur au Lac had allocated to Henry Elliott. Coyle certainly did not complain. Despite the generally gloomy season, the view towards the lake was magnificent, the interior tastefully opulent and every single item worked perfectly. He treated himself to an indecently long shower, dried off with towels that gave new meaning to the word fluffy, and emerged into the main reception room wrapped in a luxurious bathrobe bearing the hotels distinctive crest.

'The shops will be opening just about now or in half an hour,' Elliott informed him. 'I told the concierge what you wanted, and gave him your sizes.'

'Was he suspicious?'

'If he was, he didn't show it. Far too professional. Anyway, I told him you pulled out of a hunting trip because you didn't like the company, and left your gear at the lodge.'

'Actually I rather liked the company. Good men all of them.'

'When should I wake you up?'

'I'm not going to sleep yet.'

'I think you should, Coyle! You must be running on fumes!'

In response Coyle flipped open Mesmer's computer. 'There may be only a small window of opportunity here. We've got to take advantage of it. I'll take a nap when I'm done and leave for Nagelmann at 4pm.'

Elliott sensed that arguing was futile and withdrew tactfully. Mostly he wanted to think about the situation and ways he could make a difference. When the concierge rang the doorbell and delivered Coyle's new wardrobe, he thanked him and slipped him a 500 Swiss franc tip.

Then he opened his own computer and checked the news and financial sites he normally relied on for daily information. Nothing about the King of England disappearing, but plenty of speculation about whether the Rightful Tories would pull out of the coalition and bring down the cabinet.

Suddenly he felt very tired. The long night of suspenseful waiting at Brindisi airport had drained him more than he thought. He had showered and changed on arrival at the hotel, but it wasn't enough. With a resigned shrug he set the alarm for two hours and lay down on the sumptuous bed.

89. LONDON

Caroline Steele knew she had lost, and struggled hard to maintain a mechanical smile where she stood in the line of party seniors behind Brian Atkins as the camera lights came on. Inwardly she was seething from having realised that the press conference must have been called well before the decisive vote in the combined party board and parliamentary group meeting their leader had suddenly convened. There had been no proper debate. She had tried to reason with him, but he had overruled her and pushed for a show of hands right after his own speech. Amazingly, a narrow but clear majority had supported him.

Looking every inch the statesman, he stepped up to the microphone. In his carefully measured voice he thanked the press for showing up at such short notice, and made some perfunctory pronouncements about difficult times and the duty of every party to put the interest of the nation first. Then he delivered the news almost everyone in the room expected.

'Following intense deliberations with my colleagues, I have just notified the Prime Minister's office that the Rightful Tory Party can no longer continue as a partner in the coalition government. I am resigning from my post as Minister for Transport and the Rightful Tories will no longer support the Government in parliamentary votes. In fact, should the opposition call for a vote of non-confidence and an early general election, the RTP will support such a vote.'

There followed some banal sounding words about how tough the decision had been and how sometimes men and women of principle had to do the right thing. Then he abruptly thanked them all for their attention and wished them a nice day.

Caroline's fake smile died on her lips as she grasped that he was leaving it at that. Mystified, she tried to catch his eye as he fended off an avalanche of questions fired at him by the congregated journalists, with a trite 'thank you, that'll be all for now.'

Then he remembered the two secretaries who stood ready to hand out written statements, and pointed them out.

'We have of course prepared a written press release with all the pertinent information.'

This was their golden opportunity as a young party to broadcast their message into every household in the country on the back of a really important piece of news! And their leader said nothing about what they stood for and what they would be offering the voters in the election! He had managed to turn a high profile platform into a damp squid! Caroline felt herself first blush with embarrassment, then go pale with fury. Her leader had just singlehandedly turned the Rightful Tories into a historical footnote!

90. ZURICH

When Elliott woke up something felt wrong. Glancing at his watch he realized he had slept for over four hours rather the than two he had intended. He quickly established the reason. Although he had set the alarm, he had not actually activated it.

Annoyed with himself, he headed for the marble, steel and polished hardwood bathroom, where he brushed his teeth and splashed cold water over his face to shake off the drowsiness.

Then he started up his computer again and watched his favourite news site update. He read the headlines for ten seconds before dashing into the room where he had left Coyle.

He found him asleep on the sofa where he had been working his way through Mesmer's secrets. Not sure how to wake a man whose killer instincts were as finely tuned as Coyle's, he retreated to the door and gave it a couple of knocks.

Coyle sat upright as if raised by a steel spring. Seeing Elliott in the doorway he looked embarrassed.

'Sorry Henry, I must have dozed off.'

'Me too. It's nearly 3 o'clock.'

'No problem. I did what I wanted to do on the computer. Did my clothes arrive?'

'Yes they did. But there's something else. I just looked at the news.'

'The King?'

Elliott allowed himself a weak smile. 'No, his secret seems to be safe still. But bloody Brian Atkins has made his move. The Twits are pulling out of the cabinet!'

91. LONDON

The ringtone was unfamiliar and not very loud, and it came from ... under her desk!

DCS Clara Miller had to get down on her knees and extend her arm into the space between the last drawer and the floor. Her fingertips touched an object, and when she shifted to the front she was able to pull out a phone that was still ringing. She pressed the answer button.

'Hello.'

'Is that DCS Miller?' asked a male voice. Courteously, but not in the manner of salesmen. No real accent she could identify.

'Yes. Who's speaking?'

'Can you talk? Are you alone?' Something in the voice told her this was no crank call.

'I'm alone for the moment,' she replied. 'Your name please!'

'I wanted to thank you for saving Joanne Stack's life.'

'What's happened to her?'

'She's safe with a Special Unit, but if you hadn't called Sir Hugh, she'd have been passed on to LONA and probably ended up dead by now!'

'No way! Commander Reid...'

'Works for LONA! Has been on their payroll for years. I need your help again.'

'Who *are* you?'

'I'm Joanne's friend. And Sir Hugh's. I'm trying to stop LONA taking over the country.'

This was ridiculous, yet the voice was full of calm authority.

'And how do you imagine *I* can help you with that?'

'When we're finished, I'll send you a file. It contains the names of several hundred police officers who like Commander Reid have sold out to the Longbows. Another part of the file lists key people at the Home Office and

MI5 who are also in Neil Nelson's pocket. Finally you get a list of senior judges to avoid for the same reason.'

'You expect me to *arrest* all these people?'

A brief pause as he took note of and dismissed her sarcasm. 'No, but I recommend that you avoid them and exclude them completely from your operation.'

'What operation?'

'All LONA facilities must be raided simultaneously tomorrow, Clara. I'm asking you to put together an operational plan that is practical and easy to implement on short notice, but one that definitely excludes everyone on the traitors list. Can you do that?'

'I couldn't possibly authorise a raid on LONA!'

'Of course not. The authorisation will come from the Commissioner in due course, just like the order to transfer Joanne came from him. Trust me on this. You don't have to take any action until authorisation is given, but I would really appreciate an operative plan before midnight if you can manage it.'

'Can I call you back when I've seen the list?'

'Write me a message. I won't be taking calls the next couple of hours. And please keep Joanne's phone with you at all times.'

'Okay I will.'

'Thanks,' said Coyle and hung up.

A few minutes later Clara Miller looked at the names on the list and knew she had to make the most important decision of her career.

92. WORCESTERSHIRE

When Joanne arrived back at the Gamma Unit she was running on empty, both physically and emotionally. The sergeant on duty listened to her semi-coherent tale, and after only a couple of questions made two decisions. He sent a follow-up patrol to Mike Stack's cottage – this time armed to the teeth and prepared for anything the enemy might throw at them – and he ordered the house medic to put their distraught guest under sedation.

Joanne woke up with a headache and a burning thirst. Daylight was seeping in through the plain grey curtains, so she must have been out all through the night and then some. A brief inspection of the room told her she was not being held in a cell. It was more like a normal bedroom, only a bit *institutional*.

She swung her legs off the bed, observed that she was wearing what she had put on at the cottage – minus the sweater and her jeans – and started searching for the loo. Before she had taken more than a few tentative steps there was a knock on the door, and in the next second it opened. The taciturn woman she had met earlier poked her head through.

'I heard you moving about, dear.' The voice was a lot friendlier now that she was no longer a prisoner under guard. 'I'm Sally – the housekeeper.' She handed Joanne a beige robe. 'The bathroom is down the corridor, I'm afraid. Second door on the right.'

Still drowsy, Joanne mumbled her thanks and allowed herself to be wrapped in the robe.

'I'll bring you something to eat in a little while. But the Major wonders if you'd be willing to see him first.'

'Yes of course,' Joanne replied mechanically, but then the implication dawned on her. 'There're back then! How did ... ?'

'I don't know anything, dear. The Major will fill you in, I'm sure. Five minutes?'

She found the bathroom and thankfully also a brand new toothbrush. Once she had brushed her teeth she felt half human again, although it seemed her entire body still ached from the explosion.

There was only one chair in her room, so she decided to act the patient and climb back into bed. It made complete sense as every movement hurt and she felt – well, battered.

Major Harcourt knocked softly and waited to be asked in. He seemed disarmingly ill at ease interviewing a woman at bedside, and Joanne began to think that her first impression of him – as a hardened non-nonsense soldier – might not be all that accurate.

At her insistence he gave her a highly condensed version of the events in Albania. Potter's death and Wilson getting shot up cast a pall on what would otherwise have been a brilliant success. Coyle and Elliott would soon be flying straight from Zurich to London, to link up with the King there.

'Now please tell me what happened at your father's place,' he said gently but gravely, and she was momentarily shaken by the grief she saw in his normally hard grey eyes. Losing four good men in an ambush was incredibly hard for him.

To tell the story without tears would have been impossible. She spoke about her dad's nightly call to her and how she had found his phone with a bullet hole from the last shot he ever fired. She described how Frank had taken a round to the head before he even knew they were under attack, and how Ted, Tony and Bernard had been hopelessly exposed to the attackers' triangulated fire.

There was an element of retaliation in the way she had tricked her way out of the situation, but both of them knew that luck had played as much part in her survival as cunning.

'I shouldn't have regarded it as a routine clean up mission,' said Andy bitterly. In Joanne's mind he had by now morphed from Major Harcourt to Andy, a very decent man.

'How could you have known?' she defended him, but he wasn't having it.

'I was distracted by the Albania raid. Four of our finest men died because I didn't make them do a proper perimeter recce!'

They had come to the point where words become empty shells and arguing leads nowhere. Their shared grief and pain hung in the air between them, and Joanne wanted him to hold her but she couldn't make herself say it.

The long moment passed and then they were looking ahead to what had to be done. Andy explained that the King wanted a small Gamma contingent on stand-by in London in case he needed it. They would stay at an SAS safe house near Victoria Station.

'Can I come along?' she asked. 'You can keep an eye on my there just as well as here.'

He thought about it and was going to say something about rules, but realised that they were already way past any normal rules. 'No problem!' he agreed. 'You deserve to be part of the endgame – whatever it is!'

She touched him then. Just slightly on the arm, but it was a line crossed nevertheless. 'Thank you Andy!' she said very quietly.

93. ZURICH

Coyle arrived by taxi at Hannes Nagelmann's villa. He paid the driver but asked him to start the meter again and keep it running on the 100-franc note he handled over.

'If I'm not back by the time my money is all spent on waiting time, you may leave without me,' he instructed the attentive driver.

There was a doorbell on the gate and he gave it a two-second press. A clear and very professional voice announced that this was Dr Nagelmann's legal office and waited for him to state his business.

'I'm here to see Herr Dr Nagelmann. My name is Markevich.'

'You have an appointment?'

'Dr Nagelmann has assured me that I'm always welcome in his office. If you would be so good and let him know I've arrived.'

Several minutes passed and he was just about to give the bell another go when the gate clicked open. He pushed through into the courtyard and saw the main door already open for him and he recognised the severely dressed woman who beckoned him to proceed. She was one of the middle-aged office ladies he had observed on his previous visit.

Another familiar face appeared as he stepped into the foyer. It was the young bodyguard he had embarrassed, and the boy glared at him with barely contained hostility. Another heavy, whom he didn't recognise, completed the welcoming committee. Coyle gave them a glance that said *Don't even think about frisking me!*

To his surprise, the woman conducted him not to Nagelmann's office, but a small reception room in the private residence part of the villa. Small, but exquisitely furnished with antiques, classic art and an impressive collection of porcelain and silverware in glass displays.

The lawyer stood in the middle of the floor. He looked tired – and under considerable stress.

'So we meet again,' he opened the conversation and Coyle nodded. 'We have some unfinished business,' he agreed. 'Of a *private* kind.'

Nagelmann dismissed the heavies along with his assistant. He was intelligent enough to realise that Coyle wasn't there to kill him. You don't parade yourself openly in front of the staff if you are about to do a hit.

They seated themselves in surprisingly comfortable Louis XVI chairs set at a 90-degree angle.

'So what can I do for you, Mr Markevich?'

'Quite a lot actually,' said Coyle with a thin, not entirely cordial smile. 'In fact, I'm here to offer you a job.'

Nagelmann's eyebrows could hardly have risen higher. 'A job!' he exclaimed. 'You're not serious!'

'Let's call it a *position* then. You must know that I got to Mesmer last night.'

The eyebrows came down but Nagelmann's shoulders suddenly slumped. 'Copenhagen!' He pronounced it like a curse.

'The meeting was a ruse yes. I had to find Mesmer's hiding place. I tracked him to his forest lair in Albania. There isn't a lot left of the base, I'm afraid, and Mesmer is dead.'

Nagelmann looked as incredulous as Clinton Tan had been, but also close to panic.

'I didn't kill him personally if that's what you're thinking. But he got what he richly deserved. Blown to bits by his own booby-trap.'

The lawyer's jaw muscles were hard at work. Coyle guessed his was doing damage assessment in his head, and decided to help him out.

'The gentlemen from Red Moon survived – with one minor exception. Mr Tan may be an excellent accountant but he's no warrior. Getting the bank codes from him wasn't hard at all.'

By now Nagelmann had gone deadly pale and perspiration began forming on his face. 'The codes?' he almost whispered.

'I cleaned out all Mesmer's big L&O accounts. Billions as you can imagine. Only chicken feed left. And you know what I did this morning?'

There was no curiosity left in Nagelmann's eyes, only horror.

'I discovered that Mesmer had access to *your* accounts as well, Dr Nagelmann. Well, you may have some private funds as well that I couldn't get at, but I doubt they amount to the 187 million Swiss francs you now owe Red Moon.'

94. ZURICH

Coyle had not expected Nagelmann to know much about Red Moon, and this was soon confirmed. It make no sense to have a front like Nagelmann unless he was kept in the dark about the ultimate sponsors behind L&O. But he knew enough to be terrified by the prospect of Red Moon assassins hunting him down for the missing money.

'You mentioned a proposition,' he reminded Coyle, who sensed that he had the lawyer where he wanted him.

'Let me explain why I'm giving you that option. For reasons that don't concern you, I made Clinton Tan think that I'm an international master criminal and that I put together the whole operation to steal Mesmer's – well, Red Moon's – money.'

Nagelmann caught the drift. 'I could be persuaded to think that is the case,' he said pensively, but Coyle made a dismissive gesture.

'You're too intelligent and you know too much. What is your family situation? Are you married?'

'I'm divorced. And I have a grown son. He works for a company in Basel.'

'A lawyer?'

'No, he is a chemical engineer.'

'Too bad he can't take over the legitimate part of your law practice. I assume there is a legitimate part?'

'Of course!'

'Anyway, he should start looking for a job within commuting distance of this house. As of tomorrow you'll no longer be here.'

A look of disbelief. 'How could I ...?'

'This is what you'll do. First of all you download everything you have in your system about the L&O movement all over Europe. Including every payment you've ever made for political purposes. Once all that is in my possession, we together erase every single file and destroy the hard disks. Anything on paper you either shred or leave behind, I don't care. But you don't take anything with you!

'You pay off your security guys and give your office staff and domestics a nice and decent redundancy packet. Then transfer the house and any other property you have to you son, but inform him by letter. Don't call him.'

'What about my law practice?'

'Close it. Your assistants seem competent. Their last tasks for you should be to introduce your clients to other law firms and file all necessary documents to discontinue this one. Give them open power of attorney.'

Nagelmann's mind was somewhere between desperation and dull resentment of his fate, but Coyle gave no reprieve for reflection.

'Then you pack a single suitcase with whatever valuables you can carry and some personal stuff. Leave everything else behind. You won't need it.'

'Where am I going?'

'Your destination is the city of Douala in Cameroon, western central Africa. You can go there any way you like, but for your own sake I recommend a route that is hard to follow. And of course you tell *no one* where you're heading!'

'Why Cameroon?'

'Because that is where the job is. I want you to set up a legal office in Douala for the purpose of providing pro bono services to poor people and charities. You speak French of course?'

'Yes, but I still don't understand!'

'I'm giving you a chance to redeem yourself through hard unpaid work and be an honest lawyer for a change. If I find out that you're into any kind of fiddle over there, the deal is off – and I mean seriously, irrevocably – *off*!' He pointed an imaginary gun at the lawyer's head.

Interestingly, Nagelmann no longer questioned the outcome, only the details. 'How can I live and work if I don't have an income?' he argued.

'Oh you'll have plenty of money at your disposal. As long as you play an honest game, I'll make sure you live comfortably and I'll fund any sensible charitable scheme you develop. You'll report to me using this email address.'

He handed over a slip of paper, and a hoarse chuckle escaped Nagelmann as he understood. 'The L&O money!' he acknowledged.

'I'll feed it back to you bit by bit as you earn my trust. Over time 187 million Swiss francs should do a lot of good in Cameroon.'

'How long?'

'How long what?'

'How long do you expect me to stay there?'

'The position is permanent.'

'What does that mean? Nothing is permanent!'

'My deal is! You are never to set foot outside Cameroon unless I give specific permission. If I find out – and I will – that you've violated our agreement and for example travelled back to Europe, I'll track you down and kill you. If you remain in Cameroon but step out of line in other ways, I'll come looking for you there. I trust we are clear on that point!'

95. LONDON

Rita Ridgewood could not think of a good reason why she was unable to contact Craig Baines and his stakeout squad in Wales. His first report had been clear and succinct. Sergeant Stack had managed to kill their first team, but taken a round to the chest himself and lay dead on the ground. Craig and his two handpicked men would conceal themselves and see who showed up at the site.

That was yesterday. By lunchtime today she was severely annoyed at not having received any further update and started calling all three mobiles and sending encrypted messages to Baines's secure device. The hours passed, but nothing came back from the stakeout.

By early evening Rita knew she had to make some hard decisions. Sitting alone in her party HQ office, she made up her mind that sending more men to the cottage in Gwent would be foolish. She had to assume that something had happened to Baines and the others, and that *something* had to be Markevich related!

Incredibly Joanne Stack had been sprung out of Scotland Yard within two hours of Clive Reid calling to announce that he had captured her on the premises and was working on how to get her to LONA for interrogation! The Commissioner himself had intervened! At whose request? Markevich's? If so the man was connected beyond belief. No, there had to be some very powerful figure in the background. Assuming that Markevich was indeed the mysterious Bhutan agent, someone had to be running him, but who? The answer had to be in his recruitment and training. She knew that Henry Elliott had played a role, but it seemed unlikely that the business tycoon was pulling such an agent's operational strings. No, it had to be a political figure or someone very high up in the secret intelligence community.

A beep from her secure device interrupted her thoughts. A message from Reid. It took the decryption programme a couple of seconds to display the text in readable format.

There are in-house rumours of a Met operation tomorrow against LONA. Raids of party HQ, parliament offices and homes of key leaders. Tried to get more detail, but came up against brick wall. Another rumour: There is a list of officers too close to LONA and yourself.

Stunned, Rita reread the message before erasing it and running a special hard disk wipe to ensure it could not be recovered. Then she called Hannes Nagelmann's private number. After two rings, the call diverted to voicemail. It seemed too late to call his office, but she tried anyway. No reply, not even a recording.

A consummate intelligence professional, she always tried to have alternative lines of communication at her disposal. Over the past years she had tactfully cultivated Frau Ingrid Hauser, the junior of Nagelmann's office ladies. Discrete little kindnesses like theatre tickets and a couple of restaurant meals when Rita was in Zurich on business had led to a level of familiarity that included having each other's private mobile numbers.

Ingrid answered quickly, but seemed tense and only barely in control of her emotions. 'I don't know what's happening!' she lamented. 'He says it's a lifestyle change and his own decision, but I don't believe him!'

'Steady on Ingrid! Is this about Dr Nagelmann? I've been trying to call him on something rather urgent.'

There was more than a hint of sobbing in the Swiss woman's voice. 'He has stopped taking calls. Just busy getting ready to leave. All these years and now we are all losing our positions!'

'You've been *fired*, Ingrid?' asked Rita incredulously.

'Dr Nagelmann is closing his law office and leaving Switzerland. He won't even tell us where he is going. We are getting severance pay, but ...'

'Why is he doing this, Ingrid? There must be a reason!'

Now the silly cow was actually crying!

'I really don't know! This Herr Markevich came to see him earlier today and when he left Dr Nagelmann called us into his study and told us he was leaving for good. Out of the blue, Rita! Out of the blue!'

Markevich! The name hit her like a body blow. He had gone back to Nagelmann and whatever took place at their meeting, Nagelmann had crumbled. The spineless deviant was pissing off to a destination unknown and leaving everyone else to their fate!

There was nothing more to be had from the devastated Swiss woman, so she ended the call on a note of false cheerfulness. Craving a stiff drink, she thought about the bar cabinet in Nelson's nearby and invitingly empty office, but forced herself to rise about the temptation. She absolutely had to keep a clear head!

Her choices had become stark. The fact that Markevich had gotten to Nagelmann meant that everything would be revealed about how L&O had effectively *created* LONA by making outrageous amounts of money available to Nelson's fledgling group of rightwing activists. Serious in itself, but catastrophic when considered together with the message from Clive Reid. If the Met were preparing raids on them tomorrow, it meant that Nagelmann's information was already in the hands of British authorities. And a list of unreliables! Where had that come from? Only one possibility really. Highgate Security and that shithead Grant Whitmore! Markevich had absconded with Whitmore's computer and all its secrets.

Well, she had always known that taking over the country would not be an entirely risk free endeavour. At least she now had sufficient warning of the pending disaster to take some bold steps.

96. LONDON

Barry Vickerton – the man earmarked for 11 Downing Street in Neil Nelson's LONA government – was deep in contemplation of numbers he did not like but had to go along with. The payment to Brian Atkins did pave the way for LONA's rise to power, but it seemed obscene to reward that corrupt mannequin of a politician with 200 million pounds. Not that Vickerton held himself to the highest of standards when it came to fiscal propriety. He had found discrete ways of feathering the nest he eventually would settle into for his retirement. As chief financial officer of the party he controlled both their legitimate and the illegitimate funds – the latter being by far the bigger and also outside the scope of proper accounting. With all the *inducement fees* and *loyalty stipends* passing through his hands, diverting the odd hundred thousand had never been a problem. Not that he really needed the money of course. Once their party was in power, he would have license to print as much as he wanted.

There was a knock on the door, and his concentration broke. Vickerton looked up in initial irritation, but brightened when he saw Rita Ridgewood.

'What can I do for you, my dear?' he enquired solicitously. Rita was someone he both admired and felt attracted to. She sailed into the office with an air of briskness and bent close in to deliver her request.

'I need to get into the vault. Sorry to bother you Barry, but would you mind? I know it's late in the day.'

Party HQ's basement contained a vault that would not have been out of place in a city bank. The access protocol was rigid. Only the six most senior party officers and the chief clerk had electronic keys and corresponding personal codes. These had to be used in parallel with either Vickerton or Nelson himself.

'No problem, dear.' He started heaving himself up from the custom made swivel chair. 'I just hope you don't need a lot of cash. We're quite low at the moment.'

Rita patted him on the upper arm. 'I'm not looking for money this time Barry. Just some rather sensitive documents.'

They took the lift down. It was a small lift, installed mainly for Vickerton's own convenience, and rarely used by the others. The physical proximity forced on them felt awkward and Rita was relieved that she did not have to respond to any trivial banter.

They inserted their respective keys and typed in the relevant codes. Rita heard the gears in the electric lock engage, and a few seconds later a hydraulic mechanism swung the heavy steel door open.

'Well, I'll leave you to it then,' said Vickerton and made to turn away, but Rita stopped him.

'Actually, I could really use your help Barry. I'm not quite sure where I put this file.'

She walked into the vault and he followed.

'You couldn't just pull the door closed, could you? I don't want anyone looking in on us by mistake.'

Vickerton obeyed, but couldn't resist a quip. 'Let's hope it doesn't lock. We'd be stuck here together all night. That'd never do.'

Rita removed a small pistol from her purse and stepped in close behind Vickerton.

'Of course not,' she said. 'There wouldn't be enough air, so I'd have to kill you.'

Then she shot him point blank in the right temple.

97. LONDON

'An election is out of the question!' said Coyle. 'There must be another way!'

The midnight hour was approaching and of the four men gathered in the King's secret chamber only Sir Hugh Canderton was relatively fresh. The King himself, Henry Elliott and Coyle all looked drawn and exhausted, but they shared a sensed of determined steadfastness. The country was heading into a political and quite possibly a constitutional crisis – every step they took from now on might be crucial.

'I don't see how I can refuse,' countered the King. 'In theory I could ask the PM – or even one of the other party leaders – to try and put together a new coalition, but everyone knows it's unrealistic. That's why the media are already treating the election as a done deal.'

Before Coyle could respond, he noticed an incoming message on his phone and held up his hand. 'Looks like DCS Miller has come through for us,' he announced. 'Let's see what the plan looks like.'

He downloaded the file onto a memory card, which he inserted into one of the King's computers. Moments later they were able to view the contents together on a large screen.

Clara Miller's approach was both meticulous and straightforward. The main raid on LONA Party HQ would be at 10am, but smaller teams would simultaneously be entering the party's offices at the House of Commons, Nelson's own Hampshire manor, his London penthouse and the private residences of eight major party figures. She had painstakingly selected officers that were not on the Highgate list, but in some cases she had marked an individual with an asterisk to denote someone *possibly tainted by a known relationship with a person on the list.*

'Good work!' observed Sir Hugh. 'She has even included the necessary warrant applications. We can just print them out and get them signed.'

'Absolutely!' agreed the King. 'Perhaps you could take them to the Commissioner yourself, along with the plan. He'll have to line up a reliable judge, so he has to see *the list* as well.'

'Are we sure he'll go along with the plan?' Coyle interjected.

'Oh, I think he will!' said the King confidently. 'I'll call him in a moment and tell him Sir Hugh is on his way.'

Elliott offered his own armour-plated car that he had standing by, but Coyle suggested using Andy Harcourt's team instead.

'Their vehicles are less conspicuous. Besides, having a few Gamma Unit guys around you can't hurt.'

Elliott nodded his agreement, but was not quite finished. 'Can I make another suggestion though?' he asked. 'How about having DCS Miller join you at the Commissioner's? In the end, he is the one who needs to stand by the plan, so why not let him query her directly in case there's something he's uncomfortable with?'

'That makes perfect sense!' agreed Coyle, but the King suddenly looked worried.

'What if the police don't find enough evidence to disqualify Nelson and his party from the election?'

'It may take a bit of time to complete the case against the Longbows, but that's exactly why we don't want an election right now.'

'How? The PM is coming to see me at 4pm! There is no way I can refuse to meet with him!'

Coyle shrugged but his expression changed into something resembling mischievous. 'Let me see. The PM is coming to tender his cabinet's resignation, right?'

'Right.'

'So that the election can be called?'

'Right again.'

'But what if Your Majesty appoints a new cabinet there and then?'

There was a moment of stunned silence.

'Any new cabinet must have the backing of parliament!' the King objected, but Coyle seemed undeterred.

'Maybe we can arrange that,' he mused.

98. LONDON

The fucking staff didn't give him enough painkillers! Bill Utley was in constant discomfort – pain if anyone asked him – from the three bullet wounds inflicted on him at Osman Khan's house. The doctors claimed he was making good progress, but it sure didn't feel like it. The past days had been absolute agony – the nights even worse!

The only cheerful thoughts that sustained him involved what he would do – or have done – to the shooter; whether Markevich or some other equally despicable cunt. He had a feeling it was Markevich though. All the aggravation that had hit them lately seemed connected to that man. Once LONA was in power, hunting him down would be Home Secretary Utley's highest priority.

His ears picked up the sounds of the ward slowly coming to life, meaning another horrible night was almost over. Soon he would be able to pester the doctors and nurses for stronger pain medication. And as usual he was bursting to take a piss. He reached out for the call button that would – at some point – command a nurse to his bedside, but stopped when he saw the door to his private room open and a large green clad figure enter. A male nurse, but not one he had seen before.

'You awake, Bill?' asked a familiar voice.

'Johnny! What are you doing here?'

'Rita sent me to show you a piece of paper. She said you'd understand and know what to do.'

'How'd you get past the guard?'

There had been a plainclothes policeman outside Utley's room since he was admitted.

'Those idiots are never very alert this time of the morning. I just picked my moment.'

There was something vaguely amusing in seeing Johnny Gordon, LONA's most feared enforcer, dressed as a nurse. Utley's mind wandered off to Carry On movies and briefly pictured Johnny in comical drag as a slutty female nurse. Then he shook off the absurd vision and reached for the document the big man was holding out for him.

It was a single page, but totally cramped with text. The font size was incredibly small and virtually impossible to decipher. Utley first held the page at arm's length, then brought it slowly closer until just a couple of inches from his face. Hopeless! How did Rita expect . . . ?

He felt a slight sting on the side of his neck, but was so focused on the text in front of him that a couple of seconds passed before he looked up and saw Johnny dropping a small syringe with a tiny needle into his side pocket.

He tried to shout *fucking bitch!* but only produced a faint wheezing. His lungs cried out for air only to find that there was none left in the room. If Johnny had not used his massive hands to effortlessly restrain him, he would have thrashed about and maybe attracted the staff's attention before he died.

99. GERRARDS CROSS

The girls were in a bad mood. Breakfast had consisted of cornflakes, toast and incessant bickering. Lucy was the older by a year and could normally be relied on to give way, but today she responded in kind to every jibe from nine-year old Cathy. Something must have happened between the sisters last night, but Caroline knew better than to barge in with motherly arbitration. It never worked for her. Only their father could pull it off, but then he was a law professor. Unfortunately Malcolm was not at home. He was about to start the second day of an international law seminar in Geneva.

'Mrs Parker's here!' Caroline announced as she spotted her friend Claire's dark green people carrier pulling into the drive. 'Get your bags!'

As her daughters scrambled away from the kitchen, she once more appreciated how fortunate she was to have Claire able and willing to drive Lucy and Cathy to and from school. It was not much extra trouble of course – her own daughter attended the same school and was Lucy's best friend – but it was a huge help to Caroline and allowed her to just about balance her life between family and Westminster's corridors of power.

She watched her offspring climb into the people carrier and noted that their school uniforms looked *reasonably* clean and wrinkle-free, and that the two girls no longer seemed to be arguing with each other. Claire gave her a cheery wave through the windscreen and she waved back as the people carrier reversed out of the drive.

She now had eight minutes to herself before dashing off to the station. Unfortunately she had barely turned on the bathroom light when the doorbell rang. *I don't have time for this!*

The young woman on her front step looked like she had come straight from an emergency ward. Her otherwise pretty face was bruised and splattered with bandages. She was dressed in cheap and uncoordinated clothes, like she had raided a second hand shop in a hurry. Worst of all, her eyes were tired and – the word *haunted* seemed appropriate. Caroline's first thought was that she was looking at a battered women on the run from an abusive husband or boyfriend.

'Caroline Steele? I'm DS Joanne Stack.' The woman pointed to a man standing several yards back, whom Caroline had not yet noticed. 'That's Major Harcourt, security services. We need to speak with you urgently, please!'

After some waffle about IDs and *what's-this-about,* Caroline found herself back in her kitchen pouring leftover breakfast coffee for her visitors. She was not going to catch her regular train to London.

100. GERRARDS CROSS

The printout consisted of four separate pages. As she began to grasp its contents, Caroline felt a strange kind of relief that her own dismay towards yesterday's events had been justified. But most of all she felt betrayed by and furious at Brian Atkins!

If she had wanted to go into denial she could have chosen to believe that she was being shown a forgery, but there was actually no doubt in her mind. This totally explained why Brian had campaigned so hard in favour of leaving the coalition. The bastard had sold out for a lot of black money, and he had no doubt bribed key opponents on the party board.

Joanne was making exactly that point. 'We're aware that several million were paid out immediately after the L&O funds arrived in Atkins's offshore accounts, and once we've tracked down the recipients we'll know for sure.'

'Brian always kept party finances as his exclusive domain. We didn't have a lot of big donors that I knew about, so I sometimes wondered how he managed to keep us going.'

Joanne decided not to push too hard. 'We'll know more in a couple of days once LONA archives have been seized and analysed. But it does look like the Longbows were putting money into your party right from the start.'

Caroline's world as she knew it was crumbling. 'You mean even our breakout from the Conservatives could have been arranged by Nelson?'

At this point Joanne felt a sense of elation. Coyle's guess that Caroline Steel was an honest MP despite her position as deputy leader of the party was proving correct. She had not been aware of Atkins's machinations.

'We think Nelson probably did everything to weaken the existing parties and the political system around them,' she explained. 'Including supporting organised crime and terrorism!'

Caroline let out a sigh of pained understanding. 'This is all so the Longbows can do well in a general election, right? Nelson is paying Brian to clear the way for him!'

'We think LONA have some surprises planned for the campaign and believe they can get an overall majority. They've been getting almost unlimited funding from L&O after all. But not anymore!'

'Why do you say that?'

Looking over at Andy Harcourt for support, Joanne explained in brief terms what a small team of agents had done to cripple L&O.

'You don't want to know all the details!' she said in conclusion, and Caroline wholeheartedly agreed. Then she asked the question that had been troubling her almost from the start of their conversation.

'What is it that you want me to do?'

Crunch time, Joanne thought. *How can I put this the right way?*

'Knowing what you know now, Caroline – would you still have marched out and joined the RTP?'

A resigned and frustrated shake of the head.

'No, of course not!'

'What about the others? There were thirty-two of you – including Atkins.'

'I can't imagine *any* of us would! No wait, maybe Simmons and Yardley – they're both close friends of Brian's. But the others wouldn't have. I'm positive!'

'Then in principle twenty-nine of you could rejoin the Conservative Party – immediately!'

Caroline was emotionally shattered, but she had not lost her sharp mind. 'That would restore the coalition's majority in parliament!'

Joanne beamed at her. 'Can you do it?'

A fleeting moment of self-doubt. Then 'How long do I have?'

'The Prime Minister will meet the King at four o'clock this afternoon. To hand over the cabinet's resignation and call for an early general election. But because of the exceptional circumstances, the King will invite the leaders and deputy leaders of *all* parties with seats in parliament to a follow up meeting.'

This was Caroline Steele's moment and she was rising to it. 'I need to get to Parliament!' she nearly shouted, and got to her feet.

'We have transport waiting outside,' Andy Harcourt assured her.

Outside Caroline looked pensively at the strange couple protectively shepherding her towards the SUV. She wondered if they were in a relationship. There seemed to be an emotional tension between them that was hard to explain otherwise.

101. LONDON

Johnny Gordon had left the hospital a happy man. Disposing of Utley had been easy, but then Rita had given him precise instructions. She knew the ward well from her visits to her colleague's bedside.

Johnny understood completely why Utley had to be eliminated. Rita had explained that LONA was in severe crisis and might even be destroyed. That meant certain loose ends had to be taken care of, and Utley was the only one – except Rita herself – who knew the full extent to which LONA had reached out to criminal and terrorist circles. In addition, he had managed Nelson's *infiltration* project – buying the loyalty of nearly two thousand highly placed individuals in British society. Selecting the right candidates in the civil service, police force, judiciary, armed forces, intelligence community, even the press, had been a challenging task and he had done it well. Now that a *certain list* was about to be made public, Utley had to go.

Rita had called him last night and told him to pick her up in his car at party HQ. She had been waiting on the pavement and barely allowed the SUV to stop before jumping into the front passenger seat and telling him to drive on.

Then she explained the situation and told him what she wanted him to do in return for the two hundred grand in cash and small package containing half a million worth of high grade diamonds she handed him. Enough for him to disappear. Completely and in comfort.

He parked in front of the familiar building rather than operate the now once more functional underground garage door. Inserting his electronic fob into the slot by the front door he waited for the slightly delayed buzz-click before pushing into the lobby. Not surprisingly Fred had been replaced at the guard desk. Johnny nodded at the new man, whom he vaguely recognised.

'Morning Barry!' he called out cheerfully, using the information on the man's chest tag, but didn't engage in further conversation. He took the stairs rather than the lift and climbed effortlessly to the third floor.

No one paid any attention to him – he was a regular sight at Highgate – as he made his way to Grant Whitmore's corner office. The door was open, so he walked right in and closed it behind him.

Whitmore was not at his desk. Instead he had made himself comfortable sitting diagonally across a plush sofa with his bandaged foot propped up on an extra cushion. He balanced a new laptop on, yes, his *lap*, and looked up with an expression that changed from initial irritation to casual interest when he recognised the visitor.

'Ah, Johnny! What brings you over?'

'Nelson needs your advice. You've heard about the Twits, right?'

'Of course, that's what we've all been waiting for!'

'Well something strange is going on. If you don't mind clicking on their website.'

'RTP's website?'

Johnny stood behind Whitmore and bent down to point a finger at the screen – like it would help.

'Yeah, just type in *Rightful Tories* or something.'

Whitmore put both hands over the keyboard, but before he had typed a single character he felt Johnny's massive arms entwining his head from behind. The thought that flashed through his brain was one of confused unreality. He knew what *seemed* to be happening but at the same time sensed that it *couldn't*. By the time his neck snapped he still had not reached clarity.

102. LONDON

As they filed into the large room, most of them were at least momentarily taken in by the regal surroundings. Because of the numbers involved, the King had arranged for tables and chairs to be set up in one of the official reception rooms, complete with pre-Victorian chandeliers and even older oil paintings on the walls. The seating arrangement formed a shallow U with a large screen and a speaker's lectern at the open end. Everyone had an assigned seat, with a neatly printed name card. Those who wondered about the logic soon figured out that the parties were arranged in descending order in terms of their number of seats in Parliament. Not every seat was taken. Some of the smaller parties had sent only one representative, no one from LONA had turned up, and Caroline Steele's seat next to an agitated looking Brian Atkins was empty.

The meeting was due to start at 4:15. Two minutes earlier, the Prime Minister entered and took his designated seat in silence. He gave no indication of what had passed between himself and the King during their formal audience, and barely nodded towards his coalition partners.

Then, with extreme punctuality, a side door opened to admit two men. Many of the assembled leaders and deputy leaders recognised Sir Hugh Canderton, but only Atkins recalled having met the tall severe looking younger man with the sharp blue eyes at his side.

Sir Hugh stepped to the lectern and spoke into the prepared microphone. 'Prime Minister, ladies and gentlemen, I'm Hugh Canderton and in view of the exceptional circumstances we are facing, His Majesty has asked me to tell you about some important developments.'

There was a rustle of chairs shifting slightly as everyone sharpened their attention.

'As you can see, Mr Nelson and Mr Henderson are not with us today despite the fact that their party yesterday issued a statement in favour of an early general election. An election they apparently expect to win.'

He had their attention now. The room held its collective breath in anticipation.

'You all know that LONA has been pursuing a political agenda similar to other so-called Law & Order parties in Europe. What you did not know is that behind all the L&O parties there was a single secret entity that has been financing the entire movement. The rapid rise and high profile of LONA in this country was made possible by illegal contributions from L&O – we are talking billions rather than millions.'

'Excuse me!' interrupted Atkins. 'How do we know all this?'

Unruffled, Sir Hugh responded. 'Partly through a clandestine operation that penetrated L&O, partly through material gathered at police searches this morning of LONA's Party HQ, parliamentary offices and the homes of senior party leaders.'

A sense of unease seemed to be spreading amongst the audience. 'What kind of clandestine operation?' asked one of the Scottish nationalists.

'I'll get right back to that, but first you have to know that LONA used a lot of the L&O funds to buy power. That is a polite way to put it, ladies and gentlemen. What they actually did was bribe nearly two thousand people in influential positions. I'm talking ministries, police and armed forces, judiciary and especially our intelligence services. Because of this we conducted a *private* clandestine mission, authorised personally by His Majesty the King.'

The Scotsman raised his voice again. 'That's unacceptable! The King can't do that!'

There was a murmur of agreement, but quite tentative still, so Sir Hugh fixed the SNP deputy leader with a cold glare.

'Actually His Majesty's highest duty is to defend the freedom and liberty of this nation,' he retorted. 'However, the King anticipated some dissent and asked me to tell you that if the people in this room overwhelmingly disapprove of what he has done, he will step down.' After a short pause for effect, 'He has drafted a letter of abdication and is prepared to sign it.'

There were several heavy seconds of stunned silence, in the end broken by the PM. 'I'm sure that won't be necessary, and not in the national interest,' he stated and looked around the room sharply. Two left wing fringe party leaders seemed prepared to push the matter further, but sensing the mood in the room, pulled back from confrontation.

The Conservative leader and Chancellor in the redundant cabinet rushed to offer his support. 'I'm sure we are grateful to His Majesty, but all the same we'd like to know more please! Who exactly carried out this operation?'

'*I* did!' said the man with the steely blue eyes and stepped up to join Sir Hugh on the lectern. 'I gathered basic evidence of the conspiracy to destabilise British society in order for LONA to gain power as the only party capable of restoring law and order. Then an SAS Special Unit and I conducted an armed strike on the secret entity Sir Hugh mentioned. We destroyed its ability to sponsor the L&O parties. Maybe not permanently, but in the near to medium future certainly.'

'Who are you exactly?' shouted the SNP man. Sir Hugh responded before Coyle could.

'Mr Baker is someone I called into active service for this specific mission. We kept him on standby for many years in case a really dangerous and delicate situation developed. I obviously can't go into details about Mr Baker's earlier history with British intelligence.'

A murmur of vague dissatisfaction spread among the listeners, but Coyle gave them no time to become restless.

Using a remote control, he activated the display screen next to the lectern.

'What you see here is a record of actual bank transactions. We discovered them during the raid on L&O's sponsor. A renowned lawyer in Switzerland acted as clearinghouse for the payments. L&O to Nagelmann – that's the lawyer – Nagelmann to offshore accounts controlled by the parties they were subsidising. Each party had money-laundering experts to make the funds accessible. Of course it helped that a big part of the agenda was to promote crime – lawlessness creates a demand for law and order – so there were close criminal connections that could be used.'

The politicians were clearly stunned by the magnitude of the payments, and their whispered comments soon grew louder. Coyle brought up a slide he had prepared carefully.

'These payments are particularly interesting,' he emphasised. 'Actually they're pretty much the reason we're meeting here today. Notice the date, the day before yesterday. We have four transfers of fifty million pounds equivalent each. Then, as you can see, immediate transfers out of about six million.'

'Why are these especially important?' asked the Conservative leader.

'Because the cabinet lost its majority due to RTP's pullout. And we have been able to link the four offshore accounts to Brian Atkins.'

After a collective gasp, all eyes turned to the RTP leader. Atkins had turned red in the face.

'Nonsense!' he shouted, and pointed at Coyle. 'The man is an impostor! He came to see me pretending to be a *Dr Barnes*!'

Coyle used the microphone to penetrate the din. 'I did indeed, Mr Atkins. I warned you against helping LONA come to power by forcing an early election. You must have sold out just hours after we had our chat.'

'Outrageous!' cried Atkins.

'Yes it is!' agreed Coyle. 'Selling your country for money is outrageous! And illegal of course.' Behind the lectern he pressed a button that sent a signal outside the room.

The PM was staring at Atkins. 'Do you deny it?' he demanded.

'Of course I deny it! This is a frame, a bloody setup! By some deviant spook gone rogue!'

He would have rambled on, but the door opened and two women entered the room. One was tall and dark haired and wore the uniform of a senior police officer. The other was Caroline Steele.

103. LONDON

Sir Hugh introduced DCS Clara Miller of the Metropolitan Police, but was rudely interrupted by Atkins. 'Come to arrest me, has she?' he snorted. 'That's utterly preposterous, you hear!'

Clara Miller stayed remarkably calm. 'In view of the evidence I certainly have grounds for an arrest, Mr Atkins, but couldn't we just say that you'll be helping us with our enquiries?'

'Come on Brian, don't be such a *Twit!*' an irreverent Ulster Unionist cracked. Some nervous laughter broke out, and Atkins seemed on the verge of a seizure.

The DCS turned to Sir Hugh. 'There has been a serious development. When the Met raided LONA's Party HQ, the vault was locked and no one in the building could open it. Apparently one of two people has to electronically countersign. Neil Nelson himself or Barry Vickerton, the party treasurer, neither of which was available.

'Well, our officers finally persuaded Mr Nelson to accompany them from his Parliament office and the vault was opened. Inside, our officers found Mr Vickerton's dead body. It seems he had been shot in the head at close range. Apparently early last night.'

This time it was the PM's turn to register contemptuous indignation. 'Inside job or another *clandestine* operation?' he asked testily, but Sir Hugh responded immediately.

'Nothing at all to do with our operation! All our assets were busy planning for today last night. Any comment from you side, DCS Miller?'

'Actually yes. Two senior LONA figures are unaccounted for. Bonnie Stevens, Chief Whip, and Rita Ridgewood, Head of Security. Then we have the sudden death in hospital of Bill Utley, one of Nelson's closest lieutenants. We're not certain that Utley was murdered, but we're treating his death as suspicious. Sorry, just a moment please!'

Clara Miller glanced at her phone, which had alerted her to a new message. When she looked up there was a puzzled frown on her face.

'I'm getting a report of a possibly connected murder. The Managing Director of Highgate Security was killed in his office this morning. The main suspect is connected to LONA!'

'As is Highgate Security itself!' added Coyle. 'I was going to bring that up later. LONA needed an army of enforcers to keep track of, and when necessary, intimidate the people on the traitors list. A company providing security services to major hotels was a perfect front for hiring muscle – most of them professional hitmen or mercenaries.'

'So why didn't the police raid Highgate as well this morning?' asked the PM. Coyle looked over to Clara Miller.

'We didn't have enough initial evidence for that warrant, Sir,' she replied. 'Besides, Mr – Baker – assured me that we would have more than enough once we had searched Party HQ.'

'And was he right?'

'Absolutely Sir! Highgate's premises are still being searched as we speak.'

'You mentioned a traitors list,' the Conservative deputy leader prompted. Coyle looked at Sir Hugh, who gave him an encouraging nod.

'It is list of 1897 individuals who were paid regular bribes by Highgate on behalf of LONA,' he explained. 'Without a much deeper investigation we can't say how seriously these people compromised themselves and their employers – nearly all of which are in the public sector – or even if the list is complete. For all we know there may be LONA collaborators whose names for some reason don't figure on the list. But it's a very good start, as I think DCS Miller has discovered.'

'Yes I have. But of course we have to thread carefully until each of the names has been properly investigated. Publishing the list is almost as unthinkable as keeping the people on it in their current positions!'

Her statement caused plenty of concerned expressions around the room, but it was Sir Hugh who spoke.

'We'll be proposing a special investigative task force drawing on MI5 and Met resources, but to avoid the impression of a witch hunt, we must follow normal procedure for prosecution. Innocent until proven guilty! However, people in key positions must be suspended from their normal duties for as long as the investigation takes.'

There appeared to be general agreement on this point. Then Caroline Steel's voice cut through the murmurs. '*You're* on the list, Brian!'

Atkins almost rose to his feet, but restrained himself with an effort. 'That's absurd!' he protested.

'Being on the list is not in itself an offense,' said Clara Miller. 'But your name does indeed appear on the list, Sir.'

Caroline jumped in seamlessly. 'The RTP was never your idea, was it Brian? Nelson paid you to weaken the Conservatives! And now he's paying you to bring down the coalition!'

'Successfully!' said the PM in a tone of outrage mixed with regret.

Coyle tried to catch Caroline's eye. Had Joanne's talk paid off?

Atkins watched in disbelief as his deputy walked over to the Conservative leader and handed him a piece of paper.

'This is a signed statement of intent by twenty-seven of RTP's thirty-one MPs. We are prepared to re-join the Conservative Party immediately.'

'You can't do that!' Atkins yelled, but Caroline was already addressing Sir Hugh and Coyle.

'If we're accepted back, it means the coalition's majority will be restored.'

'Well, we certainly won't leave you out in the cold,' the Tory leader assured her with an enthusiastic smile. 'By the way,' he continued, 'the returning MPs will make our party the biggest in Parliament.'

It took only a second for the implication to penetrate.

'So you're claiming Number Ten?' said the PM icily.

'Absolutely! Standard parliamentary practice. In a coalition cabinet, the Prime Minister comes from the largest party.'

'Don't make the assumption that Labour will join *your* coalition!' the PM cautioned him.

Suddenly there was a tangible chill in the room. The pride and personal ambitions of highly placed politicians were bound to get in the way. With an unreadable expression Coyle stepped up to the microphone and spoke loudly enough to grab everyone's attention.

'At least two good men died and many others risked everything to rescue the country from a LONA dictatorship. Our King anticipated that the people in this room might not reach an understanding, despite the gravity of the situation. He is therefore prepared to stand in front of you and outline an alternative solution. If – and only if – you wish him to do so. His Majesty is fully aware that he is, as he put it, trespassing into political territory; meaning he can only present his plan for you to consider if you invite him to.'

As expected, there were protests from some of the fringe parties, but all senior figures in the room quickly signalled their consent. Coyle walked towards the door to fetch the King, but stopped a few feet short.

'DCS Miller, don't you think this would be a good time for Mr Atkins to go where he can assist the police with their enquiries?' he suggested.

104. LONDON

Afterwards there were diverging recollections of what the King actually said when he addressed the party leaders. No recording was made and no shorthand clerk called in to take down every word. Thus those present tended to remember the speech in different ways. Actually, everyone seemed to agree that is was not really a speech as such. The King did not mount the lectern and he did not use the microphone. He stood right in front of the assembled desks and talked to the leaders in plain words without pandering to their vanities or agendas. He never came across as a man with a plan to sell – he spoke to them as their King.

He emphasized that no one in the room could avoid guilt by association for allowing the country to get to the brink of disaster. Populist movement only become really dangerous when the established parties don't do their job properly. The Longbows had appealed to the masses because law and order had indeed deteriorated badly on the coalition's watch.

The country now needed a new and functional government – not a divisive election. It might be possible to disqualify all or most of the LONA candidates on legal grounds, but that would antagonise thousands of disgruntled activists and supporters now at loose ends, and they might well take to the streets – or worse.

Everyone also recalled that the King gave the group a name – the Buckingham Council – with the task of joining the King in his monthly meetings with the new PM, someone who would be a man of integrity and proven competence, but without political ambition.

Henry Elliott's name caused a stir of course, but many of the senior figures indicated that they saw the reasoning behind the choice. The deal was simple. Elliott would be PM for the remainder of the parliamentary period, giving his government eighteen months to heal the country and start it on the road to economic recovery. The cabinet positions would be reshuffled to compensate Labour for the loss of Number Ten, but the same parties would rule – with the exception of the Rightful Tories, who were left with only four seats in Parliament. However, the opposition parties would gain unprecedented insight and influence through the Buckingham Council.

Elliott himself would remain unaligned and take no part in the general election. To reinforce his image as transition leader, he had reluctantly accepted a life peerage and ultimately a seat in the House of Lords.

There was enduring confusion as to how unanimously Lord Elliott's cabinet was actually appointed - perhaps because the King had introduced his second newly named and intriguing construction – the Sandringham Commission.

Chaired by Sir Hugh Canderton and meeting at Sandringham House, the commission was to have two distinct objectives. Deciding how to deal with LONA and the people on the traitors list, and working out an electoral reform package that would make it more difficult for a movement like the Longbows to grab power in the future. Both were demanding and delicate tasks, and crucial to the nation's wellbeing.

There was general agreement on the standing ovation at the end, but differing impressions about who started it. The most popular version, which also found its way into the media, was that the PM rose to his feet with great dignity and put his hands together, inspiring the rest to follow suit. For her part, Caroline Steele thought the first impulse might have come from the man with the piercing blue eyes who hovered in the background.

105. CHEQUERS

The PM had invited two off-the-record guests to his official retreat for a late Saturday dinner. Coyle showed up on one of his motorbikes, the King half an hour later in a chauffeur driven Mondeo. So there would be minimum interruption by staff, Lord Elliott had persuaded his wife to remain in London for a weekend of culture, and arranged the meal around an enormous platter of cold seafood.

The mood was a positive one, but far from celebratory. Each man was aware of the many serious issues that remained. Elliott started by confirming that the special investigative task force was operational and reporting to the Sandringham Commission. Most of those on the traitors list had been interviewed.

'What about arrests?' asked Coyle.

'Only about fifty so far. It takes time to collect solid evidence. But over five-hundred have resigned and nearly a thousand have been suspended from their positions.'

The King looked concerned. 'Won't it take quite a bit of time to replace them?'

'Unfortunately yes,' agreed the PM. 'Promoting new people into the jobs can be done quickly, but bringing them up to speed takes time. And there is the connected problem of finding out exactly how compromised the system itself has become. There may be all sorts of hidden corruption we haven't discovered yet.'

'I understand Andy Harcourt and his Gamma team are seconded to the Sandringham project,' the King offered.

'Exactly! I though they'd be useful as the sharp end of the operation.'

He looked at Coyle with a hint of apology. 'I haven't involved you in Sandringham because I think you should remain our secret weapon of last resort.'

Coyle's face stayed passive. 'That makes sense,' he conceded. 'I'm sure Andy is on top of what needs to be done.'

The King looked pensive. 'Was there something not right between you two in the end? He seemed a little ill at ease when I last spoke to him.'

'He is a very decent man,' said Coyle quietly. 'Decent enough to tell me he and Joanne wanted to start seeing more of each other, and wonder if I minded.'

'What did you tell him?'

'That I'm happy for them. And that putting DI Stack on the Sandringham police team was an excellent idea. She'll work well with Commander Miller.'

'No personal regrets then?'

'None. I travel light.' He turned towards Elliott. 'As I see it, we have unfinished business in Europe with the other L&O funded parties and then with Red Moon of course. Which would you like me to prioritise, Prime Minister?'

'I'd like you to stay out of Europe for a while,' replied Elliott. 'The Foreign Office has already started the process through diplomatic channels, and I've directed our police and the intelligence services to reach out to their European counterparts. All very discretely and low profile of course. It certainly helps that we have Nelson and Henderson in MI5 protective custody. Both seem to have realised that cooperating is in their own best interest.'

Coyle indicated his contempt for both men with a dismissive sneer. 'How about Rita Ridgewood and Bonnie Stevens? Any sign of them yet?'

The PM shrugged. 'We're fairly sure they've left the country. All friendly police and intelligence services are on the lookout for these ladies, but so far nothing! They've vanished completely. And so has Johnny Gordon, by the way. The enforcer we think killed Whitmore, the Highgate boss.'

'Acting for Ridgewood,' suggested the King.

'Nelson certainly denies being involved. And claims he didn't murder Vickerton either.'

'I believe him,' said Coyle. 'He's not a hands-on killer. My guess is that Ridgewood disposed of Vickerton so she could escape with whatever money and other assets she stole from the vault.'

'It's unfortunate that those three got away,' said the King with a regretful sigh. Coyle glanced at Elliott.

'Just an idea, Prime Minister. Maybe you should have MI5 put extra effort behind tracking down their man Carpenter. Something tells me Ridgewood and her friends will want to settle their score with him.'

'Find Carpenter and wait for the LONA trio to show up. Not a bad idea,' mused Elliott. 'You could do it yourself, Coyle.'

'Perhaps. But I take it you have no objection if I make hunting down Red Moon my highest priority.'

'Won't they be hunting *you* already? Since you made them think you're a master thief who was only after their money.'

'I hope they bought that line, yes. But it won't stand serious scrutiny, which is why I should make my move soon. Any instructions about the money, by the way?'

Elliott looked at the King. 'Sir?'

'Up to you, Prime Minister!'

'Then let's keep the funds safely where they are – for the time being.'

'Only one problem with that,' said Coyle. 'If I should die in the near future, which is not exactly unlikely, the money would be difficult to retrieve. Why don't I supply both of you with the account details and access codes?'

Elliott nodded gravely. 'Good idea. Let's do it that way. That leaves only one more matter to be agreed – with Your Majesty's permission.'

'Yes?' The King looked intrigued.

'Honorary knighthoods for two football club owners.'

'One for the helicopter and one for the yacht,' Coyle suggested, earning a wide smile from the King.

'No objection from my side, gentlemen!'

106. SINGAPORE

KC Fung loved coming to Singapore. The place was clean, safe, sophisticated - and everything always worked. Even the late afternoon traffic flowed much better than in other major Asian cities, as he noted while being whisked from Changi Airport to the Shangri-la hotel in a spotless S-series Mercedes. The driver was equally immaculate in his uniform and designer sunglasses. Benny – as per his nametag – had of course greeted Fung and his travelling companion in perfect Mandarin with only the slightest Singaporean accent. Another great thing about the place – everyone spoke Mandarin here.

As chairman and principal owner of the Red Moon group, KC Fung was one of the richest men in China. That invariably meant great deference and attention from everyone around him, but also the straightjacket of protocol. Wherever he went he was *managed* by bodyguards, secretaries and other subordinates. Consequently, everything he did had to be planned and executed according to a predetermined schedule. This could be stifling for a man as intelligent and energetic as Fung.

But here in Singapore he could relax and enjoy a private weekend with his newest and most favoured girlfriend. Marilyn Mah was an exquisite creature, whose talents extended well beyond the bedroom. In fact, she was rapidly becoming a force within Red Moon's extensive international PR department, which meant that only a small circle of trusted assistants could know about her *friendship* with the chairman. Her job made her available for travel, but there were few places where the two could meet without an entourage.

Of course there were a couple of junior managers and secretaries following by taxi, but they would stay in a different wing of the hotel and only appear when called.

Fung and Marilyn would have an enormous Valley Wing suite at their disposal, and probably only leave its comforts for some delightful meals. The industrialist liked many different cuisines and thought of Singapore as the best place to enjoy truly high-class food from all corners of the planet.

He made a mental note that the Mercedes had turned into Tanglin Road, which meant they were getting close to the Shangri-la. The flight from Shanghai had landed on time, so things were going his way. There was time to try out the suite's Jacuzzi with Marilyn and enjoy a short post-coital nap before dinner.

The driver would make a left turn were Tanglin Road became Orchard Road, and then they would be at the hotel in a minute. Inexplicably however, Benny took the previous left, only a hundred yards before the proper one, and proceeded down Nassim Road. Hotel drivers didn't take the wrong turn in Singapore!

'What are you doing?' Fung protested.

'Sorry. Road works on Orange Grove Road. Must drive this way.' Benny spoke calmly, but no longer in Mandarin. He was addressing KC Fung in the Red Moon chairman's native Cantonese!

By the time Fung registered the language shift the Mercedes slowed suddenly and turned right into a set of iron gates that were swinging open. Benny drove another thirty yards up a private drive before bringing the car to a stop.

Fung tried the door but it was securely locked.

'Please stay calm,' said Benny. 'This won't take long, but we must have a talk.'

As he turned around to face his backseat passengers he removed his sunglasses, and KC Fung noticed that his eyes were piercing blue.

**** END ****

CPSIA information can be obtained
at www.ICGtesting.com
Printed in the USA
BVOW08s1752181216
471166BV00002B/142/P